T0058752

Runaway Heir

ALSO BY RUTH CARDELLO

WESTERLY BILLIONAIRE SERIES

Up for Heir
In the Heir
Royal Heir
Hollywood Heir

LONE STAR BURN

Taken, Not Spurred
Tycoon Takedown
Taken Home
Taking Charge

THE LEGACY COLLECTION

Maid for the Billionaire
For Love or Legacy
Bedding the Billionaire
Saving the Sheikh
Rise of the Billionaire
Breaching the Billionaire: Alethea's Redemption
Recipe for Love (Holiday Novella)
A Corisi Christmas (Holiday Novella)

Runaway Heir

RUTH CARDELLO

Montlake
Romance

Published by Montlake Romance, Seattle

www.apub.com

Amazon, the Amazon logo, and Montlake Romance are trademarks of Amazon.com, Inc., or its affiliates.

ISBN-13: 9781542005128
ISBN-10: 1542005124

Cover design by Eileen Carey

Printed in the United States of America

To my friends who inspire so many of my stories by
sharing their own.
Think no one would sneak to bury someone at night?
You must not know the same people I do.

Don't Miss a Thing!

www.ruthcardello.com

Sign up for Ruth's Newsletter:
https://forms.aweber.com/form/00/819443400.htm

Join Ruth's Private Fan Group:
www.facebook.com/groups/ruthiesroadies

Follow Ruth on Goodreads:
www.goodreads.com/author/show/4820876.
Ruth_Cardello

Westerly
Family Tree

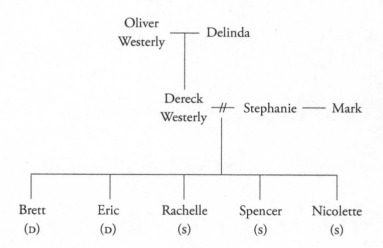

Oliver Westerly —— Delinda

Dereck Westerly —#— Stephanie —— Mark

Brett (D) Eric (D) Rachelle (S) Spencer (S) Nicolette (S)

(D): stays with Dereck after the divorce

(S): stays with Stephanie after the divorce

Prologue

Seated near one end of a table that was tastefully decorated with white linen and bouquets of wildflowers, Delinda Westerly watched her youngest grandchild, Nicolette, struggle to navigate the wedding reception. She looked positively miserable while speaking with her eldest brother, Brett. Delinda cringed when Nicolette downed her tulip-shaped glass of grappa in one long gulp.

We all love her.

That's not enough for the young. She needs the truth. The not knowing is eating away at her. It broke Delinda's heart to see Nicolette upset while the rest of the family was finally getting along.

At her side, her good friend Alessandro Andrade touched her arm, drawing her attention back to him. "Are you getting tired? Should I track down Tadeas?"

Delinda's back instantly straightened, and her chin rose with pride. "I'm perfectly fine, thank you."

Alessandro scanned the room. "Just missing your fiancé?"

"Hush," Delinda said sternly, more out of habit than from irritation. Old habits were hard to break, and lifelong ones impossible. Alessandro's mother had been one of her closest friends. He was dear to her heart, but that didn't stop her from scolding him. "We haven't made an announcement yet, and Eric and Sage's wedding is certainly not the place for it."

"Queen Delinda," he teased.

The look she gave him would have cowed a lesser man. "Tadeas is abdicating his crown. Magnus is ready, so it's time for Tadeas to . . ."

"Become a Westerly?"

With a tolerant sigh, she shook her head. Alessandro always had been a rascal, but she couldn't imagine not having him in her life. "You're incorrigible."

Alessandro studied her face for a moment. "Love looks good on you, Dee. I'm happy for both of you."

"Thank you." She gave his hand a pat. "I never thought I could feel this way again for anyone, but Tadeas makes me believe in a lot of things I'd thought were impossible." She looked around. "Like having my family all together in one place." She blinked back a tear.

"He didn't do this—you did. You set out to bring your family back together, and they're all here. I'll admit that I often didn't agree with your methods, but your heart was in the right place. I even saw Dereck and Stephanie having a civil conversation right after the ceremony." He did a mock half bow. "I'm impressed."

Delinda's gaze naturally sought out the woman who had once been her daughter-in-law. "They have a long way to go, but not yelling at each other in public is a start." She looked over to where her grandson Eric was dancing with his new bride. "I can't tell you how happy I am that Eric found Sage. I've never seen him more at ease with himself."

"Good thing you didn't have her arrested," Alessandro chided.

"Indeed," she conceded. She might have been wrong about Sage's intentions, but she wasn't apologetic about the lengths she would go to for her family. Her gaze returned to Nicolette. "Now there is only one I'm worried about."

Alessandro turned in his chair. "Nicolette?"

He sees it, too. As Delinda watched, Nicolette downed another glass of the digestif that was normally sipped slowly. Of all her grandchildren, Nicolette had been the one she'd worried about the least. From the time she'd first learned to speak, no one had ever wondered what that little one wanted. Unshakably loyal to her mother, often inappropriately vocal about her opinions, Nicolette had the heart of a Westerly. Proud. Independent. Fierce. Until her parentage had come into question and she'd withdrawn into herself. This less confident, childishly defiant version of Nicolette was heartbreaking to bear witness to. "She's not happy. Not tonight, not with her life. She's lost and scared, Alessandro."

"Have you tried talking to her?"

"Anything I say is taken as a criticism. Like the red dress she chose. I told her it was flattering and simply asked if her generation knows what undergarments are. She stormed away."

Alessandro cleared his throat. "I can't imagine why."

Placing one hand over the other on her lap, Delinda said, "I was young once. I understand wanting to shock everyone, but it's not appropriate for her brother's wedding. We all want to see her, of course, but not *see* her."

With a deep chuckle, Alessandro turned back to face Delinda. "The dress is not as bad as all that. The young nowadays show more on the beach—"

"We are not on a beach, are we?" she asked, then noticed Nicolette slipping out a side door. "Where is she going?"

"Probably to find the ladies' room."

"Perhaps." Delinda removed her napkin from her lap and placed it beside her dessert plate, preparing to stand. "I have to do something. She hasn't been herself since she found out my son might not be her father. Dereck has been trying to build a relationship with her, but she's pulling away from the whole family."

"I have an idea . . ."

3

"Who is that?" Delinda asked as she noticed a man standing on the other side of the room. "He looks like—"

"Reese Taunton? He should. That's his grandson, Bryant."

Gripping her napkin tightly in one hand, Delinda said, "What is he doing here?"

"He was in London on business, so I asked Eric to invite him."

"You obviously don't remember his family's history with ours."

"Reese was a friend of your husband."

"Friend? No. He convinced Oliver to invest heavily in a risky venture that failed. Then, rather than admit his own incompetence, he blamed Oliver." A slow fury began to build within Delinda. "Had it not been for that man, my Oliver might still—"

"You don't know that, Dee. Oliver is gone, and Reese is as well. It's time to put the past and all that anger to rest. I had dinner recently with Bryant's father, and Maddox said—"

"Why are you talking with that dreadful family?" Delinda didn't often get cross with Alessandro, but he'd opened an old wound.

"It was sad to see how much Maddox still blames you and Oliver for the change in his family's fortune. They've recouped a lot of their wealth, but the mere mention of your name was enough to set Bryant's father off."

"I hope I star in his nightmares. He's weak, just like his father was. Neither was ever able to take responsibility for their own role in what happened."

"What was Maddox's role? He was still so young, Delinda."

"And he grew up to be a spiteful man."

"You ruined his father's reputation, ensured his family was unwelcome in high society. Did you think he would thank you for it?"

"I did nothing more than was deserved."

"Maybe, but vengefulness doesn't look good on anyone, not even you, Dee. It's time to let the past go." One of Alessandro's shoulders rose and fell. "Bryant's a good boy. Hardworking. Loyal."

"Looks arrogant and cocky."

"Sometimes. Without his father's help, he started his own business and has done well. That can give a man a little swagger."

"You like him and that's sweet, but he doesn't belong here. Alessandro, I really have no idea why you can't see that."

"Several years ago his mother discovered she had ovarian cancer."

Sad, yet not Delinda's problem. "I'm sorry to hear that."

"She was very ill for a long time but didn't want to be hospitalized, so she was cared for in her home."

"Again, why are you telling me this? I no longer have anything to do with that family, nor do I have any desire to."

"Bryant had a falling-out with his father over how to care for her in the end. His parents had never divorced, but their marriage hadn't been a happy one. Bryant left his father's business, moved in with his mother, and cared for her until she died—then he built up his own company."

It was a touching story, but Delinda hardened her heart against it. She gave Alessandro an impatient look.

Undeterred, Alessandro added, "His father paid the bills, but it was Bryant who stayed by her side, who scheduled the home care. Bryant was right there holding her hand when she died."

Oh Lord. Delinda sighed. If anyone else had pleaded the case of a Taunton, Delinda wouldn't have softened in the least. There was no place in her heart for concern for one, but she did love Alessandro. Without him, she might not have been invited to Eric's wedding. If he wanted to help a Taunton, she owed it to him to at least hear him out. "Why is it so important for me to meet him? Is he in financial trouble that you feel is my fault? Is that why you brought him here?"

"This isn't about money, and he's not here to meet you."

"I'm sorry?"

"You said it yourself—Nicolette is lost. Bryant is a man who understands what's most important in life."

"No," Delinda said in a horrified voice, coming to her feet. This time Alessandro was wrong. "Absolutely not."

"Love is always the answer."

In stark contrast to the joyous music that played loudly in the background, Delinda snarled, "Get him out of this wedding and away from my family."

Alessandro rose to his feet, looking unusually stubborn. "I will not. It's too late, anyway. He couldn't keep his eyes off her when she was in the room and has been watching the door like he's awaiting her return. I'd say it's only a matter of time before he decides to . . . Yes, there he goes, off to see where she went."

"There is no way I will stand by quietly while a Taunton—"

King Tadeas appeared beside Delinda. "What did I miss? Tonight is a celebration—why do the two of you look as if you're about to go to battle?"

Delinda clutched her fiancé's arm. "Do you see that man heading out the door? Have him removed from Eric's home—this instant."

Tensing beneath her touch, Tadeas demanded, "Bryant Taunton? I spoke with him earlier. He seemed like a nice-enough young man. What did he do?"

"Nothing yet, and that's how I intend for it to stay. Will you have him removed, Tadeas, or must I do it myself?"

Tadeas looked back and forth between Alessandro and Delinda. "Why do I have the feeling you and Alessandro are not in agreement over this?"

Alessandro folded his arms over his chest. "Eric invited Bryant at my request."

Delinda's cheeks warmed, and she dropped her hand from Tadeas's arm. "Is this how it is to be? The wishes of any man will carry more weight than mine?"

"Any man?" Tadeas frowned. "Alessandro is practically a son of yours. It's not as if—"

Squaring her shoulders, Delinda took a step away. "Since neither of you care about the well-being of my grandchildren, I will deal with this myself."

Tadeas stopped her by taking her hand in his. "Your family is as dear to my heart as my own. I loved them first because they were a part of you and have come to care for them more over time. Talk to me."

Turning back, Delinda said tightly, "Alessandro has overstepped this time. No Taunton will ever be welcome near a Westerly. Ever. If Reese's grandchild is here, it's to cause trouble. I'd bet my life on it. And if neither of you will stop him—I will."

Tadeas turned to Alessandro, aligning himself beside Delinda. "Explain yourself, Alessandro."

With his classic Italian shrug, Alessandro said, "Is tonight not proof enough of the healing power of love? I didn't do more than put Nicolette and Bryant in the same room. Fate will take it from here. He would be good for her, and she needs to find her smile again. Don't we all have too much to be grateful for to dwell in the past?" He appealed to Delinda. "I would not have reached out to him if I didn't think including him would be good for everyone involved."

Leaning down, Tadeas murmured, "It sounds as if Bryant is an innocent in a possibly misguided matchmaking scheme that resembles many you yourself have concocted in the past, but if you believe he would indeed bring harm to any member of your family, I will have the boy removed."

Given time to think it through, Delinda did not want to do anything that would mar the perfection of Eric's wedding. Bryant was not his father, nor was he his grandfather. Perhaps there was no harm in letting him attend a Westerly wedding. Still . . .

"If he is anything less than a gentleman to Nicolette—"

"I will serve you his head on a platter," Alessandro promised with a wave of his hand.

"We recently outlawed that practice," Tadeas responded, as if Alessandro had meant it literally, then put an arm around Delinda's waist. "Now, how about a dance, Delinda?"

"I'm not sure you deserve a dance," she said, but a smile tugged at her lips. Tadeas would never be a man who instantly agreed with her. He had too much king in him. He did, however, genuinely care for her family, and sometimes his calmer nature was a good balance for her more impulsive one.

I might even tell him that as long as it doesn't give him a big head.

His smile told her he knew very well what she was thinking. "Sounds like I shall have to work my way back into your graces—a challenge I find I don't mind at all."

Love swept through her with the kiss that followed his words. Alessandro was right. She would have missed this moment with all the people she treasured if she hadn't begun to put the past to rest. After Oliver's suicide, Delinda had been determined that such a loss would never hit her family again. She'd fought for them, fought *with* them, to make sure it wouldn't.

It wasn't until none of her grandchildren had attended her eightieth birthday that she'd seen how, in protecting them, she had actually driven them away. Alessandro had challenged her to put aside old grudges. He'd been there on that birthday, as he'd been at so many before and each one since. His mother had asked him to take care of Delinda, and he had—as if they truly were related by blood.

At his prodding, she'd opened her heart again.

But a Taunton?

Tadeas raised his head. Alessandro had walked away. Tadeas took Delinda's hand and led her to the dance floor, twirling her around him, leaving her feeling half her age and laughing. "Forgive me yet?"

Delinda caressed his proud features with the back of one hand. "How could I not? I'm the one who doesn't deserve this dance, Tadeas. If not for you, I would have ruined Eric's wedding."

"I don't believe that." He hugged her a little closer. "If not for *you*, I wouldn't look forward to each day as much as I do." He bent to whisper in her ear. "Or each night."

She tipped her head back and smiled. "Flattery will get you everywhere."

He kissed her lips gently, and his expression turned serious. "If Alessandro is wrong about this Taunton boy, we'll nip it before it goes anywhere."

"We." Delinda repeated the word, letting it wash over her. She'd never been one of those clingy women who believed she required a man to be happy, but she had to admit it felt good to have a partner. "Nicolette is already so confused. I just wish I knew how to make things better for her."

"We can do many things for our children, Delinda, but the one thing we cannot do is live their lives for them. Make sure she knows you love her; then let her work this through on her own."

Sound advice.

"I'll try," Delinda said. Her eyes met Alessandro's from across the room. He nodded in approval. She was aware that she came across as difficult to please—and at times overbearing. Those who knew her best understood why, and they forgave her for it.

But can't I do better than that?

I'm here for you, Nicolette, and I will support your decisions—even if you do have an aversion to underwear.

Chapter One

Nicolette Westerly stepped out onto the balcony of her brother's sprawling English estate and took a deep breath. Despite how quickly the wedding had been put together, guests had flown in from all over the world. Both the ceremony and the reception had been just as beautiful and well orchestrated as one would expect a Westerly wedding to be. After all, Delinda would accept nothing less.

I should have found an excuse not to come.

As soon as the thought bubbled up, Nicolette felt guilty for even thinking it. Eric was her brother, and even if she didn't know him well, it would have been selfish to give more importance to her insecurities than his feelings. After hearing about his journey through rehab and putting his life back together, Nicolette wanted to be there for him.

She just didn't know how to be.

The evening air cooled her damp skin. A small group of people she didn't know smiled at her in greeting. She nodded toward them, then placed her empty glass on a tray and walked farther onto the balcony, seeking a corner to hide in.

"Nicolette," a male voice called out before she even had time to enjoy the peace of the quiet corner she'd sought.

Ruth Cardello

"Hey, Jordan." She forced a smile and turned to greet a man she'd known most of her life, her brother Spencer's best friend and business partner. Even in a suit, Jordan looked a little shaggy. He didn't fit in any better than she did.

Jordan didn't care, though. She envied that about him.

He was a good guy who hadn't let his success in business change him. In the past couple of years, her whole world had turned upside down, but somehow he'd stayed the same. There'd been a temptation to cling to him, and doing so, even temporarily, had brought an awkwardness to their friendship that had never been there before.

Because given enough time, I can fuck anything up.

Jordan jogged over to her, then came to a sudden stop. If he were a dog, he'd definitely have been a Labrador. His smile was easy, his manner enthusiastic.

"I saw you leave the reception," he said. "You okay?"

Nicolette couldn't meet his gaze. She released a breath that was visible in the cold night air. "I'm sorry, Jordan."

He leaned back against the railing beside her. "That you dropped off the planet after asking me to marry you?"

I'm such an asshole. "Yeah. That. I didn't want to take money from my father, but I was desperate to get away, and fulfilling Delinda's stupid marriage clause seemed like a good idea—until it didn't."

Jordan cleared his throat. "I didn't say no to hurt you, Nicolette. I said no because you've always been like a sister. I love you, just not in a way that would work with a pretend marriage."

Nicolette rubbed her hands over her face. "I shouldn't have put you in that position. Nothing makes sense to me anymore, Jordan. Not even me." She threw her hands up in the air. "Look at me. Would the old me have worn this dress? What the hell am I doing?"

His eyes widened. "Rebelling?"

She glanced down and dropped her arms the moment she realized how she'd pulled the thin material tight against her nipples. She cringed. "Worse, I'm trying to fit in, but I don't. I don't even know how to. And before you say anything about this dress, Delinda has already made her opinion of it clear."

"Your family has gone through a metamorphosis. I can see how you'd need time to catch up."

From a passing server, Nicolette snatched a drink—a tulip-shaped glass that was filled only about a fourth of the way. She downed it like a shot.

Metamorphosis was a nice way to describe how everything Nicolette had thought she knew about her family had ended up being a lie. After her mother had divorced her first husband, Dereck Westerly, she'd turned her back on both his money and his lifestyle. It was laughable, really, to hear her mother get so judgmental about him, considering she'd let everyone believe the breakup had been *his* fault, but *she'd* been the cheater, the liar, the one with all the secrets.

Nicolette's moral compass had been in a tailspin since that revelation. Stephanie Westerly, who had kept the last name, she said, for the sake of her children, had taken her three youngest and built a life for them with another man, effectively dividing the children into two separate families. Those who had stayed with their father—Brett and Eric—had been raised with nannies and limitless funds. Those who'd gone with Stephanie—Rachelle, Spencer, and Nicolette—had gotten jobs early to be able to afford to buy their own school clothing.

It hadn't been a perfect life, but it had been one Nicolette understood. Her mother was the innocent, the one to be protected and emulated. Her father was the betrayer, the one who hadn't wanted any of them enough to fight for them. Brett and Eric were snobbish and money obsessed like their father. Rachelle, Spencer, and Nicolette were hardworking, grounded, and the ones with real family values. Nicolette's life plan to work as a waitress to fund her photography obsession until it took off into a career had been perfectly acceptable.

Then Delinda dangled a financial carrot in front of her siblings, and everything changed. All any of the children had to do was get married and invite the entire immediate family to the wedding—including Delinda—and they'd receive their substantial inheritance early.

Nicolette, Rachelle, and Spencer had grown up believing there was a good chance they wouldn't inherit anything from their father's family. Stephanie had drummed it into them that money, *that* kind of money, would tear them apart.

Her warning had first been tested by Spencer, who instantly proposed to Alisha Coventry, Rachelle's best friend, because he needed the money to grow his tech company. His plan might have worked if Alisha hadn't met their oldest brother, Brett, and fallen for him instead.

Stoic, formerly reclusive Brett claimed that marriage had changed him. After twenty-something years of ignoring his younger siblings, he acted as if they'd always been close. Was it for Alisha, or was he delusional? Nicolette wasn't sure, but every time he said he cared, she wanted to call bullshit.

Spencer had felt the same, until he reconnected with his college sweetheart, and everything else ceased to matter to him. Delinda's spiteful announcement that Spencer was the product of Stephanie's infidelity was brushed aside—no longer important. He married Hailey, got his inheritance, and was living happily ever after as a rich Westerly.

Then, as if life weren't crazy enough, humble, sensible first-grade teacher Rachelle went to Europe and bagged a prince. Because *that* happens.

And now Eric, Nicolette's dysfunctional movie-star brother, had found the love of his life and was acting as if they were all one big happy family as well.

Even her parents were attending social events together again. How did that happen?

Could it last?

How had everything changed so completely? And where did that leave Nicolette?

Rachelle now glided across rooms in floor-length gowns as if she'd always been part of this sophisticated life. *I'm happy for her, but where is the sister who used to mother-hen me? The one with messy hair and an easy smile—the one I knew how to talk to. Is she gone forever?*

Spencer had taken his tech company up to a whole new level. His face was plastered all over the news, and his software was going mainstream. *A husband, a father—so busy with his own life. He used to be my rock. Is that gone as well?*

There is no one I can turn to and say, "Hey, I'm not okay with this." Spencer was at least given the truth about his parentage. What did my mother say when I asked her if Dereck was my father? She said she didn't know.

She didn't fucking know, but if I want to be sure, I could take a blood test.

If I want to know . . .

Nicolette looked around at the other guests on the balcony. Tuxes, gowns, diamonds, perfectly coiffed hair. *I'm definitely the only bare bottom here.*

Knowing doesn't require a blood test.

Seeking to numb the ache inside her, she accepted another drink from a server and chugged it as quickly as she had the last. It was then that Nicolette realized Jordan was still beside her. To break the silence, she said, "I watched a Netflix special on you. WorkChat is going mainstream. Congratulations."

"We're not saving the world like you are, but we're doing okay."

Nicolette rolled her eyes skyward. "Saving the world? Hardly. I take photographs, that's it. I've found the only job anyone could do that will never be financially profitable. Three projects later, I'm technically still an intern."

"Is that what your grandmother said to you?"

Nicolette sighed. "She didn't have to. You know that's what she thinks."

I'm the only Westerly failure.

They'd probably all be relieved if I discovered I'm not one of them.

Jordan shook his head as if he could hear her thoughts. "Anytime you want a paying job, you know you could come work with me and Spencer. There's a huge visual component to what we do. You could be part of that."

"I appreciate the offer, Jordan, but I need . . . I don't know what I need, but I know it's not here." A server came by with a tray.

Jordan shoved his hands in his pockets. "You can tell me it's none of my business, but Spencer said you didn't end up taking money from your dad and that you won't take any from him. How are you surviving?"

"I do side jobs at each site. Someone always needs a go-for."

"Go-for?"

"Go for coffee. Go for something at the store. It doesn't pay much, but it's enough to eat, and there's no guilt when I move on to the next project."

"You don't have to live like that. You're technically rich."

"No, I'm not." Her friend Kiki had pretty much said the same thing. "Can we talk about something else? Anything else."

"I get that." They stood without talking for a moment until Jordan said, "So wanna see what I'm working on?"

"Sure." She did. Spencer and Jordan were renowned for their innovations in merging AI with virtual reality. Although most of their work was for the business sector, they'd come up with some programs that were spreading like wildfire across the globe. Who didn't want to be able to walk into a 3-D simulation of a memory built from a compilation of their photographs? They created more than programs—they created experiences.

"Prepare to smile." Jordan took out his phone, snapped a quick photo of her before she had time to protest, then handed it to her. "This is you in a bikini. It's accurate, isn't it?"

Nicolette blinked a few times at the simulation of her on his phone. She could have thrown her arms around him right then. Everyone else had changed, but Jordan was still playfully inappropriate. "Really, Jordan?"

"Come on, it's hilarious. Don't you wonder what people look like in less?"

"No, not usually." Nicolette took a moment to appreciate the sight of herself with perfectly sculpted abs, then handed the phone back to him. "I wish I looked that good. I can't believe Spencer would okay that app. Didn't he make you delete your beachball-bunny simulator?"

"This is different. It's not just for men." He played around on his phone, then turned it back toward her. "Look, this is me in a Speedo."

If she'd been in a better mood, Nicolette would have chuckled. Instead, she said, "You are so bad."

He frowned. "And you're too serious. Hang on." He pulled up another photo. "I dare you to keep a straight face when you look at this."

It was Delinda in a tiny black bikini. But instead of superimposing her face on a template of a twentysomething body, her skin was wrinkled and sagging in so many disturbing places. "No. Oh my God." She clapped her hands on her cheeks. "How do I unsee that?"

"With King Tadeas in a thong?" Jordan asked.

This time Nicolette did smile. "Please, no."

Jordan shrugged. "It's a great app. Deceptively simple. There were versions of it out there already, but they didn't factor in a person's age and body type. My app can use a person's actual dimensions to come up with a realistic image. It's good enough at guessing at concealed parts that it might have forensic applications in the future. Right now it's just for amusement."

"You can create anything, and *this* is what you're working on in your spare time?"

With a grunt, Jordan put his phone back in the pocket of his jacket. "You used to be fun, Nicolette. Spencer was like that for a while. I'd show you my other app—but you wouldn't get it, either." Jordan sat back against the railing of the balcony, sulking like a child who'd just been told he couldn't go outside because it was raining.

Oh, what the hell. "What other app?"

A smile returned to his face, and he took out his phone again. "I call it my Laid-O-Meter. Upload a selfie, answer some questions, and it'll predict how likely you are to get laid tonight."

"Seriously?" Nicolette rolled her eyes again. "Are you sure that app isn't already out there?"

"Not like this. It analyzes facial indicators and body language, then combines it with the data a user provides and kicks out a reliable percentage of probability."

"I can tell you that I'm at zero likelihood for this evening."

"So test my app. See if you're right."

Simply because, as weird as their conversation was, it was preferable to returning to the reception and having another stilted conversation with her family, she snapped a photo of her face with his phone, then answered the G-rated questions that followed it. Was she alone? Did she want to be alone? Was she drunk?

Sadly, the answer to the last question was a big fat no. Maybe a little buzzed, but not the oblivion she was seeking.

Then it kicked out its prediction . . . 0 percent.

She wagged the phone toward Jordan. "Told you."

His smile was surprisingly huge. "See, it works." Then he frowned. "Zero. That's a first. That means you're not thinking about sex at all. How is that possible? I think about sex all the time."

"You're a man." She handed back his phone to him.

He whistled. "It's not a man thing, I think it's a human-being thing. You've had sex, right?"

"Of course I have." This was the Jordan she knew. Sexual, but not sexy. Like a golden retriever humping.

He cleared his throat. "The guys you've been with couldn't have been that good. If you have any questions . . ."

"Well, this is now officially awkward," Nicolette said, rubbing her hands briskly over her forearms. Hang on, maybe the drinks were finally beginning to kick in.

Jordan flushed, too. "I wasn't offering to—"

"I know." She placed a hand on his arm to stop him. "And thanks. I'm fine, really."

After pocketing his phone again, Jordan said, "You're not, Nicolette. You're not happy. I hope you find someone or something that brings the smile back to your eyes."

She hugged him a little too long, wishing she could feel something for him. *Nothing.*

"Nothing?" He stepped back and tapped her on the nose. "I know you didn't mean to say that out loud. Easy on those drinks, Nicolette."

"Oh, shit, Jordan." She reached for his arm. "I'm such a . . ."

He smiled. "We're good. I'm going to head back in—you know, to increase *my* odds." He winked.

She nodded, but as he walked away, her eyes misted over. Lonely was bad. Lonely in a crowd of those who used to be her world was worse . . . so much worse.

Still, doing anything with Jordan would have been stupid and unfair.

Tomorrow I'd feel like crap.

If only there was someone I was sure I wouldn't see again, then maybe—

Nicolette noticed a man standing just outside the door. Their eyes met, and her breath caught in her throat. *Like him. He's hot.*

And interested.

Tall with broad shoulders, he looked perfectly at home in a tux. His dark hair was cut in a conservative style that implied his second-favorite outfit was likely a business suit. The wedding-guest list reeked of dignitaries, royals, and business moguls. Which was he? When he shifted, one of his wrists flashed as light reflected off an expensive-looking watch. Even his hands were sexy. Big. Strong.

A second wave of warmth swept through her. She'd never had a one-night stand. She could count her partners on one hand with a few fingers to spare.

Maybe that's my mistake. She stopped short of a giggle and shook her head to clear it. *Or those drinks were stronger than I thought.*

I wonder what Jordan's Laid-O-Meter would say about that.

◆ ◆ ◆

Bryant Taunton's eyebrows rose as Nicolette Westerly turned away from him. He wasn't vain, nor was he used to being sized up and dismissed quite so obviously.

He took a moment to appreciate how the wind molded the brunette's dress to her perfect little body, then caressed it across her curves. Her long hair was slowly coming loose from whatever clasps had tied it back. He'd gladly help her free the rest of it.

She was easily the most attractive woman at the wedding, but that wasn't the only reason he'd found his attention returning to her again and again. He'd first noticed her during the ceremony. Rather than sitting with her family, she'd hovered in the shadows on one side of the great hall—every now and then glancing at the door as if wishing she could escape through it.

He hadn't expected to encounter anyone at the wedding who wanted to be there less than he did. When he'd received the wedding invitation from Eric Westerly, he'd thought it was a mistake—or a joke. His family had a long history with the Westerlys, none of it good.

If the Grinch married Cruella de Vil and spawned children, even that family would seem like humanitarians compared to the soulless Delinda Westerly and her clan—at least according to Bryant's father.

Turning down the invitation had been a no-brainer until Alessandro Andrade had called to personally ask Bryant to attend. Alessandro was not someone people said no to. He was a large man with a deep laugh and an easy smile, but few were better connected than he was. His eclectic circle of friends probably had him on government watch lists the world over. Dictators? They had his number. Presidents? They had a different one. Royal friends? He'd probably lost count of how many he had. If that wasn't enough, he was like family.

Bryant couldn't remember a time when Alessandro hadn't been in the background giving business advice to his father, attending the major events of Bryant's life. He'd visited his mother when she was very ill. Alessandro said that his family, those he had by blood and those by choice, were what mattered most, and he lived by those words. During the worst time of Bryant's life, it was Alessandro who had been a beacon of sanity. His view of how the world should work made sense when nothing else did.

Which made it impossible for Bryant to refuse him anything, but that didn't mean he didn't question him. "I don't understand why the Westerlys would want me there at all," Bryant had said.

"I asked Eric to invite you," Alessandro had answered. "It's time to put the past to rest. Your father still has so much anger in him."

Bryant had stiffened at the mention of his father. "Will he be there as well?"

"Would you still go if I said yes?"

He had groaned. "For you, I would. Nothing my father does affects my life one way or another anymore."

In a quiet voice, Alessandro had said, "He won't be there, but perhaps this will bring the two of you—"

"Like you said, my father has a lot of anger in him. We're both better off the way things are."

Rather than addressing that, Alessandro had said, "One step at time, I suppose. For now, I'm glad you've agreed to come."

Bryant's initial curiosity about why Alessandro had wanted him at the wedding was forgotten as he'd watched Nicolette navigate the event. She seemed happy enough when she spoke with her family, but as soon as they turned away, her smile would fade, and there was a sadness to her that pulled him in. As the youngest Westerly, and a woman, he would have expected her to be spoiled, even a little full of herself.

She didn't appear to be either.

From across the room, he'd watched the short exchange between her and her grandmother. Although he had no idea what they'd said to each other, it couldn't have been good. Nicolette had spun away and left her grandmother shaking her head.

Her brother Brett had attempted to intervene, only to be left staring after her as well.

Simply watching Nicolette walk out of the great hall was not even an option for Bryant. He did pause, however, when she stepped into the arms of another man.

If asked, the women he'd dated would likely say he wasn't the type to get jealous. He enjoyed women and they enjoyed him, but monogamy was something he'd never seen the need for. Relationships went much more smoothly when they were kept honest and open.

No expectations. No explanations required. No problems.

He didn't know Nicolette, had yet to exchange a single word with her, yet he didn't like seeing her cling to another man. Even as he told himself she was none of his business, he stood there, watching them.

When they separated, she looked like she might cry, and Bryant's hands clenched at his sides. He fought the urge to storm over and— what? Demand the man apologize to her? He had no idea what they were even discussing.

After the man had walked away, brushing past as he returned to the reception, Nicolette's gaze had momentarily locked with Bryant's. Right or wrong, he knew he had to speak with her. He went to stand beside her and mirrored her stance of looking over the balcony railing. "Trouble with your boyfriend?"

She gave him a look he couldn't decipher. "No."

Did she recognize him? "My name is Bryant." He flashed her his most charming smile.

"Nicolette," she said, then turned away from him again. The loose tendrils hanging down from her updo tickled at her deliciously long neck. He briefly indulged in a fantasy of how her hair would swing down over her shoulders as she rode him. She was hot as fuck.

She shivered as another cool night breeze washed over her. Despite how it would conceal a delightful view, he slid his jacket off and placed it over her shoulders.

She spun on him and spat, "What are you doing?"

Her reaction took him completely by surprise. He raised his hands in mock surrender. "Easy, tiger. You looked cold."

She ripped his jacket off and tossed it back to him. "I am *not* cold."

He caught it with ease. "Sorry, I thought—"

"And who does that? Who just puts their coat on someone else? Tell me, if I were a man, would you have done it?"

"No." He shrugged his jacket back on. Put that way, he felt like an ass for doing it, but who didn't want to be cared for?

This woman, for sure. God, she was beautiful. For a moment, he forgot what they were talking about. There was just her, the defiant tilt of her head, the fire spitting from her eyes, and that gorgeous rack of hers heaving in the most decadent way. He hadn't felt anything close to this since his first crush in high school. A grown man shouldn't be so easily floored.

Or he should never settle for less.

She looked down at herself, then back up at him. "This dress is perfectly acceptable." She poked her finger in his chest. Her words slurred ever so slightly. "If you don't like it, you can take your pretty little face and that designer watch and go find someone who is impressed by either. I am not."

He caught her hand in his and simply held it. *Drunk. Too bad.* In a dry voice, he said, "That's a lot of anger to direct at someone you just met, princess."

"I was wrong. You'd be a mistake, too." She shook her hand free. "Don't touch me."

He leaned closer. Her eyes darkened with what looked like desire. Had she also felt a zing from their brief connection? "You touched first." He straightened and winked.

"I did not—" She stopped, frowned, and said, "Fine, I did. Sorry."

So serious. So defensive. With a deadpan expression he hoped might lighten the mood, he said, "I wasn't complaining."

She searched his face, and in a solemn voice that implied she wasn't holding her liquor quite as well as she appeared, she said, "If I were you, I'd head back into the reception. The longer you stay with me, the less of a chance you'll have of getting lucky. The Laid-O-Meter predicted zero probability for me tonight." She made a circle with her fingers. "Zero. Jordan didn't even think that score was possible, but that's what's in here." She tapped a finger on her temple.

He barked out a laugh. Although he'd never heard of such a meter, the idea was genius. "That's a low probability." On *his* side as well, since nothing he'd imagined doing with her would happen while her judgment was impaired. He wasn't that guy. That didn't mean he couldn't talk to her, though—find out what had her looking so sad that evening.

She poked him in the chest again. "You think I'm joking. I'm not. I don't care how blue your eyes are. Are they blue?" She leaned closer. "Or green?"

"My driver's license says blue, but they're a mix of both."

She nodded, swayed, and steadied herself by placing one hand on the railing. "Sorry, I don't usually get this buzzed from a few drinks."

"I believe that's because you've been drinking grappa—it's a brandy that is sipped after a meal to help with digestion, with an alcohol content of about 30 percent."

She made a face. "It did have a burn. Sneaky little bastards, putting it in wineglasses."

He fought back a smile. "It's an Italian liquor, unless tonight's was English. They've been dabbling in production of their own variation and have come a long way."

"Of course you know that. See, that's why *you* belong here." She waved a finger from him to the others on the balcony. "They probably all know that shit, too. My favorite drinks come in individual bottles with twist-off caps." She lowered her hand and sighed. "What did you call it? Grapple?"

"Grappa," he answered absently.

"Brett would know that. I bet even Spencer does." Her shoulders slumped a little. In a broken voice that rocked straight through him, she said, "I just want to go home." Then she wiped beneath her eyes and expelled a breath.

"Where is that?" Her accent was American, but that didn't mean anything. The Westerly family had the funds to live anywhere they chose. He turned to rest his elbows on the railing. Desire to pull her to him warred with his better judgment. She was struggling with more than the liquor she'd consumed.

She looked through him, then out into the darkness. "Nowhere now."

She wasn't homeless, but he understood that a house didn't make a home . . . just like having relatives didn't mean a person had family. "You seemed to be having a rough time inside."

Shaking her head in self-disgust, she said, "I hoped I was doing a better job of hiding it. Well, it's official, this is the shittiest night of my life." She leaned forward onto her elbows as well. "I should have skipped the wedding."

Bryant had felt the same way before he saw her. "Because of the guy you were talking to? Did he say something to upset you?"

"Jordan? No. He's harmless."

"Good," Bryant said. Women didn't fuck harmless.

She scanned his face again. "*Who* are you?"

"Bryant Taunton." He waited for a sign that she recognized his last name, but none came. "I'm a friend of Alessandro and his wife, Elise."

A faint smile stretched her lips. "I like them. Really nice people. Even if they are friends with my grandmother."

"That's bad?"

"It's not good." She held his gaze. "How well do you know her?"

"This is the first social event we've both attended."

"You're lucky." She turned to look out into the darkness again. "That sounds horrible, doesn't it? I'd say I didn't mean it, but I am so done with her." She straightened, and her shoulders squared. "Sorry. I'm happy for Eric and Sage. All I have to do is smile and make it through a couple more hours."

"And maybe slow down on the grappa," he added, hoping the joke would make her smile.

She looked like she was about to say something, then decided against it. "Wish you'd said that two glasses ago. It didn't do anything; then all of a sudden—pow." The wind blew again, and she shivered. Their eyes met and held, and this time the air sizzled.

Pow.

"Sounds about right." Being so close to her was dangerous. "They're serving coffee inside. Why don't we go get some?"

Her bottom lip stuck out. "I can't go back inside. Not like this." She turned so she was leaning back against the railing and braced her hands on either side of her, tightening the thin material across her breasts, highlighting how cold she was.

Bryant groaned and looked away.

"I really messed up tonight," she said in a small voice. "I thought I could pretend everything was okay, and then I got here, and everyone was so happy that something inside me crumbled, and I couldn't do it. If I ruined any part of the wedding for Eric, I will never forgive myself. What is wrong with me?"

Bryant cleared his throat. "I don't know what you're going through, but everyone deals with things differently. I'm sure your family understands."

"You don't know my family." She laughed out a sob. "But that's okay, because I don't, either. It was all a lie. All of it. But *I'm* the problem. Me." She sniffed. "Maybe they're right and I need to just get over it. I'm trying."

He made the mistake of looking at her, and the expression on her face had him pulling her to his chest for the hug he knew she needed. He fought against his body's response to how she fit against him. The scent of her filled his senses, and he was fully aroused even as he told himself not to be.

She tipped her head back to gaze up into his eyes, looking as tempted as he felt. Everyone beyond her faded away. She licked her bottom lip, and he nearly died. "Don't look at me that way."

"What way?"

"Like you want me to do this." He brushed his lips gently over hers. She leaned into the kiss, framing one side of his face with her hand. She tasted like honey, fine liquor, and trouble all rolled into one. He raised his head reluctantly. "I told myself I wouldn't do that."

She swayed a little in his arms. "Because I had a few drinks?"

He tucked a loose tendril back into her updo. "Because when you're with me, and you will be, I want you to remember it."

The delicate hand that had tapped his chest now splayed across it in the most delicious way. "I bet you say that to all the ladies."

His mouth twitched with a smile. "All the drunk ones."

She pouted. "I cannot tell a lie—I may be just a teensy-weensy bit wasted. Don't hold it against me. I am normally very, very, very, very, very sober."

"I'm sure you are."

She gave his chest a pat. "But I am very, very, very, very, very not right now."

"I noticed."

"I would probably remember sex with you, though."

"We won't test that theory." He set her back a bit, just enough to give his throbbing cock a little space and cool air.

"That's probably for the best, because I'm a little nauseous."

He laughed. "I appreciate the warning."

"You have a beautiful laugh," she said, then brought a hand up to his mouth and traced his lips. "And really soft lips."

He grabbed her hand and brought it back to his chest. "Is there someone who could take you home? Your sister?"

"No," Nicolette said in loud whisper. "Don't let Princess Rachelle see me like this."

"One of your brothers?"

Her eyes narrowed. "Hey, if you don't want to talk to me anymore, you can go. I don't need anyone to take me home. I'll just call a British Uber or something."

"No. Someone should take you home."

Her eyes widened, and she wiggled her eyebrows. "You could."

He groaned. "Not going to happen, sweetheart."

She waved a hand at him. "That's rude. I've slept with two guys in my life. Count them." She held up one finger, then another. "One. Two. And I'm twenty-eight years old. That's less than one guy a decade. Except I started at twenty. Hold on. That's like one guy every four years. Does that sound like someone you should say no to?" She smiled up at him, and two of the most adorable dimples appeared.

"Yes?" he said with a smile. "Where are you staying?"

"With my friend Kiki."

"Let's call her."

Nicolette shook her head. "She's out with her boyfriend. She won't pick up."

"Okay, what about another friend?"

She raised both hands over her head. "Just me. I've pissed everyone off, 'cause I'm an asshole."

"I find that hard to believe."

She spun before him. "Oh yes. Take away the grappa, and I'm 100 percent an angry bitch. Ask anyone who knows me. I'm no fun anymore. Completely unlovable."

When she steadied herself by placing a hand on his chest again and smiled at him, he didn't see the woman she described. He saw someone who was hurting and losing to that pain. It brought out the protective side of him.

"Don't look at me like that," she said, running her hand up to cup the back of his neck.

"Like what?" He whispered her own words back to her, knowing exactly where this was going but not strong enough to refuse her. One more kiss, then he would deliver her to a member of her family and remove his temptation.

"Like you want me to do this." She rose onto her tiptoes while tugging his head down, and when their lips met this time, he lost his head. Her mouth opened for his, and he groaned, savoring what she was so boldly offering. He wrapped his arms around her and pulled her to him again—kissing her deeper and with less control this time.

He ran his hands over her hips and moaned as the material moved over her bare skin beneath. It was the kind of dress that should stay on, easy enough to bunch at her waist, thin enough to suckle a nipple through. Bryant reminded himself that there would be a better time and place for everything he was thinking.

He was just about to break off the kiss when she writhed against him, and his resolve weakened. *Holy fuck.*

"Excuse me," a female voice said in an authoritative tone that instantly broke the mood. "Could I have a moment alone with my sister?"

Bryant raised his head.

Nicolette stepped out of his embrace breathing as heavily as Bryant was. "Rachelle."

"Nicolette." Her very pregnant sister voiced her name in reprimand. The look Rachelle gave Bryant was not at all as friendly as when she'd been introduced to him in passing earlier. His hand went to Nicolette's back in silent support.

She elbowed his side. "Escape while you can, Bryant. The judgment train is pulling in."

"I'm fine," he said. Rachelle might be her sister, but Bryant wasn't about to walk away until he was sure Nicolette was with someone who would take care of her.

Rachelle leaned in for a closer look at Nicolette. "Are you drunk?"

"Noooooo," Nicolette said but revealed her state with that one simple word. "Okay, a little." She pinched the air. "This much."

"What are you doing, Nicolette?" Rachelle looked pointedly at Bryant. "Do you even know who he is?"

Nicolette smiled up at Bryant and gave his chest a hearty pat. "That's my new friend Bryant. Isn't he beautiful?"

Rachelle sighed. "Sure. Come on, Nicolette, time to get you out of here. You can come home with me and Magnus."

"Afraid I'll embarrass the family?" Nicolette asked with a rawness that cut through Bryant.

"Too late for that," Rachelle said, then seemed to instantly regret it.

Nicolette stepped back as if struck. "Wow, my sister really is gone. Long live Her Royal Highness Princess Rachelle."

Rachelle's face crumpled. "That's not fair."

"Don't talk to me about what's *fair*." Nicolette shook beneath Bryant's hand even as she growled the words. "*You* belong here."

Rachelle threw her hands up in the air. "I'm not having this conversation with you at Eric's wedding. And I'm definitely not having it while you're drunk. I get that you don't want to be here. We all get it. If you stop feeling sorry for yourself long enough, you might see that today wasn't actually about you."

"Stop. If you're trying to make me feel bad, don't bother. I don't feel anything right now, and it's the most beautiful thing in the world." Nicolette swayed and stumbled as she went to step away. Bryant righted her.

Chin high, Nicolette said, "I'm leaving, but not with you and your prince."

She turned those big, tortured brown eyes of hers on Bryant, and he was temporarily at a loss as to what to do, especially when he saw similar desperation on her sister's face.

Shit. I can't, little one.

"Fine. I don't need either of you." With a dismissive wave of her hand, Nicolette walked back into the house.

Bryant said, "Someone needs to make sure she gets home safely."

Rachelle gripped his forearm. "I handled that badly, but that *someone* won't be you."

Part of him couldn't blame her. He'd lost his head a little when Nicolette had kissed him. It probably was better to end their night there and then. Still, he needed to make sure she was okay. He glanced at the door Nicolette had disappeared through.

Placing her other hand on her rounded stomach, Rachelle said, "Walk away, Mr. Taunton. I don't know why Alessandro wanted you here, but he was wrong to. You'll only make things worse."

"Because I'm a Taunton?"

She released his arm. "Please. I don't want to threaten you. Stay away from Nicolette because it's the right thing to do."

She walked away without saying more.

A moment later, Bryant reentered the great hall and scanned the room. He spotted Rachelle with her husband, but not Nicolette. She wasn't anywhere he could see. Had she already left? Who would have taken her? As far as he could tell, the rest of her family was still there.

Rubbing his chin, he went over everything she'd said, and a possibility came to him that he decided was worth looking into. He'd find her, make sure she was okay, then do what her sister asked—at least until tomorrow.

Chapter Two

Nicolette was grateful the bathroom she'd found had a locking door. As she hovered near the toilet feeling queasy, she decided bathrooms were unsung heroes. Really, they didn't get enough respect. Not only did they provide a place to relieve oneself, but they were blissfully private.

Her stomach settled a little, so Nicolette put down the cover of the toilet and sat on it, smiling as she did. *I could stay here all night. Just me and this gold-plated wallpaper. I bet that is real gold.*

You can tell if a diamond is real because it cuts glass.

How can you tell if something is gold? She narrowed her eyes and rubbed her finger across one of the embossed designs.

I have to pee.

I should probably lift the toilet cover again.

A knock on the door startled Nicolette. *Crap, they found me. I have to do something.* Doing her best impression of an old woman's voice, Nicolette said, "Occupied." It was so perfect she laughed, then covered her mouth. *Double crap.*

"Nicolette? It's Bryant."

Oh, Bryant. "Are you alone?"

"Yes."

She opened the door. "I didn't throw up."

"I'm glad to hear it."

His smile was so sweet, she wanted to kiss it again. She held on to the bathroom doorknob for balance. "It was close, though."

"How do you feel now?"

She gave his question serious consideration. "I have to pee."

His mouth twisted in another smile she didn't deserve. "You might want to do something about that."

Yeah.

She got lost for a moment in those blue-green eyes of his. "I don't want you to leave."

"I won't."

She swayed a little. "You're worth coming out of the bathroom for."

He laughed. "Thanks. Now close the door, and don't forget to wash your hands."

She laughed so hard at that her stomach did a little flip. She shut the door quickly and returned to looking down at her porcelain savior.

Her stomach settled.

False alarm.

She hiked up her dress and relieved herself with a happy, audible sigh. "Are you still there, Bryant?"

"Yes."

She moved to the sink. "Listen." She turned on the water and used much more soap than necessary to wash her hands. A crazy amount that filled the sink with hilarious suds. After wiping her hands on a small towel, Nicolette threw open the door.

"Thank you," he said in an amused tone.

He was just as beautiful as she remembered.

"Now let's go find that family of yours, because it looks like the grappa is really kicking in," he said.

Disappointment slammed through her. "I thought you liked me. You would toss me to the wolves? You're heartless."

He shook his head. "It's for the best."

"For who? You? Them? Not me. I have given them enough to be mad at me for one day. I am going back to Kiki's. I called for a car. You don't have to help me. You don't even have to sleep with me. Just don't tell anyone you saw me. They're not going to worry. They probably have someone following me anyway."

"Someone following you? Like security?"

Nicolette looked down the hall one way, then the other, and lowered her voice. "Someone is always watching. It's kind of creepy, but my opinion doesn't matter." She pursed her lips as she realized how very true that was.

"You shouldn't just leave. Your sister is worried about you."

"I'll text her from Kiki's." Bryant didn't look like he agreed with her plan. That was a shame, because it meant she would have to leave him behind as well. "Goodbye, Mr. Taunton. It was nice kissing you." She stepped out of the bathroom.

He linked an arm with one of hers. "Where does Kiki live?"

Nicolette took out her phone and showed him the address. "It's not too far. I could almost walk it if I weren't in these—" She wiggled her toes, then looked down at her feet. "Oh my God, someone took my shoes."

Bryant chuckled. "Damn thieving English."

Nicolette laughed. "Right?"

"You're going to have quite a hangover, my friend."

Nicolette hugged his arm to her. "I don't care. I feel good, and I haven't in so long."

As they walked down the hall, she put the rest of the evening out of her head. It would all be there, waiting for her the next day, but right then she let herself bask in the fact that Bryant had sought her out—and was taking her home.

He texted someone as they waited for his car to be pulled around to the door; then Nicolette sank into what was possibly the most comfortable passenger seat her butt had ever made acquaintance with. The movement of the car wasn't as pleasant. Her stomach started to churn. She laid her head back and closed her eyes.

Only a moment later, Bryant was telling her they had arrived. She blinked a few times, took his hand, and followed him into an elevator, out of an elevator, and to Kiki's door.

He knocked.

"She won't be back tonight," Nicolette said, remembering what Kiki had said about staying at her boyfriend's.

He opened the door with a key she didn't remember giving him, and they both stepped inside. She reached out to steady herself by holding on to his arm. He closed the door and looked around. "Do you have everything you need?"

She motioned toward her luggage that was open beside the couch. "Everything I own is right there—so, yeah."

He looked from her to the tattered bag and the couch that was still covered with the comforter she'd slept beneath the night before. "I'm going to find the kitchen. Are you able to change into something to sleep in?"

"On my own?" She tried to wink at him but gave up as both eyes kept closing. When he didn't look all hot and bothered by the move, she shrugged, pulled away, and marched over to her bag. "Yeah, I can do that."

With him and his sexy smile in mind, she started hunting through her clothing for something that would have him looking at her the way he had earlier. Only after she'd emptied the contents of her luggage onto the floor did she remember that she didn't own lingerie. Shorts and a T-shirt would have to do, as they did every other night.

She hoped he didn't witness any part of her almost falling on her face while pulling her dress over her head, then almost giving up halfway through getting dressed again. Her stomach told her if she kept moving around, it was about to send her a very nasty reprimand. She flopped facedown onto the bedding on the couch.

Bryant was back. "Sit up, tiger. You should drink some water and take an ibuprofen."

She shook her head and groaned.

"I found some saltines," he said in a coaxing tone.

She turned her head. He had placed a glass of water beside a plate and put both on the coffee table a foot from her. It was touching in a way that confused her. She focused on his shiny black shoes. "I messed this up, too, didn't I?"

His tone was gentle. "Drink some of that water. You'll feel better tomorrow if you do."

She raised herself onto her elbows and drank some of it before putting down the glass and rolling onto her side. Although she didn't know him, she felt safe. He looked like he was waiting to make sure she was okay before he slipped away.

She pulled at the blanket, adjusting it so it both covered her and acted as a pillow beneath her head. *I should tell him it's okay if he leaves. I'll be fine on my own.*

On my own.

"Bryant?"

"Yes."

"Could you stay until I fall asleep? I don't want to be alone."

"Sure." He sat on an overstuffed chair across from the couch.

Her eyes fluttered. "And can you do me one more favor? Could you forget this ever happened? I'm going to do my best to."

◆ ◆ ◆

Bryant rose at the light knock on the door and crossed the room to open it. Looking concerned, Alessandro and his wife stepped inside.

Bryant brought a finger to his lips and motioned that Nicolette was sleeping.

"Oh, the poor thing," Elise said in a hushed tone. She was a short, auburn-haired older woman with naturally elegant taste but a relaxed manner, even in an awkward situation like this. "You were right to call us." She stepped over Nicolette's dress, giving Bryant a pointed look as she did.

"Nothing happened," Bryant said.

Alessandro clapped him on the back. "He's a good boy, Elise. You know that."

"I know." Elise ran a hand over Nicolette's forehead in a show of motherly concern. "She's just had such a rough time. It broke my heart to watch her at the reception. I wanted to hug her and tell her that she'll come out of this stronger."

"Come out of what?" Bryant asked. "Why did she feel like she didn't belong at the wedding?"

"It's a long story." Alessandro moved to sit in the chair Bryant had vacated earlier. Elise sat on the arm of it. They looked poised even amid the dorm room–like furnishings.

Elise put a hand on his shoulder. "And not really ours to tell."

"He's family, Elise," Alessandro said with his signature shrug that meant he'd already made up his mind on how to proceed.

Bryant looked from Alessandro to Nicolette and back. "You didn't ask me to the wedding because you wanted us to meet, did you?"

A smile spread across Alessandro's face. "She's beautiful, no?"

Elise gasped. "*Alessandro.* You told me you were done with matchmaking."

Alessandro shared a look with Bryant, then said lightly, "You told me to be done with it, but look at them. She needs a good man, and he needs a woman without a hundred other men in her playbook. It's time for you to think about settling down, Bryant."

"That's not going to happen anytime soon," Bryant said with confidence. Nicolette was indeed a beautiful woman, but he liked his life just the way it was. He slid his hands into his pockets. "Don't tell me anything more than she'd be comfortable with sharing. Something tells me that wouldn't be much."

"Her family is worried about her, Bryant. They laid a bombshell at her feet, and she doesn't know if she can forgive them for it. You know that feeling."

Bryant rocked back on his heels. When Alessandro spoke, he did so from a good place. If his own father ever had, they might have found a way to reconcile after his mother died. Sadly, his father's first concern continued to be himself. "I do know that feeling. I also sought escape a few times at the bottom of a bottle." He looked across at Nicolette again. Her face was peaceful in sleep. "It doesn't make anything better."

With a knowing look toward his wife, Alessandro said, "Admit it—perfect for each other. He understands her."

Elise looked skeptical. "Delinda will never accept him."

"Let me worry about Dee," Alessandro said.

Bryant raised his hands. "Whoa. First of all, I can hear you, and although I appreciate the introduction, this has trouble written all over it. I'm not looking for anything serious, and the last thing I want to do is cause problems for her."

Alessandro rubbed his chin. "Well, that settles it, Elise. He's not interested. What other single men do we know who are Nicolette's age? How about Spencer's friend—what's his name? Jordan?"

Bryant's eyes narrowed. He wasn't playing Alessandro's game. "Elise, are you and Alessandro okay staying for a while? I don't feel comfortable leaving her alone without her roommate here."

Elise walked over and touched his cheek in a way that made him miss his mother. "We'll take care of her. Don't worry."

He turned to look at Nicolette again. "She might hate me for calling you, but I didn't know who else to ask."

"We'll leave before she wakes. It'll be like we were never here," Alessandro promised, rising to his feet to give Bryant a back-thumping hug. "Now go, we've got this."

"Her family—"

"Knows we're here," Elise said softly. "Delinda was beside herself when she thought Nicolette might have left with you. We told her we drove Nicolette back. A small lie, but the only way to stop the cavalry from descending."

At the door, Bryant met Alessandro's gaze. "Don't you dare set her up with anyone."

Alessandro shrugged.

Bryant swore and closed the door behind him.

Chapter Three

The next morning Nicolette woke to the sound of knocking on the door. She rolled over and buried her face in a cushion. Whoever it was, they couldn't be looking for her. Nicolette hadn't been in London long enough to know anyone.

The knocking started again—louder than before.

"She's not here," Nicolette called out. "Try her cell."

There was no reprieve from the knocking. It echoed through the pillow she held over her head, echoed right through her hungover skull. *The building had better be on fire.*

How she'd gotten home was still fuzzy. She remembered Bryant walking her to her door. A glance at the coffee table confirmed that he'd stayed long enough to bring her a plate of crackers and water. And ibuprofen that she popped into her mouth and chased with the rest of the water.

She looked down. Her T-shirt was backward, and her shorts were inside out. Memories of struggling to get dressed quickly before he returned from the kitchen came back to her. *Well, I'm not naked, so apparently drunk me is not as cute as I thought I was.*

The knock at the door continued. She brought a hand to her aching head. She could only imagine how her hair looked. *Does it matter?*

It's probably just a delivery for Kiki. Nicolette grabbed a few bills for a tip and called out, "I'm coming. I'm coming."

Before the door was even fully open, she wanted to slam it shut. Standing there dressed in a crisp burnt-orange dress like the queen of England coming for tea, hat and all, was her grandmother. How had she even found her?

"I hope you don't mind that I dropped by without calling. May I come in?" The steel in her grandmother's eyes indicated only one response would be accepted.

"Sure," Nicolette conceded, trying to flatten the hair she felt sticking out of one side of what was left of her updo. "I wasn't expecting anyone, so . . ."

Delinda walked past her, looked around, and wrinkled her nose at the messy living room. "I had a guest room made up for you at my house across town. Both your mother and father are staying with me. I'm surprised you chose not to."

"Yeah." Exhausted and suddenly nauseous, Nicolette closed the door and rubbed a hand over her face. She must have done something awful in her last life to deserve this hell. "I hadn't seen Kiki since college. We had a lot to catch up on."

"Is she here?" Delinda asked.

"No. She went out with—"

With a wave of her hand, Delinda cut her short. "I'd rather not know." She walked farther into the apartment, moved Nicolette's folded dress off a chair, and placed it on the table before taking a seat. "So how long are you staying in London?"

"I don't know." Nicolette sat on the couch, pulling a blanket up on her lap. "I just finished a project, so I'm not sure where I'll go next." *How long is she going to pretend she's here to see how I'm doing? We both know she's itching to tell me what she thought of my behavior last night.*

"You're turning thirty, Nicolette—"

"I'm twenty-eight."

"Exactly. It's time for you to start thinking about what you want from your life."

"Why are you here, Delinda?"

"Rachelle was upset after the two of you spoke."

"The feeling was mutual."

"She's worried about you."

"I'm fine."

"Are you?" Delinda's tone cut right through Nicolette's confidence.

Flashes of the night before came back to Nicolette, and there wasn't one of them she was proud of. She owed Eric and Sage an apology. *Sorry I got drunk at your wedding. Sorry I made out with Bryant in front of your guests.*

Just sorry.

"I believe you've already learned this, but grappa is a liquor that is meant to be sipped and savored. Not guzzled like a—"

"Don't, Delinda." Nicolette raised a hand. "Please don't." The mere mention of it was enough to flip her stomach.

Delinda looked around, and Nicolette followed her gaze. The clothing she'd tossed on the floor the night before had been folded and stowed back in her luggage. Had Bryant done that? The room spun a little. *I know I didn't do it.*

Her stomach churned.

Don't throw up. Don't throw up.

Do. Not. Throw up.

Her grandmother had that oh-so-familiar tight, judgmental expression.

Nicolette squared her shoulders. *Yeah, take a good look. I'm sure I'm a beautiful sight.*

Delinda folded and unfolded her hands on her lap. "You used to call me Grandmother."

"I *used* to know we were related."

Delinda sighed. "Spencer felt the same way, but then he realized it doesn't matter."

Nicolette's hands fisted, bunching the blanket inside them. "Doesn't matter to who?"

"To whom," Delinda corrected.

That little correction was enough to have Nicolette's pride kick in. It brought back every visit she'd had with her grandmother—every time, despite hoping it would be different, she'd felt the sting of her disapproval. As a child, Nicolette had run to hug her, only to be reminded that children do not run indoors. Every achievement had been dismissed. Nothing was ever good enough. She was never right.

Maybe I don't want to be a Westerly if this is what it feels like.

"Thank you for the lesson in grammar. Are you done, or would you like to critique anything else while you're here? Don't hold back. Say you hate where I'm staying. That I look horrible. Oh yes, and you think my behavior at the wedding yesterday was not up to your standards. Say it—I know you want to."

Delinda's small frame tensed—like a snake readying to strike. "There's no need for rudeness, Nicolette. Don't let your chosen surroundings negate your good upbringing."

"You know nothing about my upbringing. So say your piece. And then, please—go. I'll apologize to Eric later, smile politely regardless of how I feel, and pretend everything is fine. But know that the only perk of discovering I might not be Dereck's daughter is that I also might not be related to you."

It was an awful thing to say, but if Nicolette had hoped for an emotional response from her grandmother, she didn't get one. Delinda's composure didn't even crack. If anything, she looked annoyed. "I *am* hard on you, but . . ." She stood and waved a hand in the air. "How could anyone be expected to condone this?"

Nicolette rose to her feet as well, walked to the door, and held it open. "Thankfully, you don't have to."

Delinda stepped just outside the door. Some of her arrogance fell away, but it was too late. "Nicolette, what I came here to say was that I—"

Nicolette closed the door in her face, and in a mockery of her grandmother's voice, she muttered, "I'd rather not know."

For several moments after the older woman left, Nicolette leaned back against the door. She'd always been the snarky one in her family, but she'd never said hurtful things or wished for anything but good for those around her. In her fantasy family, she could run after her grandmother, throw herself in her arms, and apologize.

In reality, if she did that, Delinda would probably chastise her for making a public display of herself and start another argument. It wasn't just Delinda. Lately every conversation Nicolette had with her family was stuck in some kind of dysfunctional loop.

It's me, isn't it? There is no going back. I can keep banging my head on that wall, or I can figure out what else to do.

She stumbled to her suitcase, grabbed some clothing, and made her way to the shower. When she returned to the living room, she was dressed in her normal jeans and T-shirt. The messiness of the living room disgusted her, so she threw her hair up in a ponytail and began to clean it. That was the power of Delinda. Her disapproval not only stung but lingered, changing a person's behavior. Once you saw your life through her eyes, it was impossible to go back to "good enough."

Almost thirty and I'm couch surfing like someone in college.

I couldn't afford to stay in a hotel room even if I wanted to.

She's right—is this the life I want for myself?

One phone call to Dereck Westerly would significantly change her financial situation. She'd lost count of how many times he'd offered to give her an allowance. She continued to clean as she reminded herself why that wasn't possible.

I don't want to be taken care of—like I'm a child.

Like I'm his.

Nicolette paced Kiki's immaculate apartment. She stopped in front of a mirror. Her transgressions from the night before were partially concealed by the miracle of makeup, but that didn't make Nicolette like what she saw in the mirror.

I've become the woman who leaves a wedding with a man she doesn't know and begs him to stay with her because she's afraid of being alone. A woman so pathetic and so drunk that he doesn't even want to fuck her.

That woman.

"How could anyone be expected to condone this?" Delinda's cutting remark echoed within Nicolette, filling her with the same disgust toward herself that she'd felt when she'd looked around the living room earlier.

She squared her shoulders and told herself that all she had to do was make it through the rest of the weekend. Eric and Sage had postponed their honeymoon a day so the whole family could gather at their home for brunch.

I'll apologize to everyone and just suck it up.

One more big family gathering, and I'm free.

She glanced down at her jeans. Were they suitable for brunch with this new version of her family? Probably not.

She hadn't packed anything nicer. She'd shed so much of what she owned when she started moving around.

Her credit cards were maxed out, otherwise she'd go shopping.

There'd been a time not that long ago when she would have turned to her sister, Rachelle, for advice. She might have even raided her closet, but not after last night.

I've made such a mess of everything.

Nicolette's mother had always told her that doing the right thing meant putting aside one's feelings for the greater good of the family. It was why they had gone to see Delinda even though they'd always left feeling worse for the experience. It was what kept Nicolette coming to these family events.

Now that her mother's infidelity had come to light, so much of what she'd preached sounded hypocritical. Her mother certainly hadn't let what would have been best for the family be her moral compass.

Eric had it right when he made his home an ocean away from the rest of us.

How much would he actually miss me if I skipped the brunch?

How much would anyone?

She searched her email on her phone until she found the message she'd received from a woman named Paisley Russo, who owned a bed-and-breakfast in MacAuley, Iowa. It was a small town with an uncertain future. The woman had seen an article about Nicolette's photographs being included in an exhibit in the Boston Museum of Fine Arts and had asked her if she'd photograph her town . . . help put it on the map again.

Iowa.

Nicolette needed to get away, and Iowa sounded as *away* as a person could get. The town would be the perfect place to hide. Safe. Isolated.

Paisley said people there didn't have to lock their doors. It was a place where children still rode their bikes to school, people took care of their neighbors, and strangers were potential friends. They were an open community who wanted to be known as such.

It probably wasn't the haven Paisley described, but what was the likelihood that Nicolette would run into anyone she knew there? Zero.

Nicolette laughed without humor. *A number I'm becoming familiar with.*

The email said the main income of the town had come from a factory that had closed a few years back, and now its population was dwindling. They needed to lure either a new business or more tourism into the area before the local government dissolved.

Paisley doesn't know that the only reason my photos are in a museum is because Delinda is a generous benefactor. I should tell her she reached out to the only Westerly without connections or influence.

Or I could go and use this as a fresh start. I do know how to get the press interested in a story and how to build a social media platform.

Maybe I could help that town.

Worst case? They don't pay me because they don't like my work. I don't have a lot of other options right now.

Nicolette sent a quick text to Eric that included an apology as well as a lie. She said she wished she could have made it to his house for brunch, but she had been called away early for a job.

She wrote to the woman in MacAuley to say that she would love to help the town. Despite the early hour in the US, the woman wrote back that she was thrilled and asked Nicolette when she should expect her.

Tonight, Nicolette texted.

Tonight? That's fabulous. I'll have a room made up for you. Tell me your flight information, and someone will pick you up from the airport.

Nicolette used a flight voucher to book one leaving a few hours later, then texted Kiki to thank her for letting her stay with her. She grabbed her luggage, called for a ride to the airport, and told herself she wasn't running away—she was doing what was best for everyone involved.

It wasn't until she was in the back of a car speeding toward the airport that she gave a thought to the man who had taken care of her the night before. She cringed as she remembered how he'd found her in the bathroom.

Then blushed as she relived their kisses. *I am never drinking again.*

Was he even as hot as I remember, or was I just that drunk?

She smiled with self-deprecation. *He's probably twice my age and bald. Grappa, tequila has nothing on you.*

But he sure did know how to kiss.

On the heels of that memory came the one of Rachelle finding them together, and embarrassment filled Nicolette again. *Stop.*

I want off this ride.

All of it.

Iowa, here I come.

◆ ◆ ◆

Later that day, in flight back to New York City, Bryant texted his friend and business partner Lonsdale Carver. They'd met during a robotics competition in high school and gotten such a kick out of each other's entries that they'd stayed in touch afterward.

Lon was a self-made man. He'd put himself through college and fought for everything he had. His robot designs reflected his view of life being a battleground. Want a robot that could be hit by a car, pick itself up, and make emergency self-repairs if necessary? Lon was your man.

Bryant's prototypes were more focused on improving the human condition. He'd seen up close how fragile a body could be in the end. His goal was to have a viable, affordable robotic caretaker that was strong enough to lift any body type while remaining gentle. His innovation would also create just enough AI communication skills to be a comfort to its user.

AI and robots already had a foothold in the health-care industry, but they weren't yet where Bryant imagined them going. It wasn't enough for AI to become commonplace; it needed to do so in a way that valued human dignity. Coding compassion was what Bryant was known for.

Lon: Got your notes. Sounds like the trip was worth it.

Bryant: It was. I did bring a translator, but I should have brought twenty. The meeting felt more like a conference where I was the guest speaker. They sent a crew of their top designers to meet me.

Lon: I told you that might happen. Did you at least leave with as much as you shared?

Bryant: I hope so. They're beyond us in some aspects, but we're ahead in others. Affordability will be their greatest hurdle. They want too much out of the gate. People don't mind simple in the beginning as long as it's reliable. What mattered to me was that they left knowing what I imagine will soon be possible.

Lon: You're too generous with our competitors.

Bryant: We're all going to get there, Lon. It's only a matter of time. Riku MedTech is leading the industry over there. Their caretaking robots will show up in the US market—there's no avoiding that. I can't, in good conscience, not share what I know if, by doing so, we affect the quality of care the users will receive.

Lon: Touching sentiments, but not the best way to secure our own place in the market.

Bryant: We already have more money than we know what to do with.

Lon: Speak for yourself.

Bryant: We can't take it with us. What do you want to be remembered for?

Lon: That's the point. Giving your methods away will ensure someone else will be credited for your achievements.

Bryant: I'm fine with that.

They'd had this conversation before. Conversation, not argument. They'd long ago accepted that there were some things they'd never agree on, but unlike his relationship with his father, they respected each other more for their differences. There was no better wingman.

Lon: How was the wedding?

Bryant: Interesting.

Lon: You go to a Westerly shindig, survive it, and that's all I get?

Bryant: It wasn't at all the way I imagined it.

Lon: So they welcomed you with open arms?

Bryant: Not exactly.

Lon: They threw you out.

Bryant: No, but I don't think I'll be invited back anytime soon. Alessandro had it in his head that I'd be perfect for the youngest Westerly, Nicolette.

Lon: Wtf that family hates you.

Lon wasn't wrong.

Bryant: You know how Alessandro is. He thinks everything is fixable.

Lon: Tell me you didn't fuck her.

If anyone else had asked, Bryant would have said it was none of his business. Lon was different, though. He was the closest Bryant had to family. I didn't fuck her.

Lon: Thank God. We're doing too well to invite trouble. You don't want to be the third generation that family comes for.

Bryant: I'm not my father. He tangled with them and lost. I don't care what happened before I was born. For all I know, my grandfather deserved it. God knows, my father's a dick.

Lon: Okay. So you'll be back tonight.

Bryant: Yeah.

Lon: Up for drinks?

Bryant: No. I've got a lot on my mind.

Lon: As long as it's not Nicolette Westerly.

Bryant didn't answer. He wasn't going to lie to Lon. Nicolette was exactly what he couldn't stop thinking about. He'd done the responsible thing—taken her home and left it at that. He had no doubt that Elise and Alessandro had stayed with her and that they wouldn't have let anything happen to her. They considered her family as well.

She'd be fine.

But he couldn't shake the feeling that he should have stayed. He'd slept like shit because his thoughts kept going back over everything she'd said and asking himself if he should have done more—or less.

Questions were driving him crazy, especially considering he could have had them answered by Alessandro. For all the good qualities that man had, keeping a secret wasn't one of them.

He told himself he'd stopped Alessandro from spilling the details of Nicolette's situation because he respected her privacy. The truth? That might have been part of it, but he couldn't deny that he didn't want to get pulled in deeper. Beautiful and troubled—might as well call her what she was—a successful man's Kryptonite.

Lon: Pursuing anything with her would be business suicide. I'm just throwing that out there because I like being wealthy.

His friend's seriousness belied the joke. And he was right. There were a lot of women in the world, and whatever Nicolette was dealing with, it wasn't like she was alone. Especially now that Alessandro was involved. He'd watch out for her.

Lon: Come out tonight. We'll find you someone who will wipe your little infatuation right out of your head.

Bryant: It's not like that.

Lon: Not like what?

Bryant didn't answer, because he couldn't yet articulate how he felt. Yes, the first lure of her had been purely sexual, but the reason he'd had trouble leaving her apartment had been about more than that.

Her struggle was too familiar to him for him not to want to help her.

Lon: You're scaring me, Bryant. Don't fuck with that family. With your pretty-boy looks, you can get any woman you want. You don't need this one.

Bryant tossed aside his phone. Lon was right—not about him being able to get any woman, but about the real trouble he could bring his company by involving himself in Westerly business. He took out his laptop and tried to forget the yearning he'd seen in Nicolette's eyes when she'd asked him to stay. He paused from reading an email to savor the memory of her taste, the feel of her body against his. He almost smiled as he remembered some of her snarky comments and her complete lack of guile.

How had she described herself sober? An angry bitch? Unlovable?

Was that why she was sleeping on a couch in someone's apartment on the wrong side of town?

He'd lost most of his crowd when his mother had gotten sick. Their world didn't change just because his had. They couldn't understand why he didn't want to party with them, how he could risk a falling-out with his father.

When he'd left his father's company, many he'd considered friends had stopped taking his calls. More than one had told him he'd be nothing without his father's money. Hitting rock bottom taught people a lot about both themselves and those around them.

Lon had stuck by him. He wouldn't be where he was if his friend hadn't kicked his ass out of the slump that had followed his mother's death.

Did Nicolette have someone like that in her life?

What he felt for her wasn't just sexual. Getting laid wouldn't help him forget how hurt she'd been when her sister had suggested she was an embarrassment to her family. It wouldn't stop him from wanting to tell her that she deserved to be treated better, no matter what was going on or what bombshell her family had dropped on her.

He sent a text to Alessandro to ask for her number.

He could have asked how she was, pumped Alessandro for more information about her, but he didn't. He kept his request simple and to the point, just as he intended to keep things with her.

A moment later her number was in his messages. Waiting for him.

He didn't do anything with it at first. He wanted to text what he was feeling, but they didn't know each other well enough for that.

He typed, You're not alone. But decided it was too cryptic, so he deleted it.

Putting aside his phone, he returned to reading work-related emails before picking up his phone again. He opened his messages and started a new one to her.

Hey, tiger. Hope you're having a better day. —Bryant

Chapter Four

Despite the fact that the sun was still shining, Nicolette sagged with exhaustion as she made her way through the small airport a few miles outside MacAuley. She'd made sure to hydrate on the flight, but she still had a headache. *Long day.* She blew a loose curl out of her face as she rode down an escalator to baggage claim, then straightened when she saw a very tall, heavily bearded man in a plaid shirt holding up a bright-pink sign that had her name written on it in glitter.

I like this place already.

She nodded in acknowledgment. He waved enthusiastically and smiled as if he knew her.

"It sure is nice to meet you, Miss Westerly," he said when she reached him.

"Thank you. It's great to meet you as well," she answered.

"I'm Bruce Russo, Paisley's brother. She sent me to pick you up. Let me carry your bag," he offered, slipping her carry-on off her shoulder before she even had time to formulate a response. Still smiling, he handed her the sign. "My five-year-old, Tera, made this for you. She'd be here, too, but she had chores to finish. She hasn't stopped talking about meeting you since she heard you were coming."

"Thank you. I love it. Your daughter sounds wonderful."

His smile widened. "She's a handful, but then so is her mom, and I wouldn't change a thing about either of them."

Nicolette nodded and followed him to the luggage turnstile. Where she was from, this level of warmth was reserved for friends. She wasn't sure how to respond.

As they waited for her luggage to arrive, he introduced her to some of the locals who had flown the last leg of the flight with her. There was Mia, an older woman with a friendly smile that shone first from her dark-chocolate eyes. She was fresh from Detroit, where her daughter had recently had a baby. Nicolette was treated to not only an update on how she was doing but also to several photos of the mother and child. Then there was Hayden, a young man with a classic boy-next-door face, dressed in jeans and a gray hoodie, who was going to college in Cedar Falls but had come back for the weekend to help on his family's organic farm. He missed his home but had no desire to move back after graduation. Katie and Tom, a tired yet tan young couple, had just returned from a honeymoon cruise. They loved the area and wanted to raise their children there but weren't sure if staying would be possible.

Katie said the buzz of Nicolette's arrival had reached them during their travel back. "If you can do half of what Paisley thinks you can, you'll be our hero. We took over the general store from my father a year ago. Business isn't what it used to be, because we're in a population crisis. The more people who leave, the fewer businesses can survive here, the less reason there is for anyone to move here. There was a time when we were worried we'd get too big and have all the problems of city living. Now we're worried we might disappear, right along with the value of our homes."

Nicolette felt a bit like a fraud. A hero? She was there to take photographs, maybe build a website. They were talking like she was their last chance to save the town. "I'm happy to be able to help," she said in a thick voice.

The woman turned to Bruce. "You'd better not dawdle at Paisley's, not once LeAnne hears how pretty Miss Westerly is."

Not looking worried at all, Bruce picked up Nicolette's larger bag as if it weighed nothing. "LeAnne doesn't worry about stuff like that. No offense, Miss Westerly, but I only have eyes for one woman."

"None taken. LeAnne sounds like a lucky woman." Nicolette smiled for the first time since she'd decided to come.

Bruce blushed, but not in a guilty way. He simply seemed uncomfortable with having attention focused on him. "She is. I knew she was the one for me back in sixth grade when she punched Dustin in the nose for picking on me." Nicolette's eyes must have shown her surprise that anyone would take on someone of his size. He shrugged. "I didn't sprout until high school."

Nicolette smiled again. MacAuley was a town with history, with heart. The people there seemed to know exactly who they were. They made sense like little had in a long time.

Leaving the airport was a lengthy process, as each person she'd met took the time to wish her luck and extend an invitation for her to drop by for a visit. Nicolette climbed into Bruce's truck and fastened her seat belt. The sound of country music filled the cab when he started the engine. He lowered the volume and pulled out of his parking spot. "No one really expected you to come."

"No?" His comment took Nicolette by surprise. The jovial man of earlier had been replaced by a very serious one.

"Big-city folk don't care much about what happens to towns like ours. They think going to church means we judge people, that community means we fear change. They don't know us. Everyone in this town can trace their roots to somewhere else. LeAnne and I never could afford to see much of the world, but people are people everywhere."

She'd certainly seen the truth of that in her travels. Race, language, location, and religion didn't change the fact that parents worried for their children. In every neighborhood, in every country, there were good and bad people. Kind and cruel. Poverty didn't determine the character of a person.

No matter how good of a first impression the people of MacAuley made, the same variety was there as well. *People are people.*

Nicolette respected Bruce more for being up front with her. She would give him the same courtesy. "I'm hoping I'll be able to help."

"I'm sure you will. You're already ahead of everyone else Paisley contacted. You answered her."

"She asked other people?" Nicolette felt like an idiot the moment it came out of her mouth. "Of course she did. It makes sense that she would have."

I'm here not because the town thought I was more qualified than anyone else—I'm just the only one who answered. She looked out the window, escaping temporarily into the blur of the cornstalks they passed.

Bruce cursed. "Now I've hurt your feelings. I meant that we appreciate you putting your life on hold to come out to help us."

"I didn't walk away from that much."

"Weren't you in London attending the wedding of Water Bear Man? What's it like to have a brother who is a Hollywood superhero? It must be a whole lot more exciting than anything you'll find around here."

Without looking away from the cornfields they passed, Nicolette shrugged. "My brother did just get married in London, but I couldn't scramble out of there fast enough. You know how annoying family can be."

He was quiet for a moment. "My mom always said family is a lot like the seasons. Some are more pleasant than others, but the year wouldn't be as colorful without all of them."

"Yeah, well, my mom said a lot of shit she didn't mean, too." The silence that followed Nicolette's declaration stretched on long enough to give her plenty of time to regret venting. "But yours is probably an amazing woman."

"My mother passed away when I was in high school. She was an incredible person, and I'll miss her until the day I join her."

Well, that confirms it. I'm an asshole in Boston, London, and now Iowa. "I'm sorry, Bruce." She took a deep breath. "I'm tired. Please don't listen to anything I say."

Bruce didn't respond until he parked in the gravel driveway of what looked like a residential home. It was a three-story white farmhouse set against the backdrop of overgrown fields. On the front there was a quaint covered porch with an American flag flying from one of the posts above a carved wooden sign: **PAISLEY'S B & B**.

"Miss Westerly—"

"Call me Nicolette, please."

"Nicolette, Paisley and a lot of people in this town are going to open their homes to you because they believe you're here to help. Are they wrong to? Do you intend to promote our town, or are you running away from something . . . or *someone?*"

It was a fair question. She wasn't technically *running* away, but Nicolette had absolutely come to Iowa mostly because she'd needed to get away. *If I were the person they think I am, I wouldn't be here. I would be off somewhere saving the world instead of hiding from it.*

This isn't going to work.

What did I think coming here would do? That I'd suddenly be a better version of myself? That I might actually do something right for once?

She turned to look him in the eye. "You're right. I accepted this job because I wanted to get out of London."

"You in some kind of trouble?"

"No. I'm just looking for a place to clear my head. I don't know if I have what it takes to help this town, but I'd like to try."

He rubbed his chin through his thick beard as he considered her words. "I guess that's all anyone can do."

As Nicolette slid out of the truck, her cell phone fell from her pocket and bounced on the dirt of the driveway. She picked it up and dusted it off but didn't turn it on.

Bruce stood beside her, having taken her luggage. "Did you crack the screen?"

"No, thankfully."

He looked from it to her face. "Don't you think you should turn it on? Tell your family you made it here okay?"

She tucked the phone back into her pocket. Just before she'd taken off, she'd sent a message to her mother so her family wouldn't worry, but she'd also written that she needed space. Then she'd turned off the phone. By now her messages would be full of everyone's opinions about what she'd done. She wasn't ready to justify her decision to come to Iowa yet or apologize again for leaving early. She just wanted to *breathe.* "They know where I am." *Sort of.*

Bruce didn't say more on the subject. He carried her things up the steps of the bed-and-breakfast and swung the screen door open while calling out, "Paisley."

The woman who came rushing to the door to greet them was a strawberry blonde with freckles who looked about Nicolette's age. Beautiful in a wholesome way. "Bruce, I told you to call me when you were on your way. I haven't put the meat loaf in the oven." She wiped her hand on her apron, then shook Nicolette's. "I'm horrible with time. Hope you're not too hungry. It'll be a little bit before it's ready."

"I'm fine either way," Nicolette said to be polite. She was starving.

"Well, come on in," Paisley said with a wave at the hall behind her. "You must be exhausted after flying all that way. I have a room all set up for you. It's the first one on the right at the top of the steps. Go up, relax, and I'll call you when dinner is ready."

"That sounds lovely."

A little face stuck out from behind Paisley. Her hair color and features were similar enough to Paisley that she guessed they were related. "Is that Water Bear Man's sister?"

Eric often said he couldn't escape his on-screen persona. She definitely saw what he meant. "Hello there, I'm Nicolette Westerly."

The little girl stepped closer with more confidence. "I'm going to marry your brother when I grow up."

"Oh, hon, that's so sweet, but he just got married."

"To who?" the child demanded, hands on hips.

Whom. Nicolette winced as she heard her grandmother's voice correct the child in her mind, then did her best to shake off the effect it had on her mood. "To a woman named Sage. There will even be a Mrs. Water Bear Man in his next movie."

"Is she old?"

"Pardon?"

The little girl tilted her head to one side and spoke as if she were explaining something that should have been obvious. "I still have to grow up. If she's old, she might be gone by then."

Paisley burst out laughing. "Bruce, that's your daughter."

"Your niece," Bruce countered and adjusted the bags he was holding so he could take his daughter's hand. "Tera, it's not nice to wish death on anyone."

Completely unrepentant, little Tera said, "She shouldn't have married my husband."

Paisley laughed again, and this time Nicolette joined in. Her time in MacAuley wasn't going to be boring—that much was for sure.

"Let's get you settled in," Paisley said.

Nicolette reached to take one of her bags from Bruce, but he shook his head. "You can take her, though," he said with a smile, holding out his daughter's hand.

Not expecting her to accept it, Nicolette offered her hand to the young child. Tera took it and guided her into the house, chatting as they went. "Do you think Water Bear Man will come here? Could you ask him to? Can he really fly, or is that just in the movies? If you call him, can you tell him I love him?" She stopped walking abruptly. "I don't care if his wife gets mad at me. I loved him first."

Nicolette chuckled.

"What are you laughing at?" Tera demanded.

Young pride. How could she explain how cute Tera's declaration of love was without denting it? "Sorry. I was thinking about something else."

"You're tired," Tera said in a tone her mother probably used. "Aunt Paisley told me you would be. She told me to not bother you. Am I bothering you?"

"Not at all," Nicolette said, because Tera's hadn't been a question that allowed for a negative response.

"Aunt Paisley said your sister is a princess. Does that make *you* a princess?"

"No." The last conversation she'd had with Rachelle came back to Nicolette with painful clarity. Things were getting worse between them. *I'm happy that she found love—happy that she found it with someone who fit perfectly into our family.* Rachelle was a worrier, always had been. When she worried, she hovered and came across as a little judgy.

I know she's only trying to help.

Neither of us handles conflict well.

I owe her an apology, too.

Tera studied her face. "Don't be sad. You might be old, but you could still find a prince."

In a knee-jerk reaction, Nicolette snapped, "I don't want a prince. It's not always about the prince."

Eyes wide, Tera put a hand on one hip and said, "You're cranky. You need to go to bed early."

Nicolette slapped herself in the forehead. *It's pretty bad when a five-year-old has her shit more together than I do.* She nodded. "I'll do that, thanks."

A short time later, Nicolette sat on the edge of the bed in the modest room. By Westerly standards, it wouldn't have been a suite, but Nicolette had stayed in much worse. It was clean. The bed seemed comfortable—and, hey, it wasn't a couch.

I'm already turning things around.

There was a knock on the door.

Nicolette rose to her feet and walked over to answer it.

Paisley had a tray of food. "You're welcome to eat downstairs, but I thought you might want a little downtime tonight."

After accepting the tray and placing it on the edge of her bed, Nicolette said, "Thank you so much. I'm more tired than I thought I was. I might just eat and pass out."

"You can put the tray outside your door, or leave it in your room and I'll pick it up tomorrow." Paisley lingered at the door. "There is something I thought we should discuss."

"Yes?"

"Your arrival came so quickly that we . . ." Paisley made a pained face. "We didn't cover compensation. I don't actually have any money to pay you. You're the only guest I've had in months. I should have said this up front. I know you don't need the money, but you probably expect something. If there is any way that we could consider your room and board your payment, that would be a huge relief to me."

"Room and board will be fine," Nicolette said. *I'll make it work somehow. Maybe I can go without a phone. Or find something part-time in town.*

Looking around the room, Paisley said, "I'm sure you're used to much better than this . . ."

"It's perfect, Paisley. Truly warm and welcoming."

The smile returned to Paisley's face. "Thank you. That means a lot to me. Sorry about Tera. We're all pretty sure she'll be the town administrator one day."

"I have a niece like that," Nicolette said. Spencer's adopted daughter was similarly spirited. She hadn't spent much time with her, but once she got herself back on track, she might see about changing that. No matter how things shook out, Spencer would still be her brother. "Her name is Skye."

"Will it be hard for you to be away from your family?"

Nicolette shrugged. "I don't see them much."

"Oh." Paisley looked uncertain about what to say next.

"Thank you for bringing my food up," Nicolette said.

"You're welcome." Paisley took the door handle in her hand. "There's an office downstairs that I cleared out when I heard you were coming. Consider it exclusively yours while you're here."

"I will. Thanks again."

There was an awkward pause before Paisley said, "You don't know how much it means to us that you're here. The state is considering closing our high school and busing the kids to other towns. That might not sound like the end of the world to someone who hasn't grown up here, but it's the beginning of the end of our community if it happens. If there is anything you need—anything at all—don't hesitate to ask. We don't have much, but we pull together and make amazing things happen when we have to."

Nicolette didn't doubt that for a second. Paisley also deserved the truth. "I thought this was just about taking some photos and building a website."

Paisley looked away, then back. "You're a Westerly. Just being here has people talking about MacAuley. And you must know everyone who is anyone. I can't wait to see what you can do."

"Me too," Nicolette said with a forced, bright smile.

"See you in the morning." With that, Paisley closed the door.

Returning to her spot on the bed, Nicolette picked up her phone and turned it on. The list of messages matched her expectations. Her mother said she was too old to be acting this way. Nicolette didn't bother to answer. She wouldn't write what she wanted to say—that in the race for maturity, she was still ahead. Rachelle apologized. Nicolette responded with the same. Brett offered to send her cash. She lied and said she didn't need it. Spencer offered to fly her home.

Home? Where is that? I used to know.

She thanked him for the offer and promised to visit him soon. The next message surprised her.

Hey, tiger. Hope you're having a better day. —Bryant

She almost deleted it but instead read it again—and again.
Tiger.
Not "Hey, sexy."
Or "Hey, hot mama."
Just *tiger.*
"Easy, tiger." His voice still rang clear in her memories.

She flopped back on the bed, closed her eyes, and let herself be on the balcony with him again. In the middle of what had otherwise been a disaster, there had been a sweet spot when she'd felt—happy?

The alcohol had started to sweep through her, just enough to quiet her demons and let her enjoy being a woman flirting with a handsome man. *He can't be ugly. I didn't imagine those eyes, those abs, that killer smile.*

The night might have gone very differently if her buzz had leveled off there, but she'd guzzled those drinks, and when their effects hit—they'd hit hard.

Was I really in a bathroom barefoot? Eww.

At least it wasn't a public one with stalls.

In her mind, she used Delinda's voice to mock herself. *"A lady would never lower herself to that."*

Was that the moment Bryant decided not to stick around?

I have some ego, don't I? Did I think I'd wake up and find a man like that just hanging around, making me breakfast?

She opened her eyes and read his message again. Hey, tiger. Hope you're having a better day. —Bryant

Her fingers poised over the phone screen. What do you say to a man you threw yourself at while drunk? Thanks for folding my underwear instead of taking advantage of me?

Hope you're having a better day as well?

How about: Please stop writing to me because it only reminds me of how badly I handled myself at Eric's wedding?

I didn't come to Iowa to waste my time thinking about a man who probably believes I always act that way.

Luckily, that's not something I need to feel bad about. He's not part of my life.

I don't even want to know how he got my number.

She deleted his message.

Bye, Bryant Taunton.

Trust me, I just did you a favor.

She was about to drop the phone beside her when it rang. *My mother. Great.* What was the likelihood that she would get the hint if Nicolette didn't pick up? *Zero.*

Nicolette put her on speakerphone. "Hi, Mom."

"I was worried when you didn't answer my text," her mother said.

"I didn't know what to say." That was honest enough.

"This weekend was a celebration, not a funeral. You couldn't wait one more day to start your new job? Everyone was disappointed."

"I apologized to Eric. He understood."

"Well, I don't, so explain it to me. We just went through hell with Eric. There's no shame in admitting you have a problem. That rehab in Vandorra did wonders for him."

Oh my God. "No, Mom. I don't have a drinking problem." *I only drink when I'm with my family. No family, no problem.*

"Are you behaving this way because you want to punish us? Me? Or is it a cry for attention? Is that why you hooked up with Bryant Taunton? You know your grandmother is furious that you did that. If you were trying to piss her off, you found her button."

Nicolette threw an arm over her eyes. *Breathe.* "I'm tired, Mom. Can we continue this conversation later?" *Like never?*

"What are you doing in Iowa, Nicolette?"

"A job. I told you."

"What *kind* of job?"

"Does it matter? I'm working."

"Are you lying? You're not with—him, are you? There are many things I don't side with your grandmother on, but that family is trouble. I'm sure you'll tell me you don't care, but Maddox Taunton, Bryant's father, is a horrible human being."

"According to you, isn't that everyone with money?"

"Nicolette." What else could her mother say? "You don't know the history our family has with theirs. You need to be careful around them. I don't know why Eric invited Bryant, but he was wrong to. The Tauntons would love to strike back at Delinda and your father. Ask Brett—he'll tell you that Maddox never stopped trying to make trouble for our family. I wouldn't put it past him to have Bryant use you in some sick revenge plot."

Those types of problems hadn't been a topic of discussion until recently. What happened to the mother whose greatest concern was whether Nicolette was practicing piano enough? That's the mother Nicolette missed. Not this one. And how could she worry about ancient history when the present was still in chaos? "You've been spending too much time with Delinda, Mom. You're beginning to sound like her."

"I'm worried about you. We all are. Do you want me to fly out there?"

"No," Nicolette said in a rush. "Mom, I'm fine. I'm not drinking. I'm not hanging out with a Taunton. I'm taking photographs for a website about a town. Please. I asked you for space, and that's all I need. Just time to think some things through."

"I do love you, Nicolette."

"I know you do, Mom. I love you, too. I just need time."

Nicolette hung up after promising to call soon. She lay there on her bed for a long time simply looking up at the ceiling.

What the hell was between the Westerlys and the Tauntons?

She went back over the whole night with Bryant. If he'd really wanted to get back at her family, he would have slept with her.

Or maybe he didn't sleep with me because he wanted to gain my trust so I would go along with his revenge plot.

Mwah ha-ha.

My family is fucking crazy.

◆ ◆ ◆

Back in New York, Bryant returned from a jog and took a long shower in an attempt to fill some of an evening that was dragging. When he was toweling off, his phone beeped with a message from Lon. He'd sent the view from a VIP section of this month's hottest club. The floor was full of beautiful women, but Bryant wasn't tempted.

He threw on some lounge pants, grabbed his phone and laptop, and crashed on his leather couch. Despite his productive intentions, he sat there staring at the dark screen of his computer without turning it on.

Nicolette hadn't responded to his text. She might simply not want to talk.

Or she could be upset with him.

Or having another rough day.

He needed to know, so he texted Alessandro. Anything new with Nicolette?

He prepared himself for what Alessandro would most likely say— that she was fine and out with some new guy. His phone rang.

Alessandro said, "I hate texting. So. Nicolette didn't answer you?"

"She did not."

"That's a shame. I thought the two of you had a real connection. I was hoping you'd tell me she's safe."

"Wait. Why wouldn't she be safe?"

"She was supposed to spend the day with her family but didn't show. Instead, she sent her mother a text about starting a new job and flew off to Iowa."

"Iowa? I thought she worked with international organizations to promote their causes."

"She did. So what is she doing in some small town where she knows no one?"

"Starting a job?"

"But what kind? We don't know these people. She's vulnerable right now. For all we know, she was lured out there by some wacko who's going to hold her for ransom—or worse."

The mere thought of either had Bryant's full attention. "What do you need, Alessandro?"

"Fly out there, check out the people who hired her."

"Like a background check?"

"We've done that. No, I mean look them in the eye. See what your gut says about them. I'd never forgive myself if anything happened to her."

"What are you not telling me?"

"I may have admitted to Delinda that Nicolette left the party with you. She called me, asked how her granddaughter was, and how I ended up being the one to take her home. I couldn't lie to her the way Elise did. A stretch of the truth is one thing, but she's known me too long for me to be able to sustain a lie."

"And you think that caused trouble for Nicolette?"

"I underestimated how deep this goes for Delinda. Oliver was her world. When the deal he and your grandfather entered into tanked, Oliver killed himself. Your grandfather lost a fortune; Delinda lost her husband. What others see as Delinda being overbearing, I understand as her response to fear. Oliver didn't come from money. He was thrown into the family business—sink or swim—and he sank. She blamed herself for not preparing him for the responsibility of it. She pushed her son and still pushes her grandchildren because she fears that if she doesn't, they'll fail—and she'll lose them the way she lost Oliver."

"Tough love."

"Tougher than Nicolette can handle right now. I thought if you were the one to bring a smile back to Nicolette, Delinda might see that the past should be put to rest. I'd hoped the same would be true for your father. The Westerlys and the Tauntons have both done wrong, and they've both suffered. I wanted to make things better, but I may have made them worse."

"I don't understand how I'm not the last person you think should go after Nicolette."

"Because she needs someone on her side, someone she can trust. Someone who won't leave her at the first sign of trouble. You're that kind of man."

"It sounds like what she needs is a friend."

"Then be that to her. Make sure she's in a safe place. For me."

Bryant sighed. How could he say no? "Did I mention she didn't answer my text? She might not want to see me."

"Pretend to be there on business."

"Sure, because I go to Iowa all the time. That's believable."

"If you don't want to do it, just say so," Alessandro said, and the sharpness of his tone caught Bryant's attention. Alessandro was an even-tempered, easygoing person. His patience was endless. For Alessandro to lose his cool even a little meant he really was worried.

"Of course I'll go. I don't know how I'll explain my presence there, but—"

"You'll think of something."

"Send me copies of the background checks you've had done and any info you have about anything else regarding where she went. I'll fly out first thing tomorrow."

"Thank you, Bryant. This is the right thing to do."

Is it? Bryant wasn't so sure, but that wouldn't stop him from going. Like Alessandro, he'd never forgive himself if something happened to her.

After ending the call with Alessandro, Bryant texted Lon. I won't be in the office tomorrow. I'll probably be back the day after.

Lon texted back, Everything okay?

Bryant: Yes, I need to take a quick trip to Iowa.

Iowa? Wtf? Before Bryant had a chance to answer, Lon continued on. She's in Iowa, isn't she?

Bryant: Yes. Alessandro asked me to make sure she's okay.

Lon: Why?

Bryant: He's concerned and that's enough for me.

Lon: Sure. We are so fucked.

Bryant didn't answer because he knew it didn't make sense to see Nicolette again. Lon's concerns were based on the real possibility that Delinda would try to blackball him, just as she had his father. The difference? Tech giants didn't care about what was said on the society page. They made their billions digitally and their connections very differently.

Sure, some might decide not to work with him so they could stay in Delinda's good graces, but many more would rather follow the holy dollar than be invited to a gala.

Let her come for me. She'll see what my father did—threats don't work on me.

An email came in from Alessandro that had all the information Bryant required to plan his trip. Nicolette was staying in a small bed-and-breakfast in MacAuley. A quick phone call confirmed there was a room free.

Perfect.

There was a small airport just outside town. He arranged for a pilot as well as a car and closed his laptop.

Iowa, here I come.

Chapter Five

Long after speaking to her mother, Nicolette had gone over what she'd said. One message resonated—her family was worried about her.

I'm a little worried about myself. I wouldn't have agreed to come if I'd known what they thought I'd be capable of doing. I take pictures—some would say not even that well.

What the hell do I know about promotion?

She'd considered taking Paisley aside and confessing everything. *That I came here because I was looking for a place to hide out. That I'm a big, fat fraud.*

Somewhere around midnight, she started to push back against those insecurities. *Westerly or not, I'm a reasonably intelligent person. There's no reason I can't take photos, build a website, and figure out a way to promote it. People probably do it all the time—regular people, like me.*

I'm sure I haven't pissed off everyone I know. Once I get the website up, I'll call in some favors.

I can do this.

The next morning, Nicolette showered, dressed, and set up her laptop on a rolltop wooden desk in the small first-floor office Paisley had said she could use. Paisley had left a note with the name and number of a woman who'd offered to show Nicolette around. Nicolette arranged to meet her early in the afternoon, then tucked her hair up into a loose bun that she secured with a pen, and cracked her knuckles.

Any good plan starts with gathering information.

The history of MacAuley was similar to many of the towns in the area: once booming with industry, now a shell of what it once had been. With a population of just under six hundred, it was definitely small. Still, many towns of that size were not only surviving but thriving in Iowa. Nicolette was determined to understand what they were doing that made a difference.

What would need to change for young people to decide to either stay or return?

There had once been two grocery stores, three restaurants, a bank, a movie theater, and a bar. Tourism came to this area of Iowa, but not to this town. Nicolette pored over traffic routes, travel sites—everything and anything she could find online about the area.

What did people come to Iowa looking for? How were other towns making themselves visible to tourists? Nicolette took notes on the websites she came across, looking for anything MacAuley might have in common with them. By lunchtime, she decided MacAuley wasn't known for anything and had nothing that stood out as different from anywhere else.

There must be something here that is unique.

I need to go see more of the town, meet those people Bruce said are willing to open their homes to me. That's the only way I'll find out what makes this town special.

She stood and stretched. Her stomach rumbled, reminding her that in her haste to begin, she'd forgotten to have breakfast. Although she'd heard Paisley moving about the house, she hadn't yet run into her.

As if on cue, Paisley appeared at the door with an apologetic smile. "I missed you for breakfast, and then I didn't want to disturb you. I should have asked you last night if you wanted me to bring something to your room."

"No worries. I usually skip breakfast anyway."

"Well, if you change your mind, tomorrow it's at eight a.m. downstairs, or anytime in your room if you tell me ahead of time." She snapped her fingers. "Before I forget to say it . . . you're already good luck for us. I have another guest checking in today. No one for months, and now two."

Nicolette tensed. *Please don't let it be Delinda.* "Another guest, that's great. Who is it?"

"A man from New York. I've never heard of him, but he's in the area on business, something about scoping out potential sites for his robotics company. Imagine that—imagine if we had a big business relocate to our area? That's what we need—jobs. And he's staying here. Thank God you are, too. Do you think you could schmooze him a little? I should ask Bruce to keep Tera away for a couple of days."

"No, you shouldn't. Your niece is a hoot. And I can't imagine a child could say anything that would sway a businessman one way or the other."

Paisley chewed her lip nervously. "You're right. I don't want you to think I don't adore Tera. It's just that she can be a handful. This is important."

"Be yourself, Paisley. Whoever this guy is, he puts his pants on one leg at a time just like us."

"You're so calm." The woman swallowed visibly.

"People are people, right?" Nicolette joked, and a smile returned to Paisley's face.

"I'm sure he has a Realtor to show him around the factory. All you'd have to do is make MacAuley sound like a good place. People with money listen to people with money."

"I don't—" She almost said she didn't have money, but the truth wouldn't help Paisley or her town. The Westerly name did carry some weight. Could it help MacAuley? Would using it for good be the ultimate act of hypocrisy? "I look forward to meeting him."

"He's arriving soon." Paisley was still smiling, oblivious to where Nicolette's thoughts had gone. "Our luck is finally turning around. I can feel it."

The yearning in Paisley touched Nicolette's heart. A factory opening in MacAuley would mean jobs. Jobs meant income. Income meant that people would move back to the area. It was a much more powerful solution than trying to draw the attention of a few tourists. "I was planning to meet Mrs. Nelson, but I can do that afterward. She offered me a tour. Do you think she'd like to give him one as well?"

"I'm sure she would, and that would be perfect. Oh God, look at the time. I need to finish setting up his room. And decide on dinner. I was nervous enough when it was just you." Paisley rushed over and swept Nicolette into a hug. "I've got a really good feeling about this. Thank you." With that, she bolted back into the hallway.

"I haven't done anything yet," Nicolette said to an empty office.

She headed to the kitchen and stopped. *I should have asked Paisley if she minds if I rummage through the fridge on my own.* Her stomach rumbled again. *I'm sure it'll be okay.* She made herself a sandwich and salad, poured herself a glass of water, and headed out of the kitchen with her lunch. She was standing in the hallway, debating if taking her food out onto the porch would require a light jacket or if the fall day would be warm enough for a T-shirt.

A knock at the door was followed by a ring of the doorbell. Nicolette was in the process of hunting for a place to put down her plate when Paisley sprinted by her.

"I'll get it," she said. "That must be him. Bruce was supposed to call me." She shook her head in frustration, smoothed down her apron, and squared her shoulders, then looked pointedly at Nicolette's food.

"Oh, right." Nicolette stashed her plate and glass on a table in a room just off the hall, then went to stand beside Paisley, who still hadn't opened the door. She put a hand on her arm. "It'll be fine. You have a beautiful place and a great little town. He's going to love both."

With a nod and then a brave smile, Paisley threw open the door. "Mr. Taunton, welcome to Paisley's B & B. I'm Paisley. But you probably guessed that. Did Bruce find you? Of course he did, or you wouldn't be here, would you?" She came to a nervous stop and glanced at Nicolette for support.

Unfortunately, Nicolette was still trying to come to terms with the fact that the man Paisley wanted her to schmooze was someone she thought she'd never see again—the same man her mother had warned her about.

And sober Nicolette found him just as good looking as drunk Nicolette had. Could a man be beautiful? He was, with the kind of perfect, chiseled features that any artist would appreciate. *What is he doing here?*

How did he find me?

Alessandro?

His evil, revenge-plotting father?

Nicolette shook her head at that last thought.

Whatever had brought him to MacAuley, she was pretty damn sure it hadn't been a desire to look at an abandoned factory. Even while part of her reveled in the idea that he hadn't forgotten her, another part of her resented his intrusion.

He'd lied to Paisley and built up her hopes needlessly. Now, instead of enjoying getting to see MacAuley and meeting the locals, Nicolette's day already needed damage control.

"Please, call me Bryant. And your brother very kindly offered me a ride, but I had already arranged for a car." Dressed in dark slacks and a black button-down shirt, he was an unwelcome, dangerously handsome sight. His gaze locked with Nicolette's, and for a heartbeat he looked guilty as sin before smiling like a man who was used to being easily forgiven.

Bastard. If this is some kind of game to him, he does not know who he is messing with.

"What a surprise to see you again, Bryant."

Paisley's head snapped back and forth. "You know each other?"

"We've met," Nicolette said in a tight tone.

"That's great," Paisley said with some uncertainty.

"It is." Bryant stepped into the house and placed a suitcase beside the door. "An unexpected pleasure."

"Unexpected for sure. It feels like I just saw you."

"Feels the same for me."

When Paisley closed the door, Nicolette caught a glimpse of her worried expression, and her stomach twisted painfully. Anger and frustration washed over her. *I thought you were a good guy. What are you doing here, Mr. Taunton?*

She forced a bright smile. "I was just about to have lunch. Would you like to go out somewhere, Bryant? Get something to eat in town?"

So I can get the truth.

And you can learn what I really think of your arrival.

◆　◆　◆

"Great idea. I'm starving," Bryant said, feeling pretty good about how his plan was rolling out. Like Alessandro, he wasn't a good liar and had been taken by surprise when the owner of the bed-and-breakfast had asked him what was bringing him to MacAuley. He'd said looking at local abandoned manufacturing sites just to say something, not because he had any interest in them. No harm done. People considered property all the time with no expectation of a deal coming from it.

Nothing he'd read in the background checks had raised red flags, nor had anything he'd seen on the drive in. The town appeared safe enough, if a little outdated. The same could be said for the bed-and-breakfast. Both felt stuck in an earlier time. Still, nothing to imply that Nicolette was in any danger. He wouldn't be satisfied, though, until he got a better sense of the people she'd connected with in MacAuley.

On the good side, she was taking his arrival better than he'd expected. Alessandro had said she'd turned off her phone. For all he knew, she might not have even seen his message.

"I'll take your things to your room," Paisley said.

"Oh, I can do that." Bryant bent to pick his bag back up, but Paisley snatched it from him.

"No, go and have lunch. I was just finishing up your room anyway. Everything will be all set by the time you get back."

"Thanks," Bryant said absently. His attention was riveted to the brief displeasure that crossed Nicolette's face before she smiled and waved goodbye to Paisley. Had he imagined it? He followed Nicolette down the steps, held open the car door for her, then slid into the driver's seat, buckled in, and started the engine. "So where would you like to go?"

She folded her arms across her chest. "Do I look stupid to you?"

Uh-oh. He hadn't made it to the age of thirty without learning what that tone meant. "No."

"Then let's drop the story of how meeting me here was a coincidence."

"Alessandro asked me to check in on you." Bryant braced himself for her response.

She let out a harsh sigh. "Alessandro? Why?"

"He's worried about you. When you skip out the way you did, you can't expect no one to be concerned."

She turned to look out her window, waved at Paisley, who had come out onto the porch of the B & B, and said, "Could you please drive away before she comes down to ask us if there is a problem?"

"Sure." He pulled onto the road. "I'll just pick a direction, and we can stop at the first restaurant we come across."

He glanced at her while he drove. If looks could kill, he would have been dead already.

"Just pull over. We're not actually going anywhere."

He did, then turned to face her. "You're obviously upset."

She threw a hand up. "Damn straight I am. I want to help this town. I have a plan to. You coming here is messing that up."

"I don't understand."

She pinned him with her gaze. "Tell me, are you seriously looking into purchasing property and potentially relocating some of your business here?"

Okay, this was awkward. "No."

Nicolette leaned forward and covered her face with her hands. "I knew it. I'm the opposite of a good-luck charm. I don't know if you're here because you like me, or because Alessandro really sent you, or for some other nefarious reason, and I'm not sure I care."

Bryant drummed his fingers on the steering wheel while he unpacked all she'd said. "The truth matters. At least, it should."

"Says the man who lied about why he's here."

Damn, she sliced through bull like a hot blade through butter. Another man might have found it intimidating, but Bryant liked that she didn't cut him any slack or worry about impressing him. "Nefarious? Is that the impression I left you with?"

She shook her head. "No, I don't know why I said that. I just don't understand what you're doing here or the reason for your cover story."

"Full disclosure, it all started with that red dress. I haven't been able to get you out of my head since."

She turned in her seat to face him. "Did you seriously just say you flew to Iowa because of what I wore to the wedding?"

The sizzle in the air told him he wouldn't get smacked for the truth. "It was one hell of a dress."

She choked on what he hoped was a laugh. "Well, I'm sorry to disappoint you, but it didn't even belong to me." She took in her jeans and T-shirt with a wave of her hand. "This is what I normally wear."

His grin only widened. "Not disappointed."

She folded her arms across her chest. "I don't care." The flush on her cheeks belied her words.

"While we're sharing openly, you're fucking hot when you lose your temper. I'm not suggesting you wouldn't benefit from an anger-management course, just saying it's a good look."

She frowned. "Are you *trying* to piss me off?"

No, he was trying to get her to laugh, but it was no easy feat. "Would you believe that I'm doing it with absolutely no effort?"

"You're an ass," she said, but there was something in her eyes that told him he was gaining ground.

"Maybe, but at least you don't have to wonder what I'm thinking. Whoops, there, I just pictured you naked. Now what were we talking about? Quick, before . . . Oh, damn, I just did it again. It's difficult to sit this close to you and concentrate."

A corner of her mouth twitched as if she was about to smile. "Not funny."

He was close to winning, and it had his blood pumping. "Not even a little? Oh, crap. In that one you were in the buff, but your skin was green. I must be watching too much sci-fi."

This time she did smile. "Green, huh?"

He reached out and touched her cheek gently. "You are stunning when you're angry, but when you smile—I can hardly breathe."

"Bullshit," she said, but didn't pull back from his touch.

He took her hand and laid it flat on his chest. "Feel that? It hasn't done that since high school."

"What—beat?" she asked, but her own breathing was becoming less even.

I shouldn't do this—it's not why I'm here, but she's hell on my resolve. "No, try to leap out of my chest. I knew you'd be trouble."

She pulled her hand free. "I wouldn't be if you hadn't followed me here."

"Or if you hadn't asked me on a date."

"I didn't."

There was a spark in her eyes when he riled her up and when they flirted. He was willing to do more of both if it kept the sadness from her expression. "You did ask me to lunch."

"Because I wanted to get you alone."

"Exactly."

Her bottom lip jutted out just a little, a hint of what he'd seen from drunken Nicolette, and it was adorable. "Not like that."

"Then you told me to pull over. I know this is awkward to discuss, but I don't want you to think I'm easy."

He wondered if she knew she was smiling even as she narrowed her eyes. "Your virtue is safe with me."

Time to go in for the kill. "Now, if you want to fuck *tomorrow*, I'd be fine with it."

A reluctant chuckle rang out of her. "Good to know." Then her expression sobered as she shut him out again.

A short silence followed.

Bryant spoke first. "What are you thinking?"

Alessandro's words came back to Bryant then. *"She needs someone on her side, someone she can trust."*

I want to be that person. "All joking aside, you have no reason to trust me, Nicolette, but I'm a pretty decent guy. Not perfect. My friends would tell you that I work too much, forgive too easily, and my poker face is absolute shit—but at the end of the day, they're willing to overlook all that, because when I care about something or someone, I'm all in. Right now, I don't know you very well. I have no idea what you're doing out here, but if there's a way I can help you with it, all you have to do is ask. Tell me to leave and I'll go, or let me in and watch the magic begin."

"Magic?" She withdrew behind cynicism again.

"How else would you describe the way everything changes when two people start caring about the same thing? Things start happening. Barriers fall away. More people join the cause, and suddenly the impossible is a reality. Magic."

"Is this the bullshit that usually gets you laid?"

He grinned. "Normally all I have to do is show up, but get your mind out of the gutter. I'm sharing a life philosophy with you. Good things happen when you realize you're not alone."

She turned away.

He started the engine and pulled out onto the road. "Let's get something to eat."

"You still want to go to lunch?" She gave him a confused look that was priceless.

"Don't you?"

"I don't understand what is happening here."

He wiggled his eyebrows. Her eyes narrowed. "You're looking for deeper?"

She clasped her hands on her lap. "So I'm a challenge to you?"

If she needed more, he'd give it to her. "What if I told you that I've been where you are, and I'm paying forward what someone else did for me."

She turned to look out the window. "Where I am? You don't know anything about me."

"So let's change that."

They rode for about a mile without speaking. When they came across a diner, he pulled into its parking lot. It was blue and silver with frosted glass squares in place of solid walls. Nondescript and familiar all at once. "If you want me to drive you back to the bed-and-breakfast, I will." He released his seat belt and turned toward her. "Or let's go eat, because I'd love to hear about what you're working on and anything else you want to share."

When her eyes met his again, they burned with whatever was tormenting her. "Because you want to *help* me?"

Nicolette didn't give a man an inch, but that was okay. Bryant wasn't a man who required the easier road. Life wasn't easy. It was often harshly unfair, but how a person responded to adversity spoke to their character. That belief was the cause of the rift between Bryant and his father. His father had stood by his wife during the first part of her fight with cancer, but when she'd been diagnosed as terminal, he'd retreated, claiming it was too hard to watch the woman he loved suffer and waste away.

Bryant knew the truth—the fate of the family business trumped the fate of the family.

His father's greatest achievement was the rebuilding of the Taunton fortune, but it should have been learning how to bathe his wife so Bryant and strangers wouldn't have had to. Hard to see his wife's beauty and health waste away? For Bryant, the harder-to-stomach sight for his father should have been looking at himself in the mirror.

Alessandro had asked Bryant to make sure Nicolette was safe. Bryant was there to protect her, but she was also hot as hell, and that was messing with his head.

"I never thanked you for taking me home," she said, pulling him back to the present. "That whole night wasn't one I'm particularly proud of."

"We've all been there at one time or another. As long as it doesn't hit social media, it never happened, right?"

"I like that." She smiled briefly, then was quiet for a moment. "I know I have everyone back home worried, but this was actually a good move for me. I've been traveling so much this past year and working on things that often didn't go anywhere. It was time to reassess and make some changes in my life. When I got an email from Paisley asking if I could photograph the town and build a website for them to help bring tourism here, it was something concrete I felt I could do."

"And it got you out of London."

"Yes, and mostly it got me out of London. I didn't understand how much of an impact they thought I could have until I was already here. The local government is considering closing up shop and letting MacAuley be absorbed by surrounding municipalities. That didn't sound tragic to me until I saw how much it means to Paisley and the others. I'm their Hail Mary pass. If nothing changes, this will soon be a town that used to be. I don't know if I have what it takes to make a difference here, but I'm going to try."

There was a beauty to her honest take on her motivation as well as her desire to do something good. She'd admitted that she'd chosen Iowa because she hadn't been happy where she was, but she wasn't merely hiding out. Or whining about how unfair life was. Her yearning to do better for herself included doing good for others. "That's a lot of expectations to pin on one person."

She lifted and dropped a shoulder. "I'm the only one who answered."

Humility. There was so much more to this woman than she let the world see, and he wanted to be the one she trusted with all of her. "Do you have a strategy yet?"

"If I can find something that sets the town apart, I could pitch a photo series to national magazines. Some towns in the area are part of organized wine tours that funnel the tourists through certain places. I'm hoping to create a kick-ass website, put together a media packet, and pull in favors from anyone and everyone to create buzz about the town."

"That sounds like a solid plan. Have you thought of asking your family to get involved?"

She shook her head and looked away. "No. We're not exactly on great terms right now. Hopefully time away from them will ease some of that."

She'd just said that she'd spent a lot of time traveling. Time away from a situation rarely improved it. "Then Iowa sounds like a good place for you."

"Yeah, except now I have to explain *you*."

"Because Paisley thinks I might bring business to the area." He grimaced.

"Until I tell her otherwise, you're the potential answer to her prayers."

He was in an uncomfortable spot, but one that he'd created for himself. "It was supposed to be a harmless cover story. We're not currently looking to relocate production."

Nicolette met his gaze. "I'll think of something to tell Paisley. She'll be disappointed, but you weren't part of the original plan anyway."

"I could stick around and help out."

Her hands were gripped together so tightly her knuckles were white. "No," she said firmly and without the apparent need to think it over.

Another man might have given up there, but Bryant couldn't. She might not be in physical danger, but she was suffering. "Let's go in and get something greasy and bad for us," he suggested. He opened his car door and waited for a sign that she was willing to join him.

She searched his face, then seemed to relax a little. "Okay." He rushed around the car to open her door before she had a chance to. They stood there for a moment, simply looking into each other's eyes.

She slipped her hands into her pockets and hunched her shoulders a bit. "I actually love diners," she said. "Where I grew up, there was one in an old-fashioned trolley. The line to get in was always out the door because they made the best pancakes. The menu changed every week, and I remember running up to the chalkboard to read the new options, so excited each time. Life was really simple then. I miss that."

He placed a hand on her back and guided her across the parking lot. "My mother and I would leave the city every Sunday morning and just drive around, stopping at whatever diner we came across. Those are some of my best memories with her."

Nicolette tensed beneath his hand. "She's . . . ?"

"She died years ago. I still sometimes pick up the phone to call her, then have to remind myself we don't yet have the technology to reach where she is."

"I'm sorry," Nicolette said with her heart in her eyes.

"Don't be. She was an incredible person, and I'm lucky to have had the time with her that I did."

"And your father?"

"Total dick. Still very much alive."

Her eyebrows rose, and a small smile stretched her lips. "Doesn't sound like you forgive as easily as your friends think you do."

He stopped to open the door of the diner for her. "I've forgiven him for what he did, but I can't stomach who he is. It took me a while to realize that staying angry with him was hurting me more than it was him. Now I put my energy into positive things and don't try to change what doesn't want to be changed."

A waitress came over and led them to a booth. Once seated, Nicolette picked up a laminated menu and asked, "Do you ever see your father?"

"A couple times a year."

She pursed her lips. "That's all I can handle with my family, but it wasn't always like that. We used to be so close."

"My father and I were never close, not even when we all lived in the same house. My mother was the only bond we really had."

"I'm sorry," she said softly. She fell silent for a moment. "If you're really interested, I'd like to talk to you more about what I'm planning. Your ideas on how I could improve my strategy could be helpful."

"Sounds like a great first date."

Her mouth dropped open; then she laughed. "This is not a date."

"Then I should definitely stop picturing you naked."

She laughed. "I go back and forth between wanting to thank you and smack you."

"We could try both," he joked, then shot her what he hoped was a sexy wink.

Nicolette laughed again, and her cheeks flushed.

She was 100 percent adorable and dangerously addictive.

I don't want to go back to New York. Not yet.

Come on, tiger, let me help you save this town.

Chapter Six

Maybe it was because she was so hungry, but the BLT she bit into was sheer heaven. Just the right amount of crispy bacon, perfectly toasted bread, and firm tomatoes, with a dash of mayo.

Was it her loneliness that made Bryant's company just as wonderful?

She deliberately didn't meet his gaze while they ate. He had her all tangled up inside. Her embarrassment over their first meeting still nipped at her heels, but it also felt really good to see him again.

She wanted to be angry with him. She didn't want to think about her family and the disaster she'd been at the wedding. Bryant brought that all to the forefront. He'd also set up a situation with Paisley that would either be incredibly awkward or involve lying. She didn't want either to be part of this fresh start.

She caught his eye for a moment, and her heart did a funny little skip. Was he really there simply because Alessandro had asked him to check in on her?

He didn't look like someone who was plotting against her or her family. When he'd said he didn't see his father, he'd seemed genuine enough. So he was simply a guy who cared about how she was doing, or he was a really good liar.

There was definitely a cockiness about him, but it was surprisingly sexy. He caught her watching him and smiled. He was too damn good-looking, and he knew it. She watched him take another bite of his burger. The muscles of his arm bunched, and his shoulders flexed beneath his dark shirt when he reached up to wipe the side of his perfect lips. Their eyes met, and he smiled again. This wasn't a man who stumbled over himself to impress a woman. What had he said? He simply showed up. Yes, she could see how someone like him wouldn't have to do more than that.

Not my type.

I definitely shouldn't want to lean over and lick that crumb right off his bottom lip. His tongue darted out, claiming the treat for itself, and she choked on her water. *Holy shit.*

The pretty waitress who had taken their order was back, batting her eyelashes at Bryant while asking if everything was to his liking. His? Talk about being obvious.

She obviously hasn't heard how important I am.

The waitress didn't spare Nicolette so much as a glance. *Understandable, I guess.* Men like Bryant didn't eat in diners in the middle of Iowa. They weren't in London or Boston, either. They were in movies. They modeled underwear. He was an opportunity too good to pass up.

Bryant fielded the woman's blatant adoration with a polite smile that had Nicolette's heart doing a crazy dance in her chest. He wasn't interested in the waitress.

She tempered her excitement by reminding herself why he was there. Alessandro had sent him. Okay, so he'd flirted with her, but a man like him did that as naturally as he took a breath.

She pushed her empty plate forward, took another sip of her water, then twirled the glass in her hand before finally meeting his gaze. "Thanks for lunch. This wasn't actually a bad idea."

"Easy on the compliments, or I might start to think you like me."

"I don't." She hated that her cheeks warmed. *What am I? Five? Stop being an idiot.* She took a calming breath. "But I don't dislike you."

He pounded his chest with a fist. "Words that warm my heart."

She rolled her eyes.

"Hey." He leaned forward. "So tell me about this traveling you did. You worked for Photographers Without Borders. Would I have seen any of your work?"

His question was an unwelcome splash of reality. "Probably not. Some of it went out in flyers a while back, but my most recent stuff didn't end anywhere."

"Why not?"

She shrugged, not really wanting to think about that, either.

"Tell me," he insisted.

"Has anyone ever told you that you're pushy?" She shook her head.

He glanced skyward as if taking her question seriously. "Pushy? No. Irresistible. Kissable. Seductive." Then he flashed that oh-so-perfect smile at her. "You know, all the stuff you told me I was when you were drunk."

"Grappa goggles," she joked, but she was having difficulty looking anywhere but into those beautiful blue-green eyes of his. It was too easy to imagine his strong arms lifting her so she could straddle his waist while he kissed her neck and tore at her clothing.

"Good one." His deep laugh fit perfectly with the rest of him. Of course, he would have the kind of laugh that made women turn to see if his face matched the image it projected. Strong. Young. Sure of himself.

After a moment, he said, "So why wasn't your recent work used?"

Nicolette tore her gaze away from his and took a moment before answering. She hadn't talked about it to anyone yet. The idea of spilling that story to Mr. Dreamy Eyes wasn't tempting.

Hi, during our first meeting I got shitfaced and passed out. This time, I thought it would be a nice touch to vomit my insecurities all over you and send you on your way.

That's how I roll.

Yeah, no.

"Things just didn't work out the way I thought they would."

"Are you going to tell me, or do I have to stare at you for an awkwardly long time until you crack under the pressure?"

A smile tugged at Nicolette's lips. *He's not staying. Does it really matter what he thinks of me? Coming to Iowa was about finding me again. Maybe it's time to say it out loud.*

"When I joined Photographers Without Borders, I thought I'd be doing something important. Saving the world—that kind of stuff. I had two assignments in Africa and one in South America. I saw so many people in need."

"But?"

Just say it. Let it out. "Even though I was there, they didn't let me do anything. I was really a glorified coffee maker. I found out why during my last assignment. They were drilling water wells to discourage the use of the contaminated river water. I took so many amazing photos, but not one made their website. When I asked why, my supervisor said I was only there because my grandmother had been generous with her support. However, when it came to choosing which photos to use, he needed to choose the best, and they weren't mine." Those words cut just as deeply in her memories as when she'd first heard them. "As an added kicker, he told me to relax and enjoy the fact that my photos would always make their way into museums and art exhibits regardless of my lack of talent—my grandmother would make sure of that."

"What an ass. Was that before or after you turned him down?"

"I didn't—" She thought back to the number of times he'd come to her tent to ask her a question or had requested she stop by his to pick something up. "I don't know. Nothing ever happened between us, but he may have wanted more."

"That's how it sounds."

"He was right, though. I do have photos in a museum that probably don't belong there."

"Don't let that douche squat in your headspace."

She lifted and dropped a shoulder. "He didn't say anything I didn't already know."

Bryant raised his hand for the waitress to approach. "Blueberry pie with ice cream?" he asked.

"Sure."

"Sugar makes every pity party more bearable."

"You wanted to know," Nicolette said with sarcasm.

"I did—I do." He ordered two coffees and the dessert, then turned his attention back to Nicolette. "Just calling it what it is."

She shook her head. "Thanks. I feel so much better." *What did I really think would come out of sharing that story?*

He held her gaze, and although she wanted to, she couldn't look away. "No, you don't, and you won't until you do something to prove that asshole wrong."

"Like save a dying town?" she asked just above a whisper.

"Exactly like that."

The waitress returned with the pie and two cups of coffee. After she left, Nicolette said, "I'm going to do it."

"I know you will."

Nicolette filled a teaspoon with sugar and dumped it into her coffee. "You have a lot of faith in someone you just met."

"I have good instincts."

She laughed without humor. "Really? Lucky you. Most days I can't even figure myself out."

"You don't seem that complicated to me. You don't like where you are in your life, and you're looking for a way to change that."

"It sounds a lot better when you say it than it does in here." She motioned toward her head.

"Then you need to see yourself through my eyes." He cupped her face and caressed her temple with his thumb. "Because the woman I'm looking at is incredible."

If it were possible to bottle a moment and save it forever, she would have chosen that one—the feel of his hand on her face and the overwhelming sensation of being accepted just the way she was. "I want to be the person you think I am."

His thumb came down to trace her lips. "You already are."

"I'm not." Nicolette sat back, pulling away from his touch. "Not yet." She rubbed her hands over her face. "I'm sorry. I came here to clear my head, and this is—this is nice, but—"

"But?"

There was no good way to articulate her inner panic. He was saying everything she wanted to hear, and that was part of the problem. It was too perfect. "I need—"

"Yes?"

To start making better decisions. "You to drive me back, then leave."

"Okay." He straightened, waved for the check, and paid it. His expression remained carefully blank as he stood.

She joined him. "I'm sorry." A pang of guilt held her temporarily rooted to the spot. He'd come a long way to make sure she was okay. He'd listened while she talked about a problem that didn't seem as bad now that she'd said it aloud.

Am I a fool to tell him to go? That thought was interrupted by the waitress handing Bryant a napkin with her phone number written on it. He accepted it, then stood there, looking down into Nicolette's eyes. For a moment, time stopped.

Would he pocket it?

What was he thinking?

He dropped the napkin on the table and gave her a long look. A lump rose in Nicolette's throat. *I wish I believed in happy endings.*

She turned and walked out of the diner ahead of him.

◆ ◆ ◆

Bryant started the car engine and waited. He turned with the intention of making a joke that might lighten the mood but stopped when their eyes met. There were so many layers to her, and he wanted to know all of them.

His phone beeped, but he didn't answer it.

With almost comic timing, hers announced an incoming message as well.

Then his.

And hers again.

Neither of them reached for their phones.

"Well, we're popular," she said lightly.

"So it would seem," he said. "Not curious about who is trying to contact you?"

"Not really. I have a pretty good idea of who it would be and what they'd say. I'm not ready to have those conversations."

His phone beeped again. "Me either."

Her eyes flew to his. "Who are you avoiding?"

"Someone who doesn't understand why I'm here."

"Really? That's exactly who I'm avoiding. So who thought you shouldn't come to Iowa?" He loved that he had piqued her interest.

"My business partner, Lonsdale Carver. I have a few projects on the table that I put on hold."

"To find me?"

"To see you again."

Her cheeks went the most beautiful rosy color again. She opened her mouth as if she were about to say something, then closed it again without voicing a word.

She doesn't trust me . . . yet.

He took out his phone. "I have an idea. I don't want to answer Lon. You don't want to answer whomever is writing to you. We should help each other out."

"How?"

He held out his phone. "You answer one of my messages, and I'll answer one of yours."

"No."

He shook his head in mock disappointment. "And here I thought you were so brave."

Nicolette took out her own phone and checked who had written to her. Her sudden smile became pure trouble. "Fine. Welcome to my world." She handed him her phone and held her hand out for his. "One message."

"One message."

She held up his phone, which was still dark until it recognized his face and opened. "Not worried about what I'll find on here?"

"I'm an open book." Besides, he was more curious about what was on hers. "Ready. Set. Read."

He should have known. The last message had been from her grandmother.

Delinda: We need to talk.

Following his gut, he decided to keep it simple and wrote: I love you. I'll call you later.

Nicolette's whoop stole his attention from her phone. "Sandra wants to know when you'll be in Cincinnati again. She had a filthy dream about you that she wants to act out."

This might not have been my best idea. A moment like this called for a man to either fold or go all in. "Be kind. She's always been good to me."

Nicolette frowned. Was it too much to hope she might be jealous? "You really don't care what I say to her as long as it's nice?"

Goodbye, Sandra. Cincinnati was nice, but I have a feeling I'll be moving on now.

"Relationships don't have to end ugly. I've never understood the desire to destroy someone just because things didn't work out. We've never been serious, but I wouldn't want to see her hurt."

While looking down at the phone, Nicolette said, "I feel bad now. I don't want to hurt her, either."

"Then go to the next message."

She touched the screen, then rolled her eyes. "Kim wants to know when she'll see you again. Texan nights are hot, but hotter when you're there. Seriously? Do you have a woman in every state?"

"No." Then he grinned. "There are some states I've never visited."

"That's disgusting."

"Not if you do it right. Oh, you're talking about my lack of monogamy? I never promised them more than a night of intense pleasure, and evidently, I live up to my own hype."

She lowered the phone. "So when you came over to me at the wedding, you were looking for Miss London?"

Sometimes the less a man said, the better. "Maybe you should give my phone back."

"No," she said, moving it into her other hand, the one on the far side of the car. "You said I could answer one message. You never stipulated, though, how many I could read before deciding which one to respond to."

Damn, a loophole he hadn't considered. Now that he thought about it, there wasn't anything on his phone that would improve her impression of him. He was a healthy male who had engaged in a satisfying amount of casual sex. Nicolette didn't need more confirmation that his cock worked. "Here, take your phone back."

She smiled. "Oh no. This is too much fun." She read through a few more messages; then her cheeks reddened again, and she shot a glare at him.

That's not good.

"Lon wants to know if you've gotten laid yet. Real nice." Her expression turned confused, then softened as she worked her way back through the conversation he'd had with Lon. When she finally lowered the phone, she searched his face without saying anything at first. "And he said that your father is not happy that you're with me."

Great. How does he even know I'm here? Alessandro? "My father is never happy."

"My mother was worried when she heard that we'd left the wedding together."

"Because I'm a Taunton."

Nicolette tapped her fingers on her knees. "She has this crazy idea that you'd pretend to be interested in me only to get close enough to hurt my family."

Well, no wonder she wants me to leave. "And what do you think?"

She searched his face. "I don't know." She handed his phone back to him. "I'm not a good judge of much anymore." That sad look had returned.

He had no idea how to make her smile this time. "I'm sorry to hear that."

She looked down at her phone and read the message he had written to her grandmother with a combination of confusion and irritation in her eyes. "I knew this was a bad idea. Oh my God, she'll probably come here now. We don't use the *L* word."

"Maybe you should."

"You don't understand." Nicolette's eyes narrowed. "Delinda is an emotional shark. You can't show weakness around her. As soon as you do—she'll shred you."

"And your mother is worried about me?"

She crossed her arms over her chest and challenged, "Didn't you say your father's a total dick? Maybe you should worry about your own family before you worry about mine."

So defensive. Too bad I see past that to the fear behind it. "I wasn't judging you."

The corner of her mouth curved with a hint of a smile. "I was totally judging you."

Ah, there she is. That's the snarky woman who could laugh even when she's hurting. No grappa necessary. "You're right. I don't have much of a relationship with my father anymore."

"I'm sorry."

"It is what it is."

She uncrossed her arms and leaned toward him ever so slightly. "Do you mind if I ask what happened?"

He shrugged. That time in his life wasn't something he ever spoke of. It had happened. It was done.

She touched his arm. "Are you going to tell me, or do I have to stare at you for an awkwardly long time until you crack under the pressure?"

Cute. Maybe the truth would help her trust him. "My father and I had a falling-out when my mother became very ill. Call it an irreconcilable difference of opinion." He wasn't going to say more, but she was watching him so intently he thought she might be looking for answers to her own questions in his experiences. If all it did was show her that she wasn't the only one who struggled with family issues, his story was worth sharing. "My mother was a kind, gentle soul. I don't know what she saw in my father, but she loved him. He said he felt the same, but it didn't show in the way he retreated from her when she needed him the most. That's not love—not any kind of love I want in my life."

She nodded. "That's how I feel about my mother and how she cheated on my—her first husband. She took a vow. Didn't that mean anything?"

"When did you find out about that?"

"When Delinda told Spencer that his father was the man my mother left Dereck Westerly for. Spencer's older than I am. You can imagine what my first question was."

"So is Dereck your father?"

"That's literally the billion-dollar question. Or would be if I wanted his money. My mother doesn't know. She left Dereck twice." A tear escaped and ran down her cheek. She wiped it away impatiently. "I'm a cliché. I used to sit on our porch when my father was scheduled for visitation and wait all day for him to show up. He never did. My mother would take us to see him sometimes, but I wanted him to come to me. Even though I was little, I knew what it meant that he didn't." She shook her head. "I used to have this fantasy of him driving to my mother's house and demanding to see me. Back then, I believed my mother was blocking him from visitation. The truth is, he probably didn't want to see me. He doesn't know if I'm his, either, so why should he care about me?"

"I'm sorry."

She sniffed. "No. I'm sorry. You were talking about your mother, and I went off about myself again."

"You need to let it out. Have you talked to your family about how you feel?"

"I've tried. They tell me it doesn't matter, but it matters to *me*. Mark, my mother's second husband, was a great guy. I still miss him, but he never felt like my father. In my heart, Dereck was my father even if I never saw him. What if I'm wrong and my real father died without ever knowing I was his? What if the man I thought was my father didn't come because he had no reason to?" She let out a shaky breath. "I could get a blood test and know for sure, but—I'm scared. It's not about the money. I want—"

"A dad," Bryant said in a low tone.

Her eyes flew to his. "Yes. Pathetic as that may sound, I want him to walk up that driveway and demand to see me." She wiped another tear away. "God, I'm such an idiot." Her hand curled into a fist on her lap.

He laid his hand over hers. "Then I am as well. I don't talk to my father. When we don't speak, I'm not angry. So we don't speak."

Her hand opened, and her fingers laced with his. "Well, we're quite a pair. I did run away from London. I'm not proud of that, but it's not the first bad decision I've made. I just want to do better from now on, you know? I want to like the person I see in the mirror."

"You will, Nicolette." He gave her hand a supportive squeeze.

A look came into her eyes that he couldn't resist. He tipped her chin up with his other hand and kissed her lightly, just a brush of his lips over hers, then tucked a loose tendril of hair back behind her ear.

She looked adorably dazed. "I'm meeting a retired couple on Main Street. They said they had something to show me. Would you go with me?"

"What are their names?"

"Shelby and Jackson Nelson."

The Nelsons. Everything he'd read in Alessandro's background check made them sound like nice-enough people. "I'd love to."

"This doesn't mean I've changed my mind about you staying . . ."

He started up the car. One thing at a time.

Chapter Seven

Talk about not knowing what I want—I just told him to leave, then asked him to stay, then made sure he understands he's still leaving.

Nicolette studied Bryant's profile as he drove. He glanced her way and laid a hand on her thigh in a move that may have been meant to comfort her but instead sent waves of heat rushing through her. The touch of a stranger shouldn't feel this good—this right.

He can't stay. He looked her way again, and the desire in his eyes shook her confidence in that claim. *I'm 75 percent positive he can't.*

His hand moved a little higher on her thigh. She squirmed, fighting an urge to encourage him to keep going. Memories of the kisses they'd shared the night of the wedding came flooding back. She could feel his hands moving over her, remember how good his excitement felt surging against her stomach. Her sex tightened in anticipation of his touch as she imagined his strong fingers undoing the fastening of her jeans, slipping beneath her panties and between her folds.

Oh God, he was barely touching her, and she was already on fire for him. It was crazy.

He pulled into a parking spot on Main Street. She scrambled out of the car and onto the sidewalk before he had a chance to say anything. *Pull yourself together, Nicolette.*

He was beside her in an instant, while she was still trying to shake herself free of the fantasy of the two of them rolling naked in the park behind them. Or fucking against a wall in an alley between any two buildings.

"You okay, Nicolette?" he asked.

She raised a hand and motioned like she'd gotten carsick. No way was she about to explain what she was actually suffering from. She'd never considered herself a sexually adventurous person. She normally couldn't turn off her brain enough to really let go. Thinking wasn't a problem with Bryant. All he had to do was look at her, and her body made a strong argument for acting first and thinking later. She now understood how couples might choose a stairway, hallway, closet.

It was exciting to think she was capable of that kind of abandon.

But it was equally terrifying.

Getting drunk had felt good, but she'd paid for it the next day. That was the problem with giving in to something she knew she shouldn't—there were always consequences. Always.

She took a deep breath and met his eyes. "Sorry, just got a little dizzy there for a minute."

He leaned closer with concern. "That could be something serious. Has it happened before?"

Finally, something she could be honest about. "No, this is a first." She straightened. "I'm fine, though. All I needed was some fresh air."

He didn't look as sure. "Your cheeks are flushed. Why don't I take you back—"

"No," she said firmly. "I'll feel better once we're walking around."

He looked as if he wanted to argue the point, but he didn't. When she started walking, he fell into step beside her and placed a hand on her back. It was an intimate gesture that she was getting used to from him. Slowly, gently, he was laying claim to her.

And I shouldn't be okay with it, but Lord help me, it feels good to be wanted for the person I am—not for who they think I am or for who they hope I'll become.

Just me.

As they walked, she tried to focus on why she'd come to Iowa. MacAuley was a quaint town. Both sides of the street were flanked by brick-front buildings from the 1800s. Some were still in use; others were boarded up. It had the feel of a place that had once been an important local community. Trees lined one side of the street, giving refreshing shade to those on the benches below them.

"Feeling better?" Bryant asked as they made their way down the street.

She nodded, not yet ready to talk. She was still working through her thoughts. *We are two single, consenting adults. Maybe I'm doing what my family constantly accuses me of—making a big deal out of nothing. I want him. He wants me.*

A night with him might be exactly what I need to get my mojo back. One night.

He took her by the arm, bringing her to a halt along with him. "We talked about some pretty heavy things earlier. Are you okay?"

In a move that surprised her as much as it did him, she silenced him with a body-to-body, arms-around-his-neck, close-in kiss. All the emotion of the day came out in a glorious release of passion. For just a moment, the wayward daughter who had left her brother's wedding without saying goodbye disappeared, along with the culmination of every time she'd disappointed herself or her family. Instead, she was a woman cuddled in the arms of the man she wanted—pure, primal, freeing. She dug her hands into his hair, writhed against him, and moaned with pleasure.

"Should we say something or come back?" a woman asked from beside them.

"If I go home, my ass is staying on the couch," a man answered.

Nicolette and Bryant broke off the kiss and stepped back from each other like two guilty teenagers. Bryant looked as shaken by their kiss as Nicolette felt.

They looked at the older couple, then back at each other. A slow grin spread across Bryant's face.

She forced herself to hold his gaze. Kissing him had only confused her more. *I came here to find myself, but I could lose myself in something that powerful. Then what?*

He turned to greet the couple who were still standing there. "You must be the Nelsons. My name is Bryant Taunton. I'm a friend of Miss Westerly's."

"If that's what you want to call it," the man said in a dry tone. He was well over six feet and thin, with a neatly trimmed salt-and-pepper beard.

"Jackson, stop. We were young once, too," the woman at his side said as she held out her hand for Nicolette and Bryant to shake. Her golden-brown hair was swept back in an ivory flowered headband that matched her dress. She could have stepped out of a 1950s sitcom. They both could have. "I'm Shelby, and this is my husband, Jackson."

"Nicolette. Thank you so much for coming out to meet us." She and Bryant shook their hands.

Shelby tucked herself comfortably into the circle of her husband's arm. "Paisley speaks highly of you. We hope we can be of some help today."

Bryant's hand returned to the base of Nicolette's back. She glanced up at him. There was a twinkle in his eye that hadn't been there earlier.

"They don't want a tour, Shelby."

Nicolette gave herself a mental shake. No matter where things went with Bryant, she couldn't let him distract her from the reason she'd come. She tore her attention from the man beside her to reassure the Nelsons. "I'm sorry. Please. Can we start over? I really do want to see what you have to show us."

"Me too," Bryant said with conviction.

Shelby nodded and waved a hand. "Main Street is pretty much what you see is what you get. We don't have a movie theater anymore, and the bank manager said it's only a matter of time before this branch closes. Everything is relocating to where more people live, but we still have some local shops. But if business returned to this area, the infrastructure is there for a booming Main Street."

Together, they walked down the street. Nicolette stopped in front of the large glass window of a toy store. "These are incredible. Everything looks handmade."

Jackson said, "It is. The Bakkers are third-generation Dutch American toy makers. No plastic. No computers. They make toys your grandchildren will save for their own children."

"Do you mind if I steal that quote?" Nicolette asked. "When I create a website for MacAuley, that would be the perfect way to describe the Bakkers' shop."

"Great idea." Bryant moved to stand beside her. "You don't see workmanship like that anymore." He peered closer. "And the prices are outrageously low considering the work that must have gone into making each item."

"There's no one here to buy them," Jackson said.

"There are people who would snap up their entire inventory," Bryant said.

"We just have to find them and put the Bakkers on their radar." Nicolette typed Jackson's quote into her phone as she spoke. "'Toys your grandchildren will save for their own.' That would resonate with suburbanites."

"I'd raise the prices, use organic materials, and market them to people in cities as well. With the right spin, there's no reason those toys couldn't fly off the shelves."

With a huge smile, Shelby chimed in, "They're such good people. I'd love to see that happen for them. Now, if you like handmade, you'll love Smits's furniture. The two families moved to this area around the same time and have been in a sort of quality-of-workmanship competition since. We've been spoiled by both. We grew up with toys by the Bakkers and furniture by the Smitses. You won't find better anywhere."

Nicolette took a moment to appreciate the display in the front of the furniture store as well. "They don't have a website, either?"

"Don't believe they do," Jackson said while scratching his beard. "I made one for the Bakkers a few years ago, but it never went anywhere."

Nicolette took a photo of a long wooden table. "It really is all about getting the word out. I know a lot of people who would love that table. If the Smitses want, I'll make some phone calls. I'm confident that they'd have a waiting list of clients."

Bryant leaned in and said, "You can do this."

"I can." When he looked at her like that, everything felt possible. Was this the magic he'd referred to at the diner? Two people caring about one thing . . .

Was it really that simple?

The next building was Lily's Breakfast Nook. Shelby said, "This is where you'll find the ice cream kids fly home for. Banana splits the size of your head, with every flavor you can imagine. Be careful, though— one taste and you'll wonder what every other ice cream is missing."

"Can I steal that quote as well?" Nicolette asked in excitement.

"Of course," Shelby said, looking pleased.

"You're a walking advertisement for the town," Bryant added.

Jackson hugged his wife. "Easy on the compliments. Her head needs to fit through our front door." He softened his words with a kiss to her temple.

Shelby smiled up at Jackson. "I love this town. Can't imagine living anywhere else. Love you, too, but that doesn't mean I won't clock you."

They shared a laugh.

Nicolette and Bryant did as well. The Nelsons were as easy to like as their town.

Before moving on, Nicolette scanned the restaurant's signage. "It doesn't say anything about ice cream."

"Doesn't have to. Everyone knows they sell it."

"Everyone will," Nicolette said, typing notes.

"We'd ask you to our place for coffee after this, but my daughter moved home with her husband and kids. They're only home until one of them finds a job—for now, our place is a bit of a zoo."

Jackson nodded. "*Zoo* is the right word. They brought their pets with them. Two dogs. Two guinea pigs. They had hamsters, but someone left the cage open, so I don't know if they now count as pets or pests. I'm pretty sure they have a nest under the refrigerator."

Nicolette could imagine it perfectly. "That happened when I had hamsters as a kid. By the time we found them, they'd had babies. That was how we learned that Chuck and Norris weren't both males, like the pet store had claimed."

Bryant leaned down. "Chuck and Norris?"

Nicolette smiled up at him. "I wanted to grow up to be a badass."

"Why do I find that so easy to imagine?" Bryant joked.

"Anyway, that's how we got Vin and Diesel, but we had to keep them in separate cages, because my mother said we'd surpassed her quota of rodents."

"Smart woman," Jackson grumbled.

Shelby laughed. "He's just grumpy because he's the one who bought them for our grandkids."

Jackson shrugged. "Before I knew they'd be under our roof. And don't think I haven't heard about it every day since. Those little bastards mock me from under the fridge, but wait until I catch them. We'll see who laughs last."

Shelby hugged her husband's arm. "Miss Westerly and Mr. Taunton didn't come all this way to hear about hamsters. Paisley said you might be able to bring business or tourism back to the area. How can we help?"

Nicolette put aside her insecurities and charged forward. "There are towns just like MacAuley that are doing well in Iowa. What most of them have in common is that they are known for something special. Whether it's their historical buildings or their wine, they have something that stands out. Once I discover what that is for MacAuley, I can help you build an online presence. There is a tourism stream that comes to Iowa each year—the question will be how to divert them here. What can they find in this town that isn't anywhere else?"

"I don't know if this is what you're looking for, but I have an idea," Shelby said. "It's on the other side of the park."

Jackson cocked his head to one side. "The cemetery?"

"I've never heard of one like ours," Shelby said.

Nicolette and Bryant exchanged a look. "What's different about your cemetery?" she asked.

"You have to see it to appreciate it, but it's not much farther." Shelby pointed to a place just beyond the trees. "My father used to be the groundskeeper, so I know all the stories."

"People like history. Just look at all those DNA sites," Bryant said. "And ghost tours are popular. It's worth a look."

Shelby and Jackson led them to an area closed off by low wrought iron fencing. About an acre of land was filled with neat rows of head-stones, sixty or so. The stones were faded, old but not weathered away like some of the historical sites on the East Coast. At first glance it wasn't an impressive sight—nothing that would put a town on a map.

"If this were a tour, it would have to start with the Clarks." She stopped near a headstone in the far left corner of the cemetery. "A hundred years or so ago, this land belonged to the town and was part of the park we just walked through. Mr. Clark had a falling-out with the local church because of some harsh things the priest said about a young unwed mother. Mr. Clark thought it was horrible that a mem-ber of their community would be treated to such a public humilia-tion. He and his wife took in the woman until she found a job and could support herself. She wasn't the only person the Clarks helped when the church turned their back on them. No one was too poor, too drunk, or too different for them to care about. 'People is people.' That's what Mr. Clark used to say. No one knows exactly what happened between him and the priest, but they had an awful argument. When Mr. Clark died, the church said he couldn't be buried at their cemetery. Mrs. Clark wanted to bury him on their land, but the town wouldn't allow that, either. Angry with the church and the town, she had this stone made and hired some local boys to dig a hole and put up the headstone." She laid her hand on the top of the stone as if it were an old friend and read, "'Here lies a good and humble man / Who always went to Mass / Don't like him here / You can kiss his ass.'"

"Is that really what it says?" Nicolette walked to where she could read the epitaph for herself. "Oh my God, that's awesome. I can't believe the wife wasn't forced to move him."

Shelby's eyes widened, and she became more animated. "They were going to. The town administrator said he would not only have Mr. Clark moved, but he would have whoever was responsible for the illegal burying arrested. He jailed the widow when she refused to tell him who had helped her. He had the police question everyone in town. It got really ugly. Something like that pulls townspeople together. No one would dig Mr. Clark up. The town administrator hired an outside contractor, but before the job was completed, the administrator died suddenly. He didn't have any family, which might have been for the best, because the night before he was scheduled to be buried in the church cemetery, someone stole him and buried him here—right beside Mr. Clark. The stone appeared the next day."

Bryant was standing beside the headstone Shelby pointed to. He bent to read the words engraved there: "'He lived without pity or remorse / So we buried him here of course.'" Bryant coughed on a laugh. "That's karma for you."

Shelby continued in an excited voice. "And a crime. No one knew what to do. The sheriff said he'd have both men moved out of the park, but then he fell very ill. That's when people started saying Mrs. Clark had put a curse on her husband's grave. Anyone who tried to dig him up would end up buried next to him. The sheriff said he didn't believe in curses, but he was scared. He released Mrs. Clark, made an announcement that he planned to leave the Clark grave alone, and he got better within days."

"How did it become a full cemetery?" Nicolette snapped a photo of the first two stones. Then stepped away to look at another headstone. Was it too much to hope they all told a story? The next stone read, STEVEN MILLER, 1898–1918. "This one is from during World War I."

Shelby walked over to join Nicolette. "Steven Miller. He died in Belleau Wood, France, but his family paid to have him brought home. He could have been buried in a military cemetery, but he'd told his best friend exactly what he wanted if he fell in battle and wrote his own epitaph. What could the town do—deny a hero his final request? No way. So he had the first legal burial here."

Nicolette touched the engraving on his stone as she read it aloud. "'If I fall, take me to the park / Bury me next to my first hero, Mr. Clark.'" She took a photo of that stone as well. "Do you think he was one of the ones Mrs. Clark hired to bury her husband?"

Shelby nodded. "My father thought so. Mrs. Clark was the next in town to die. Someone buried her beside her husband. No one ever admitted to it, but people had bigger worries. The war ended. Some of the boys were buried abroad. Some were never found. It was a sad time. People kind of forgot about these plots until one morning someone was walking through the park and they noticed a fresh grave with no headstone."

Bryant walked with Nicolette to the next headstone. He read it. "'Gertrude Peterson, 1896 to 1935.' That was during the Great Depression."

"Her epitaph is a meat-loaf recipe," Nicolette said in surprise.

"It sure is," Shelby responded. "The stone wasn't added until almost a month after she was buried. Her family couldn't afford a proper burial, but Gertrude was known as one of the best cooks around, and her family had her secret recipes. They say they traded one for a head-stone. It was a fair trade. Many of the local families still serve her meat loaf at the holidays."

Nicolette took a photo of the headstone. "This is fascinating."

"I'm glad you feel that way. You can sample her food at Lily's Breakfast Nook." Shelby touched the top of the stone. "Gertrude was the unwed mother Clark had helped. She had twin daughters: Lily and Lucy. They're buried here as well. Best recipe for apple-pie moonshine you'll ever find, but you have to read both stones for the complete directions."

"Moonshine? Do the locals still make that as well?" Bryant asked with a smile.

"Bet your ass we do," Shelby said proudly.

Jackson chimed in, "We'll send a bottle over to you."

"So that's it? It just became a cemetery naturally after that?" Nicolette asked.

Shelby waved a hand toward the park. "Not quite that simple. The next town administrator had a problem. He didn't want people to think they could just go around burying bodies wherever they wanted to, but he'd also heard about the curse. He tried to gift the land to the church, but they refused it. Eventually, he sold it to the Russo family for a dollar, just to get the problem off his docket. They put up the fence and had it declared the Friendship Cemetery. Paisley's grandfa-ther made three stipulations for being buried there. The person had to be from this town, they had to be buried at night in an unpublicized ceremony, and their epitaphs had to be witty."

"Makes you wonder what's in the water 'round here, doesn't it?" Jackson asked. He flashed a toothy smile. "I'm from McGregor. We didn't do shit like this."

Nicolette met Bryant's gaze. He had that look in his eyes again, the one that sent a flutter through her stomach. "Pretty interesting, right?"

"Very," he agreed.

Nicolette turned to Shelby. "Have you thought of doing a paid tour?"

Shelby shook her head. "Oh, I can't imagine charging for stories everyone has heard."

"Everyone who lives here might know them, but tourists wouldn't. This is great. It's different. It's unique. People travel to see things like this."

"You really think so?" Jackson asked, looking skeptical. "Half that shit might not even be true." Shelby smacked his arm. He shrugged. "No offense, but your father liked two things: drinking and telling tall tales."

Shelby stormed over to a headstone several aisles away. "Keep talking like that, Jackson, and this will be what I have written on your stone."

Nicolette glanced at Bryant. Jackson and Shelby made marriage look easy, but that wasn't her experience with it. Her parents had been a good example of how love could tear people apart—for decades. What little experience Nicolette had in the relationship department hadn't done much to change her opinion that happily ever after was a myth.

Jackson read the stone aloud. "'He finally found peace, and so have I.'" He smiled as he looked around. "Really nice. Hang on—as long as we're stealing quotes, I know the one that fits you." He scanned a few of the stones, then called out, "Here it is: 'Beloved wife, wish you were still here / Without you, who will bring me a beer?'"

Bryant laughed. "This needs to be a tour, and you should do it together."

Jackson strolled back to his wife and put an arm around her. "What do you think, Shel? Might be fun."

Shelby tipped her smiling face up at him. "Hon, I'd insult you for free, but if there's also money in it? I'm in."

He kissed her temple. "Such a sweet, sweet woman I married."

Nicolette snapped a few photos of the couple, wanting to capture the warmth of that moment. They turned from laughing with each other to smile at her. She told herself it was for the website, but she also wanted to hold on to the image of them looking at each other like couples should.

I want that.

She met Bryant's gaze again. *What is wrong with me? I hardly know you.* Nicolette forced herself to turn away. She snapped more photos of the cemetery. As she spun to get a new angle, she caught Bryant watching her and snapped a few photos of him. He had the same look in his eyes that he'd had the night he stepped out onto the balcony in London.

That's lust.

Don't confuse it with more.

Her body didn't care about the distinction. It hummed for him, warming as if he were already caressing it. Her lips parted when she relived the feel of his mouth claiming hers.

He winked, and she realized she'd stopped taking photos and was simply staring at him through the camera lens. She lowered the camera. Her hands were sweaty; her heart was going crazy. Holy shit, was this how it was supposed to be?

The moment was broken by the sound of Shelby's phone ringing. "Okay. Okay. Calm down. We're five minutes away. Don't touch anything." She ended the call, then took Jackson by the arm. "Don't be upset, but the kids were having guinea-pig races in your office, and one of them got wedged behind your desk."

"One of the kids or one of the guinea pigs?" Jackson asked.

"Oh my God, I didn't ask. I just assumed it was one of the guinea pigs." She waved to Nicolette and Bryant. "Call us if you have any questions or if there's anything we can do."

"We will," Nicolette said. "And thank you for meeting with us."

"Thank you," Shelby answered. "I hope it was helpful."

"What would be helpful would be if we knew who the hell is stuck behind my desk," Jackson grumbled. "Or where our daughter and her husband are."

"Oh, hush. I'll call them as you drive," Shelby said. "They probably went to the store. The kids are old enough to be home alone."

"Good luck, and nice to meet you both," Bryant called out as the couple began to walk away.

They both waved without breaking their stride. Jackson's voice carried back to them. "Tell Paisley if my grandkids broke my new computer, she's getting four new guests, pets and all."

"He doesn't mean that," Shelby added with a final wave before they both climbed into a car.

Alone with Bryant again, Nicolette didn't know what to say at first. Finally, she said, "Wasn't that amazing?"

Bryant stepped closer. "Yes, it was."

A battle raged within Nicolette. She didn't want him to leave, but she wasn't ready to ask him to stay. "Paisley will be disappointed when you leave."

"What about you?" He touched her cheek gently.

She tensed so much, she shook beneath his caress. "This is too fast for me. I'm still wrapping my head around being in Iowa and thinking I could make a difference here. I like you, but I can't figure out what you're doing here."

He pulled her gently into his arms. "Is it so hard to believe I might simply like you?"

Her mouth went dry, and she could barely breathe. "Yes."

He leaned down, the warmth of his breath a caress of its own on her cheek. "All it took was one look, and I couldn't get you out of my head. It's as simple and as complicated as that."

With her heart beating wildly in her chest, Nicolette said, "I want to believe everything you're saying, but things like this don't happen to me."

"Until now." He bent closer until his lips hovered just above hers. "My favorite word has three letters."

"I'm sure it does," Nicolette joked in a husky voice.

"*Yet*. It's a powerful word."

Mesmerized, Nicolette began to melt against him with *powerful* thoughts of throwing her arms around his neck.

"Try it," he coaxed. "Nothing like this has happened to you—yet. That one little word makes everything that might seem impossible suddenly very . . ." He brushed his lips over hers. "Very possible."

He tucked a hand behind her head and deepened the kiss. Their tongues met briefly, circling intimately before he raised his head. "So sweet," he said.

She wanted him in a way she couldn't remember ever wanting another man, but that's what scared her. She hadn't come to Iowa to hook up with someone. She'd come to work on herself, and she had a chance to do something good for the town.

Bryant was a distraction from both of those goals. She pushed out of his arms and took a step back. "I can't do this. I know I'm sending you mixed signals, and I'm sorry. It's better if you just leave."

◆ ◆ ◆

Bryant didn't call anyone on his flight back to New York. He sent Alessandro a text stating that he'd met with Nicolette and she was in no danger. Done.

He hit the gym hard that night, but it didn't help him sleep. No matter how he'd felt, leaving had been the right thing to do. She was not only attracted to him, she was also vulnerable and alone. Another man might have used that to his advantage and probably fucked her.

Sex, like success, was easier when one didn't give a shit how anyone else felt.

That wasn't who Bryant was or how he wanted to live.

As he tossed and turned that night, he went over everything she'd told him. Tortured himself with every touch, every kiss, every time she'd smiled at him. He was far from ready to give up on her, but he'd also heard her.

She had things she needed to work on before she could move forward with anything else. It's what he'd said to Alessandro—she needed a friend. He hadn't meant to kiss her, to push her for more. When he was with her, it just happened.

He finally gave up and called her.

"Hello?" She picked up on the third ring in a groggy voice that told him he'd woken her. He looked at the digital clock beside his bed. *Midnight, even with the time difference. Shit.* "You were sleeping."

"People do that at night."

She didn't sound irritated, so that was something. "How did it go with Paisley?"

"I told her you had to return to New York. She didn't ask why, and I didn't offer more than that."

"I should have spoken to her myself."

"I appreciate that you didn't. I don't want to lie to her, but I also don't want her to know that I'm not exactly the Westerly she thinks I am. She's not dumb. She knows we know each other. It's best to leave it at that."

"What are your plans for tomorrow?"

She hesitated. "You're really interested in this?"

"I am. If you want to share it with me."

That question hung in the air. He held his breath, waiting, not at all sure her answer would be the one he hoped to hear. "I do."

He closed his eyes and let her voice wash over him. She'd made plans to meet the Bakkers and the Smitses. At his prodding, she described her initial phone conversations with both and how she'd already started compiling a list of contacts she had who might be able to help her spread the word about both businesses.

She'd been right to ask him to leave. He could already hear her confidence building as she spoke about the ideas she had for the town.

"What about you?" she asked. "What are you working on? Is it something you're excited about?"

The question was one women didn't normally ask him. Now that he thought about it, he didn't share much of his personal life with them. They had fun. They went out. They fucked. They made plans to see each other again. They didn't ask him about work or how he felt about it.

"I am excited about my current project. The codes I'm writing today may become the basis for how machines care for people in the future. It's easy to write a program that allows a machine to manipulate something in its space. We're entering into an age of robotics, whether we want to or not. In our lifetimes we'll see automated health care. What will it look like? Will it be intuitive as well as prescriptive? Will it value human dignity? I'm doing what I can to make sure it will."

"Did you—did you take care of your mother when she was very ill?"

"I did, and it changed the way I look at everything. There's so much in life we can't control. I couldn't cure her. I couldn't make my father want to be at her side. But I could make sure she knew I cared, that she wasn't alone. Robots will never replace the human element, but they will be there, filling in, taking care of those who have no one. It's not possible for a robot to provide real comfort to the sick . . . yet."

"Yet. That might be my favorite word now as well."

He chuckled. "It's a good word. You've got a big day tomorrow, so I'll let you go back to sleep."

"Bryant?"

"Yes?"

"Thank you for coming to check on me. And thank you for leaving when I asked you to. I'm not used to people respecting what I say."

"You should never settle for less than that from anyone. Respect is a complicated thing. Right after my mother died, I didn't like much about myself or my life. I had ugly fights with my father, and we both said some hateful things to each other. I gave his opinion of me weight it didn't deserve. I became pretty much the person he said I was. My friends deserted me. I started drinking heavily. I didn't respect myself, and because of that I didn't get a lot of respect from anyone else. Lon explained that to me one day, but not as nicely as I'm saying it now. Don't let anyone disrespect you, Nicolette. Not your family. Not that voice in your head that wants to tell you you're not good enough. No one."

"Will you do me a favor, Bryant?"

"Anything."

"Will you call me again tomorrow night?"

He promised he would and fell asleep with a smile on his face.

Early the next day, on the way to his office, Bryant had an epiphany. Some relationships weren't fixable, but some were. When Bryant had been at his worst, Lon hadn't just told him that things could be different—he'd shown him. He dragged Bryant out of the house to meet people and essentially forced him to start making connections again.

Sometimes people needed a nudge.

He texted Alessandro again, this time asking for Delinda Westerly's phone number. He expected to field questions, but Alessandro merely sent the number. He could have flown up to Boston to meet her, but if he was right, Delinda was in need of a nudge as well.

She picked up on the first ring. "Hello?"

"Mrs. Westerly, this is Bryant Taunton."

The line was dead silent for a moment.

"To what do I owe the pleasure of your call, Mr. Taunton?"

"There is something I'd like to discuss with you. I'm free this afternoon. Are you available to fly down to New York? If so, how does three o'clock sound? We could meet at my office."

"Excuse me. I must have misheard you. Did you just suggest that I come to you?"

"I did."

She made a sound akin to a gasp. "My dear man, I would not so much as walk to my door if I knew it was a Taunton knocking at it."

"That's a shame. It'll definitely make this harder."

"Make what harder? Choose your next words carefully, Mr. Taunton. I am not a woman to be trifled with."

"Delinda. May I call you Delinda?"

"No."

Ouch. As Alessandro had said, Nicolette and Delinda were similar in ways neither of them likely saw. Both stubborn. Both proud. One would need to bend. "I believe I know how to help you mend your relationship with Nicolette. I look forward to speaking with you about my idea."

"This ridiculous conversation is over. Good day, Mr. Taunton."

He said, "I'll text you the address of my office."

"Hell would need to freeze over before—"

"See you then. Oh, and feel free to bring your fiancé. I enjoyed speaking to him at the wedding." With that, Bryant hung up and smiled.

Lon's voice broke in from the doorway. "I didn't expect to see you in the office today."

"I didn't expect to be here."

"So it didn't work out with the Westerly woman?"

"Something like that."

Dropping into a chair in front of Bryant's desk, Lon crossed his legs at his ankles. "Too bad. I know you liked her. Well, luckily you're not short on alternatives. I might take the yacht out this weekend. You in? We could head over to Bermuda. Don't you have a friend out there? Monique or something?"

"Monica."

"She was hot. Might be just the thing to cheer you up."

"Thanks, but I have something I'm working on."

"You do? What trumps Bermuda?" His eyebrows rose, then furrowed. "Not Iowa again."

Bryant shrugged. There was no reason to deny it.

Lon tapped the side of his head with one finger. "What is it about this woman?"

Drumming his fingers on the table, Bryant ignored his friend's sarcasm. "I don't know. I've never felt like this before. I can't eat. I can't sleep. I'm here, but I can't concentrate."

"Hang on. I'm ready to diagnose. You're suffering from a condition many men deal with on a regular basis—it's called, 'She said no.' You haven't encountered this before, so you don't have the antibodies to fight it, but don't worry—it's curable. You just need to fuck someone new."

"That's always your suggestion."

"It always works."

"Not for me. Not this time."

"Walk away, Bryant, while you still can."

"Too late. Her grandmother will be here this afternoon, so don't plan any meetings with me around three."

Lon sat forward. "Hang on, who will be here?"

"Delinda Westerly."

"Here. She's coming here? To our office?"

"Yes."

"Why?"

"I asked her to."

"And just like that, she agreed to fly down?"

"Not exactly."

"What did she say?"

"Something about hell freezing over first."

"Um, that's a no, man." He rolled his eyes skyward.

"She'll be here. I'm following my gut on this one. When am I ever wrong when I do that, Lon?"

"You're playing with fire, Bryant. All joking aside, you piss Grandma Westerly off, she won't hesitate to destroy you and our company. I know this Nicolette woman has you by the dick, but you're not thinking straight."

"All I'm doing is helping Nicolette reconcile with her family."

"Is this payback for that time I had your secretary move your car every day to make you doubt your sanity? Because that shit was harmless. This is serious. Are you fucking with me or having a breakdown?"

"Relax, Lon. I know what I'm doing."

"Because you're a relationship guru? How often do you speak to your own father?"

That took a little of the wind out of Bryant's sails. "This is different."

"Is it? Family sucks, Bryant. Your family. My family. *That* family for sure. If you think she doesn't like you now, wait until she finds out you're meddling in her shit. There are some things you just don't do." Lon stood.

"We'll have to agree to disagree."

"Will we?" Lon took out his phone and sent off a text. "I just asked your father if he'd meet us for dinner."

Bryant surged to his feet. "Why the hell would you do that?"

"So you can reconcile with him," Lon said, his voice thick with sarcasm. He waved a hand over his shoulder as he walked out of the office. "Not grateful? Your girlfriend, a.k.a. the woman who will probably take out a restraining order on you right before her family comes for us, won't be, either."

Chapter Eight

Nicolette and Paisley took up a booth in Lily's Breakfast Nook with two bananas buried beneath an obscene amount of ice cream and toppings. They had spent the morning together, visiting with business owners on Main Street. The toy-making Bakkers had taken careful notes as Nicolette shared the ideas she had for promoting their store. The furniture-producing Smitses had welcomed her ideas as well, but they were a laid-back clan who were quick to crack a joke. Both families seemed to adore Paisley, giving Nicolette the impression that Paisley was the main reason she was being welcomed so warmly to the town.

Although Paisley's parents were no longer living, people Nicolette met throughout the day mentioned them and the kind acts they'd done. For many of those whose children had moved away, Paisley seemed to have taken on that role. They nagged her about not going to see them enough, asked her when she was going to settle down so they could have babies to dote on . . . all the things Nicolette imagined normal families did.

That was what the town felt like to Nicolette—a family. No wonder Paisley was fighting to save it.

MacAuley was *home* to her.

Watching Paisley was a humbling experience. She'd lost both of her parents but hadn't let that break her. MacAuley was slowly being strangled by a lack of opportunity, but she didn't lose faith in it.

Nicolette remembered a time when her life had felt that unshakable. No matter how bad a day she had at school, she knew Rachelle and Spencer would have her back. A kiss on the forehead from her mother magically soothed most wounds. Her stepfather was just a man her mother had fallen in love with after divorcing her father.

How had they moved so far away from that? Was there any way back?

Nicolette looked across at Paisley. *If we're going to be friends, she deserves the truth.* "Paisley, Bryant didn't come here to check out the abandoned factory."

Without looking up, Paisley stirred two flavors together with a spoon. "I guessed that as soon as I saw the way he looked at you."

Nicolette's cheeks warmed. "I felt awful that you'd had your hopes raised like that, but I didn't know how to tell you the truth."

Paisley looked up and gave Nicolette a sad smile. "Did you break up?"

"We were never a couple." Nicolette choked on the words. She told herself she was being ridiculous. She'd made the right decision.

"Oh, but Shelby said—" Paisley stopped, covered her mouth, then smiled sheepishly. "Small town."

Wow, I guess so. "No. I hardly know him."

"Really? Because when he left, you looked . . ." Paisley's voice trailed off. "I'm sorry. It's none of my business."

Nicolette filled her mouth with enough ice cream to instantly give her a headache, groaned, rubbed her head, put her spoon down, and took a deep breath.

Paisley reminded Nicolette of the friends she'd walked away from when she'd left her hometown. She'd thought they'd changed once they found out her family was rich, but sitting with someone as genuine as Paisley made Nicolette wonder if the fault hadn't been hers.

When Spencer had first found out that Dereck wasn't his father, Nicolette had gone into an angry tailspin. She'd expected her friends to stick by her even as she'd spun out of control. *Did I drive them away because I was afraid they'd leave me, too?*

Did I do the same to Bryant?

His words from the night before came back to her. *"I didn't respect myself, and because of that, I didn't get a lot of respect from anyone else."* Bryant understood her almost better than she understood herself. *Because he's walked this path?*

He's looked in the mirror and hated the person looking back at him.

Nicolette didn't respect herself. She was untalented, scattered, self-destructive. Not good enough to be a Westerly.

She remembered a word she'd used to describe herself to Bryant—*unlovable.*

How did the voice in my head get so cruel?

Paisley was humble, but she didn't put herself down. *Maybe liking myself starts with being honest about who I am—embracing the good and the bad.* "Paisley, I'm not who you think I am."

Paisley's eyes rounded. "You're not Nicolette Westerly?"

"No, I am. I'm just not rich."

"But I thought—aren't you—how—"

"I literally have fifty dollars to my name. Well, forty after this."

Placing her spoon beside her bowl, Paisley leaned forward and lowered her voice. "I thought you were related to the Boston Westerlys. The famous ones."

"I am. I think. But maybe not. I don't know what I am anymore. It's complicated. If I misled you about my relationship with them, I was wrong."

"Are you saying you're not a photographer, either? That those weren't your photos I saw in the museum?"

"No, those were mine."

"How about the website you promised to make? Are you saying you can't do it?"

"No, I can. I do know how to build a social media platform."

Paisley tipped her head to the side. "So what's the problem?"

"I thought . . ."

With a shrug and a smile, Paisley said, "That anyone cares how much money you do or don't have? Look around. We're all just scraping by. You came, Nicolette. Yes, I asked you because I thought it might help if you were someone famous, but you're the only one who cared enough to try to help at all. That's what matters."

Nicolette sat back, feeling a weight lift. *She saw me—me—and stayed.*

Paisley, I'm going to save this town for you.

"I have so many ideas already about what we can do to bring in tourism. I'm going to start making phone calls this afternoon. Before you know it, this restaurant will be full. You may miss the peace and quiet."

"You really think so?"

"I do. If you want, I can show you how to design your own website. You'll want one for your bed-and-breakfast, too."

Paisley chewed her bottom lip. "Now that I know you're broke, I feel bad about not paying you."

"Don't. All of my gigs so far have been volunteer. I always find a way to support myself." She looked around. The old her would have waited tables and been proud of the paycheck she took home, no matter how small. Independent, determined, with a passion for capturing the essence of a moment in a photo—that's how she used to describe herself. *I'm not afraid of a hard day's work, and I love taking pictures. That's who I am.* "Do you think they need waitstaff?"

Paisley wrinkled her nose. "I know they do. You won't make much. That's why they can't keep anyone."

"I don't need much."

"Then I'll talk to Lily for you. I'm sure she'll hire you."

"There really is a Lily? I didn't think there would be. So the woman I saw in the kitchen . . ."

"Yep. Lily. I would have introduced you, but she was baking, which is why we served ourselves. Every generation of their family has had a girl so far that they named Lily, and she always took over the restaurant. Unless something changes, that will end soon, too. The youngest Lily is off at college, but she says she's not coming back. Her mother died giving birth to her. People think Iowa's greatest export is corn or pork—it's our college-educated kids. Can't blame them, I guess. They have to go where the opportunity is."

"She might change her mind when this place is booming."

Paisley's smile widened. "I hope she does."

The door opened. Bruce entered with a dark-haired woman and his daughter. Tera scooted into the seat next to Nicolette. The brunette took the open spot next to Paisley, and Bruce pulled up a chair at the end of the booth.

"Well, hello, Nicolette Westerly." Holding out a hand for a friendly shake, the woman continued, "I'm LeAnne, Bruce's wife."

"*My* mom," Tera said, thumbing her chest. "That's the important part."

A general chuckle came from more than one at the table, Nicolette included. She said, "Nice to meet you, Tera's mother."

"Nice to meet you as well," LeAnne answered. "Where's your man today? I heard he was a real looker." Bruce frowned. She kissed his cheek and added, "Not as handsome as my guy, of course."

He shrugged as if he hadn't been bothered, but pleasure lingered in his eyes.

"He left last night," Paisley said, then stopped as her eyes widened. "He came to see Nicolette, not the old factories."

"That's a shame," Bruce said.

"What an asshole," Tera said, and all adult eyes flew to her.

In a loud whisper, LeAnne said, "We don't swear, Tera."

Tera shot a conspiratorial look at Nicolette. "She means me. Dad swears all the time. You should hear him when he gets stuck behind a tractor."

Bruce smiled and wisely changed the subject. "So, Nicolette, how did you like the tour of the cemetery? The Nelsons thought you were great."

"It was amazing. That cemetery could be a real tourist draw. Iowa is considered one of those flyover states, but—"

Paisley made a disgusted sound. "I hate that term. It's right up there with the hollowed-out middle of the country. I don't go to Florida and call it the country's penis just because it looks like one." She looked at Tera. "Block your ears. I'm venting."

Tera rolled her eyes like the teenager she would one day be, and said, "See what I mean? If I said that, I'd have to go to church twice that week."

Nicolette bent down so she was eye level with the child. "You should try being raised with the grandmother I had." In a mimic of Delinda's voice, she said, "Sit up straight, Tera. A lady shouldn't have the posture of a drooping flower. Elbows off the table. We don't want people to think you've never been to a restaurant."

Tera belly-laughed.

Nicolette continued with her impression of her grandmother. "Tera, a lady's laughter is never heard across a room."

Paisley nodded at Bruce. "She sounds like Grandma Perry. Remember how she had the reflexes of a ninja if we tried to steal a snack before supper? Ouch. I can still feel the smack of her hand across the back of mine."

Bruce rubbed the back of his hand in memory but smiled. "I miss her."

"Me too," Paisley said with a sigh. "She made the best rhubarb pie."

"Did I ever meet Grandma Perry?" Tera asked her mother.

LeAnne took her daughter's hand. "She died when you were almost two, but she adored you." A memory misted her eyes. "No matter how sick she was, she wanted you on her lap when you visited. You even had this little hand move you made just for her." She held her hands out in front of her like a child begging to be picked up. "The night she passed, you stood up in your crib and made that motion in the air. I swear she visited you. Do you remember that, Bruce?"

Bruce leaned over and kissed his wife's hair. "My family always was nicer than yours."

She laughed and swatted at him. "Jerk."

Paisley chuckled, but a brief sadness flashed in her eyes. "Bruce and I lost our parents, Nicolette. Car accident. Grandma Perry took us in. We didn't make it easy for her, did we, Bruce?"

He shook his head, seeming to follow the same trail in his memories. "We sure didn't. Don't know if I ever thanked her for not giving up on us. Even at the end, I thought she couldn't die. She was larger than life." He cleared his throat. "I like to think she's watching over us. Smacking the hand of anyone who'd mess with us."

A quiet fell over the group. Nicolette realized then that she had the same view of Delinda. Even though she was in her early eighties, she was invincible. If news came that Delinda had died, Nicolette's last memory of her would be slamming a door in her face.

She remembered something else Bryant had said. After his mother died, he'd become the person his father had accused him of being.

I've said some ugly things to my family. They've said some ugly things to me. Is that how I became someone I don't recognize? Did I let what I'm afraid they think of me . . . become me?

Looking around the table, Nicolette was overcome with gratitude. She'd never been one to believe in fate, but she found herself saying, "I was meant to come here."

Tera clapped her hands. "So I can finally meet Water Bear Man."

"Oh Lord," LeAnne said with a laugh. "Here we go again. Nicolette, I tried to tell her that your brother is a huge movie star. Someone like that would never come to MacAuley."

"He would if you asked him." Tera turned pleading eyes on Nicolette.

What would the old me have said? The truth—without the shame attached to it. "I honestly don't know if he would, Tera. We're not close."

"How are you not close to *your brother*?" Tera asked, as if Nicolette had just claimed she didn't require oxygen to breathe.

LeAnne intervened. "Tera, it's none of our business."

Putting her hands on both hips, Tera countered, "It's my business. I should know what kind of family I'll be marrying into."

Bruce mussed his daughter's hair. "This is our darling at five. Will we survive her teen years?"

Paisley winked at her niece. "You just keep being you, Tera."

Tera beamed.

Would Eric come if I asked him? I won't know unless I try.

And I'm going to start making changes in my life right now, today. "I'm going to apply for a waitressing position at this restaurant," Nicolette blurted out. She held her breath and waited for how Bruce and LeAnne would respond.

Bruce frowned, then called out, "Lily! You back there?"

The woman Nicolette had gotten only a glimpse of earlier came out of the kitchen. She was older than Nicolette had expected—short of stature but muscular of build. Her short bob of curls was gray. Her apron had turned a similar gray from flour, like she'd been pulled away from baking. She smiled and said, "I'm making bread. What do you need, Bruce?"

"This is Nicolette Westerly. You know, the one Paisley asked to come and promote our town. She's looking for a job. You need a waitress?"

Lily walked closer, wiping her hands on a dishrag as she did. She looked Nicolette over with a critical eye. "You got any experience?"

"I do," Nicolette said. She'd had some sort of job for as long as she could remember.

"I thought you was rich," Lily said. "You Westerlys are always in *People* magazine."

"It's complicated, but I do need a job," Nicolette answered.

"I don't have time for complicated. I promised a batch of biscuits to the Nelsons. You want a job—you're hired. You annoy me, you're fired. Any questions?"

Nicolette pressed her lips together to hold back a smile. Was there anyone in the town she wouldn't instantly fall in love with? "Should I start tomorrow? What hours will you want me for?"

"You come when you want. I don't have time to babysit you. Are we done? Because if I burn those biscuits, I'm not going to be happy."

"Oh yes. Go. Sorry. And thank you."

Lily walked away grumbling that Nicolette was welcome.

Paisley was the first to speak after she left. "She likes you."

"I hope I don't annoy her," Nicolette joked. She looked around the mostly empty restaurant. Only two other tables were full, and one of them was cleaning off their own plates in the sink and stacking them in a dishwasher. Now that she thought about it, she remembered seeing them take their own sandwiches from beneath a glass dome on the counter. She watched a man open the register and put a few bills inside. He looked up, waved to their table, and walked out. "Is it always like that? Do people get their own food, clear their own tables, and then pay out their checks themselves?"

LeAnne nodded. "Lily's husband used to do all that, but after he died, we all just started helping out. It's not like we don't know everyone who comes in here. If you put in your order the day before, she'll have it ready for you. If you want something special, you make it yourself."

"Doesn't sound like she needs a waitress," Nicolette said. Or like any restaurant she'd ever been to. She looked around again, feeling like she might be taking advantage of Lily if she took the job. "I'm sure I can find something else."

Paisley, LeAnne, and Bruce exchanged a look. Paisley said, "Lily doesn't pay a salary. You'd work for tips only."

"Oh." Well, that would be interesting. There was only one other full table in the restaurant. It wouldn't be the most profitable gig she'd ever taken on, but even a little inflow of cash was better than nothing. "I feel better about it, then."

The door of the restaurant opened, and Paisley whistled. "Another boyfriend, Nicolette?"

Nicolette swung around. Her hand went to her chest when she recognized the tall man in a light-gray suit who started waving as soon as he spotted her. What was he doing there? "No, Jordan's a friend."

"He's cute," Paisley said in a dreamy voice.

To Nicolette he was a piece of life outside MacAuley arriving before she was ready to face it. She didn't want to start doubting herself or hear about how everyone was disappointed in her. Like a butterfly hiding in a cocoon, she wanted to transform and emerge only when she was ready.

Jordan walked over to the table; his open, friendly smile bloomed. She couldn't resent his arrival. "Hey, Nicolette."

"Hi, Jordan. Everyone, this is my brother's best friend. Jordan, this is . . ." She introduced Bruce, who stood up to shake his hand. Then LeAnne, her daughter, and finally Paisley.

Jordan pulled up a chair and planted himself beside Bruce. "So this is where you're hiding out. I went to the bed-and-breakfast first and was going to wait there, but . . ." He shrugged.

"How did you know we were here?"

"I tracked your phone," Jordan admitted with a sheepish smile.

"That's a real thing?" Paisley exclaimed. "I thought that was just in the movies."

Never one to miss a chance to share technology, Jordan whipped out his own and leaned in to show Paisley how easy it actually was. "If you have physical access to the other person's device, it's super simple. If not, it's a little trickier and a lot less legal, but I can send instant downloadable code that opens a person's phone." He handed his to Nicolette to pass on to Paisley. "Check it out. I can now track you."

Great, Jordan, creep out my new friends.

"But you don't even know my number," Paisley said.

"Don't have to. You're running apps that allow my phone to recognize, then access, yours. People don't read the fine print on most of what they download. Those apps are collecting data. All I do is tap in to the stream."

Paisley exclaimed, "That's the coolest thing I ever heard. So you're a programmer?" She handed the phone back via Nicolette.

Jordan's chest puffed with pride. "I am. Would you like to see one of my other projects?"

No, Jordan. No. "Jordan, I don't think that's a good—"

"I'd love to," Paisley said, with enough enthusiasm that there was no use trying to stop this insanity.

Jordan went to kneel in the booth behind Paisley. He nodded toward Tera. "Some aren't appropriate for all ages, but this one is." He shook his shaggy head of hair. "At least I think it is. No one is naked."

Nicolette covered her face with her hands. Things had been going too well.

"That's hilarious," Paisley said with a laugh. "And it looks like me. Do Bruce. I've always wanted to see him in a pink bikini."

Nicolette lowered her hand when Paisley burst out in another round of laughter. She turned the phone toward Tera. "That's your father, Tera, in a string bikini."

Tera laughed, too, and said, "Oh my God."

LeAnne was laughing so hard that tears were rolling down her cheeks. "This is the best app ever. How does it know you have love handles, hon?"

Bruce rolled his eyes and sucked in his gut.

Jordan went on a wordy explanation of the coding required to accurately represent a person's body. To Nicolette's surprise, Paisley seemed genuinely interested and amused.

The feeling appeared mutual. She'd never seen Jordan glow before, but as he huddled with Paisley, he did. So did she.

Huh.

With eyes huge with admiration, Paisley said, "What an amazing app. I bet it could be used in forensics as well. Or fashion. Most apps just put a person's head on someone else's body, but this would show a woman how she'd actually look in a dress. It would make online purchasing so much easier."

"Fashion." Jordan snapped his fingers in the air. "I hadn't thought of that. You're a genius."

Paisley blushed. "There aren't too many stores around here, so I buy online. I hate returning something when it doesn't fit me the way it did on the model."

"I can't imagine anything not looking good on you," Jordan said, then went deep red.

Jordan and Paisley?

Yeah, I can see it.

Tera broke in. "Are you really Water Bear Man's best friend?"

Jordan looked momentarily confused, then shook his head. "No, I'm a friend of Nicolette's other brother, Spencer."

Tera frowned. "I'm never going to meet him, am I?"

With a smile, Paisley clarified, "My niece wants to marry a superhero."

"Not any superhero—Water Bear Man."

"He's married," Jordan said.

"She's hoping to outlive his first choice," Paisley added.

Jordan chuckled and wagged a finger at Tera. "I like the way you think. Anything is possible."

Tera wagged a finger right back at him. "It's not polite to point, you know."

"Are you married?" Paisley asked, then looked mortified that she had.

Eyes glued to hers, Jordan shook his head. "Totally single."

LeAnne picked up her purse. "Tera, why don't we see if Kimmie is home? You could ride your bikes for a while."

"Kimmie went to see her grandma with her mom."

"Well, then, let's go see if any of your other friends are around." LeAnne stood. "Ready, Bruce?"

"Go on ahead. I'll be one minute," Bruce said without moving.

LeAnne waved to everyone, promised to call Paisley later, told Nicolette it was great to meet her, and led Tera out of the restaurant. Bruce cleared his throat. "Hey, Jordan?"

Jordan looked up from his conversation with Paisley. "Yes?"

"The sheriff is our second cousin. If anything ever happened to Paisley and I were to . . . let's just say . . . break every one of your bones . . . he'd help me hide your body."

Jordan nodded once.

Bruce stood, clapped Jordan on the back, and walked out without another word.

Looking embarrassed, Paisley said, "Don't listen to him. My brother's just being an idiot."

Jordan slid into the seat beside her. "No, he's being a good brother. If I had a sister, I'd like to think I'd be the same way."

Paisley batted her eyelashes at him. "Will you be in town long?"

Jordan blinked a few times. "I hadn't planned to, but I don't need to rush back."

Paisley smiled.

Jordan smiled.

Seated across from the lovebirds, Nicolette smiled, too, because she'd always hoped Jordan would find someone nice. Paisley was the kindest soul Nicolette had ever met. She felt like she should give them time alone, but first she had to ask, "Jordan, what are you doing here?"

Jordan glanced at Paisley, then at Nicolette, as if unsure if he could speak freely in front of her.

"It's okay," Nicolette said.

Jordan let out a sigh. "Your family is worried about you, and you know how they can be. I thought I should come here first and scope things out."

Nicolette sighed and slumped. "I told them I'm okay. I just need a little time on my own to think some things through."

"The whole 'Is he really my dad' thing?" he asked.

Jordan would never be accused of being subtle. "Yeah, and some other things."

"You probably don't want me to hear this," Paisley broke in gently. "Why don't I give the two of you some time to talk?"

Right then Nicolette realized she wanted Paisley to know. "No, Paisley, stay. You've been so kind to me. You have a right to know which Westerly you're dealing with—if I even am one." The last part still stung. She gave her the abbreviated version of how her family had become fragmented and the decision it had left her with. "I can't bring myself to get a blood test. Isn't that crazy? I mean, I want answers, and that's how to get them. I just haven't been able to do it yet."

"You're scared," Paisley said.

Tears filled Nicolette's eyes. "I love him. He'd probably be relieved to learn I'm not his, but as long as I don't get the blood test, there is still—"

"Hope," Paisley finished for her. She placed her hand over Nicolette's. "No wonder you needed time away to think. Your heart must be being pulled in all different directions."

Wiping the corners of her eyes, Nicolette put on her brave face. That's exactly how she felt. She used to know where her loyalty belonged, where *she* belonged. She wasn't sure of anything anymore. "It'll all work out. Coming here was a good move for me. For now, I'm going to concentrate on helping you."

Jordan's attention flew to Paisley. "You? What's wrong?"

She waved her hands and shook her head. "It's not me, it's the town." She explained the dwindling population and lack of local jobs. "I wrote to Nicolette asking if she could help get us back on the map, and she came. She's the answer to our prayers—a real miracle."

Nicolette added, "I don't know about all that, but I'm going to do everything I can." She briefly outlined her idea about using social media as well as blog posts to build interest.

"I'd like to help," Jordan said. "If that's okay with you, Nicolette. This is your project."

Round eyed, Paisley looked as if she were holding her breath.

In that moment, Jordan reminded Nicolette of the town. He was odd, but when someone needed him, he was right there stepping in and showing he cared. There was real beauty to his friendship that inspired Nicolette.

She hoped he'd never change.

MacAuley was a strange little town. They buried people at night in parks, but they also took each other in and even washed their own restaurant dishes. Community. Family.

Maybe finding her transformation wasn't something she had to do alone. "I'd love the help, Jordan. Paisley, is there room for him at your bed-and-breakfast?"

Paisley looked Jordan over and spoke with some hesitation. "It's nothing fancy. Just a few rooms in the house my grandma left me."

"Does it have internet?" Jordan asked.

"Of course," Paisley said with an easy smile.

"I'm in," Jordan declared; then his attention returned to Nicolette. "Is there a third room? Before I forget to tell you, Nicolette, your grandmother plans to fly out here. I thought you should know—in case you need to prepare yourself."

"She's coming *here*? How do you know?"

"Spencer told me he was trying to talk her out of coming, but your grandmother is a lot like you. Once she gets an idea in her head, there's no changing her mind."

"I am not like—"

"Jordan, you flew all the way out here to warn Nicolette?" Paisley spoke over Nicolette.

"She's like a sister to me," he said. "I don't have family of my own."

Paisley melted a little. "That's beautiful."

He leaned closer to her. "*You're* beautiful."

They both flushed and looked away before staring into each other's eyes once again.

Nicolette gathered up her purse. Her mood had just tanked. No need to kill theirs as well. "I'm going to walk around and take some more photos."

Neither looked up as she stood. No Laid-O-Meter was required to guess where they were headed.

"I'm sure I can find a ride back to the house if you forget me," Nicolette joked.

Nothing.

It was impossible to be upset when they both looked so smitten.

Nicolette stepped out onto Main Street and into the sunshine, letting it warm her face. For just a moment, she embraced the feeling before reality came crashing back in.

Delinda's coming here?

Shit.

Chapter Nine

At exactly two fifty-five, Bryant closed down his computer, stood, and stretched. He hadn't heard from any of the Westerlys, but he was confident Delinda would make their meeting.

She'll be here . . . if Alessandro is right about her, if she really does love her granddaughter.

Two fifty-six.

Bryant's phone beeped with a message from Lon. Is she there?

Bryant: Not yet.

Lon: You know you're delusional.

Bryant: She'll be here.

Two fifty-seven.

Two fifty-eight.

Bryant checked his phone. No messages. He opened the door and asked his secretary if anyone had called. Nothing.

Two fifty-nine.

Lon: No way. A helicopter just landed on our helipad. I'm going up to check it out.

Bryant: It's her.

A few minutes later. Lon: It's her and she has a king with her.

Grandma, I like your style.

Bryant: King Tadeas. Nice guy.

Lon: We're headed down to you. She just told me to stop texting because it's rude.

Bryant: So stop texting.

Lon: Good luck. She looks pissed, but I don't think it's at me.

The door of Bryant's office swung open. Delinda swept in on King Tadeas's arm. Her eyes narrowed as soon as they settled on Bryant.

"How kind of you to meet me at the helipad," Delinda said.

Lon lingered in the doorway. If he was worried, it was needless. Unlike how he'd felt about respecting Nicolette's privacy, Bryant had had no qualms about calling Alessandro for tips on how best to handle her grandmother.

He stepped forward to offer his hand in greeting to the king. It was the greeting Tadeas had offered him when they'd met at the wedding. "Thank you for coming."

King Tadeas shook his hand, clasping it in his. "Good to see you again, Bryant." In a low voice, he added, "Tread lightly, son."

Bryant motioned toward the seats. "Please, take a seat. Are either of you thirsty? Hungry?"

Delinda settled into a chair, chin high, hands entwined on her lap. "Don't waste our time, young man. If you have something to say, say it."

King Tadeas laid a hand over his fiancée's in support. "It's been a difficult few days. We're all understandably a little tense."

Fair enough. "I went to Iowa to see Nicolette."

"How is she?" Delinda asked in a rush before composing herself and adding more calmly, "I didn't realize you knew her that well."

"Alessandro asked me to check in on her."

With a disgusted sigh, Delinda said, "Alessandro will hear an earful from me about that, but right now, what is it you think you know that I don't?"

Bryant sat on the edge of his desk. "She loves you."

Delinda pinched the bridge of her nose as if his words had instantly given her a headache. "Tell me I didn't fly all this way for nothing."

Bracing himself with a hand on either side, he didn't let her tone deter him. "But you're not the one she needs right now."

"And you think *you* are?" Delinda asked in a tone so haughty Bryant almost smiled.

Now I get the king thing. He's probably the only man she doesn't scare the piss out of.

Besides me.

But I know this is an act. Thank you, Alessandro. So bring your best, Delinda. I'm not here to fight with you. And even if you can't see it yet, we both want the same thing.

"I'm not who she needs, either—not yet. Your son is. He needs to go to Iowa to see her."

Delinda looked close to telling Bryant that what her son did was none of his business; then her face crumpled. "She said she wants to see Dereck?"

I know I'm treading into a gray area, but she needs to know. "Nicolette said she's been waiting her whole life for him to come to her. It's why she won't get a blood test—she's afraid of losing him before she ever really had him. He needs to go to her just like any other dad would."

"Dereck loves her. He always has. No test result would ever change that," Delinda said in a thick voice, and her eyes misted.

Bryant leaned forward. "Nicolette doesn't know that. Part of her is still that little girl waiting for him on her mother's porch. If he doesn't show up this time, I don't think he'll have another chance to."

He took heart in the time Delinda paused before responding. "I was planning to go to her tomorrow. I'll make sure he's with me."

Deep breath. "He should go alone."

There goes that chin again. Damn, she's as proud and as prickly as Nicolette.

"Although I appreciate you bringing us the insight you gleaned from visiting with my granddaughter, I don't require any further advice from you regarding my family, thank you."

Go big or go home. "You do. You and Nicolette are too similar to work this out without intervention. You're both proud. Stubborn. Easily hurt. I don't know what it looks like when the two of you are together, but I'm guessing it's not pretty."

Delinda rose to her feet. "Tadeas, do you hear the way he dares to speak to me?"

Her fiancé grimaced.

She turned on him. "You agree with him?"

With a slight incline of his head, he said, "I've seen you and Nicolette attempt to connect. It is, as he said . . . not pretty."

With a huff, Delinda said, "Because she takes everything I say as a criticism."

Although Bryant hadn't seen them together, he took an educated guess and said, "And how do you take what she says?"

"If you heard her tone . . ." Her voice faded away, and she sat down again. How could people not see that Delinda's formidable days were over? Her frame was frail. The hand that came to her mouth shook slightly before she clasped it again on her lap. She was not nearly as tough as she wanted others to believe. "Am I supposed to pretend I agree with all of her choices?"

"That depends on whether or not you want to be part of her life."

A silence fell over the room.

Tadeas took Delinda's hand in his. "What is your horse in this race, Bryant?"

"I like Nicolette. I want to see her happy, and I believe that starts with Dereck." Lon's warning echoed in Bryant's mind, but this still felt right. "Then you."

She shook her head as she processed what he'd said. Looking pained by the idea, she asked, "Then *you?*"

He leaned forward and looked her directly in the eye. She wouldn't respect less than the truth. "Maybe."

A small smile lifted the corners of Delinda's mouth. "She sent you home, didn't she? A lady never makes the chase too easy for a man. Nicolette does have some of me in her."

Tadeas laughed. "These Westerly women are trouble, Bryant, but the kind of trouble that makes life worth living."

Delinda beamed. "Keep talking like that and I'll show you trouble."

"Don't make promises you're too old to keep," Tadeas teased.

With her sparkly, unexpected laugh, she transformed before his eyes into someone Bryant could like. Similar to her granddaughter, she kept the best of herself hidden.

They fit, this proud woman and her king. Tadeas stood taller when she looked at him. He was at her side, but not to control her or even necessarily to protect her. He was there because there was nowhere else he wanted to be.

Bryant understood that feeling—had from the moment he'd laid eyes on Nicolette. He knew that he belonged with her. The feeling couldn't be explained, nor could be it be ignored. It just was.

Delinda's attention returned to Bryant, and she pursed her lips. "Was this the only reason you asked me here?"

Bryant held her gaze with ease. "Yes."

"You couldn't have said all this over the phone?" she asked, watching him closely.

He shrugged. "Would you have heard me out?"

Tadeas coughed and covered his mouth as if concealing a smile.

"I never thought I would say this to a Taunton," Delinda said while holding Tadeas's hand, "but I like you, Bryant. Although I don't know what I think of the man standing in the door like a toddler avoiding bedtime. Lonsdale, did your mother never teach you that it's rude to eavesdrop?"

"My mother was a prostitute," Lon said without missing a beat.

Delinda opened her mouth to say something, closed it, pursed her lips, then said, "Well, it's never too late to learn good manners. Come in or step away."

Lon stepped inside like a man walking to his own slaughter. Did Delinda even see how she made people feel inferior? Was he wrong to encourage Nicolette to let such a woman back into her life?

An emotional shark who circled, waiting for a sign of weakness.

Lon was a badass. Always had been, always would be. Why would such a man find it difficult to look Delinda in the eye?

The answer came to him in a blast of clarity. The one time Lon had described his deceased mother, he'd been drunk and had said he'd been raised by a string of strangers his mother had shacked up with. He'd never known his father.

Lon thinks she is better than he is—that he deserves whatever criticism she doles out. Just as Nicolette does. Just as I once did with my father.

"Delinda," Bryant said with a clap of his hands, "I have an idea."

"Is it really as exciting as all that?" Delinda asked.

"It is," Bryant assured her. "I know how to help you now."

"Excuse me?" Up went the older woman's chin.

"Don't go getting all defensive—I'm on your side. Look at Lon's face. Now, you don't know my business partner, but I've never seen that expression on him."

Lon's hands cut through the air. "I'm outta here. Bryant, we'll regroup tomorrow."

"Wait," Bryant said, halting Lon before he reached the door. "Please."

Tight faced, Lon sat down. "This had better be important."

Bryant sat in the chair beside him. "It is, trust me."

"Only for you," his partner said with frost in his tone, but it was an endorsement Bryant didn't take lightly.

"Delinda, you love Nicolette, but she doesn't feel it when you talk to her. I propose you practice on Lon before you go see her."

Delinda turned to Tadeas. "I was mistaken. This is ludicrous. We shouldn't have come."

He folded his arms across his chest. "We should hear him out."

"I don't have time for games—"

Bryant spoke over Delinda. "It's not a game. More like a crash course in how to speak to certain people—to Nicolette."

Delinda rose to her feet. "This is not only a waste of time, but also insulting. Tadeas, I'm disappointed that you don't see that, but—"

"If you run away, how do you expect to convince Nicolette she shouldn't?" Bryant asked. "Lon is cursing me out in his head right now, but he's still here. He knows I have his back, as I know he has mine. That's what Nicolette needs with you. But to get there, you have to change how you talk to her."

His friend shook his head. "He's disgustingly optimistic, but I wouldn't be where I am without him."

"Nor would I," Bryant said. "That's the point. Lon is a brilliant, successful businessman with a heart of gold. And, believe it or not, Delinda, he wants you to approve of him."

"I do not," Lon said in a breath.

"Just like Nicolette does. Talk to him. Say something nice. Make your mistakes with him, not her." Bryant smiled. *This is genius.*

"No way." Lon stood. "If you think I'm going to sit here while she insults me as a stand-in for some woman who isn't even your girlfriend, you invited the wrong person to your therapy session."

"She won't insult you," Bryant said. "That's the point."

The look Lon gave Delinda hinted at a deep pain. "You don't even know me, but you think you do. Well, guess what? I don't give a flying fuck what you think of me."

Tadeas rose to his feet. "That's enough, son."

"Yes, it is." Delinda stood as well. Bryant tensed. He hoped he wasn't wrong about her.

Lon remained where he was, glaring down at the tiny woman as she approached him.

She held out her hand.

He appealed to Bryant.

Bryant shrugged. He had no idea where Delinda was headed.

Expression unchanged, Lon enveloped her hand in his scarred one.

Delinda gave it a visible squeeze. "Don't go. I'm a work in progress. You don't get to my age without making a good amount of mistakes, and I've made more than my share. I'm learning to be softer, less controlling. If I said something that offended you, I apologize. Let's start over, shall we?"

Lon's expression remained skeptical. "Sure."

"Stay and we'll have a chat?" She flashed him a bright smile.

His eyebrows rose, and he disentangled his hand from hers. "I have a meeting in five."

With a frown, Delinda turned to Bryant, who motioned for her to take it down a notch.

"I'm grateful for whatever time you have," she said, making her way back to her seat. She patted the chair Tadeas had vacated. "Be a dear and come sit beside me."

As he walked by, Lon mouthed to Bryant, *You owe me*, then sat next to her.

Feeling a bit like a referee, he said, "Delinda, Lon won't tell you if you make him uncomfortable. He'll hold it in until he can't anymore; then he'll start swearing and storm out. Your goal is for that not to happen."

Lon rolled his eyes heavenward. Delinda did the same. Could they do this? Yes—if they could get past the walls they both protected themselves with. "Now—"

"I do not require coaching to be cordial," she snapped.

"Not cordial—warm, supportive. Imagine it's Nicolette sitting here. What would you say to her?"

Neither Delinda nor Lon spoke for long enough that Bryant was beginning to think he'd misjudged both of them. Maybe Lon couldn't see past the first impression Delinda gave. Maybe she could acknowledge her behavior but couldn't control it. Or neither had any desire to.

The king came to stand beside Bryant in silent and welcome support. It wasn't that Bryant couldn't see that sometimes situations were unfixable. His mother's condition had been long and undeniable proof of that. But the only way any of her pain and death made sense was if she—he—everyone was part of a greater design. He didn't believe he could change the world, but he could make his small corner of it better. That had to be what life was about.

Watching Lon and Delinda sit in prolonged silence was enough to shake Bryant's optimism. Lon had made a good point—Bryant had issues with his own father. Was it blind arrogance to believe he could heal anyone else's relationship?

Sometimes no matter how hard you try, you lose.

He was preparing to release his two unwilling experiment participants when Lon let out a sigh and flexed his shoulders. "I'm going to need a safe word. I don't want to lose my shit on a little old lady."

The "little old lady's" eyes widened. "Safe word? Like in those naughty books?"

Bryant held in a laugh. It wasn't easy. Harder still when he met Tadeas's identical expression.

"No," Lon said; then he almost smiled. "Okay, maybe a little like that. I'll let you practice not insulting me if you stop when I say the word *watermelon.*"

Delinda folded her hands on her lap. She opened her mouth to say something, seemed to think better of it, and closed her mouth again. She raised a hand as a thought came to her, then lowered it again.

"You can do it, Delinda," Bryant said.

"I don't recall ever giving you permission to use my first name," she snapped at Bryant.

She hadn't, which was exactly why he'd done it.

He was beginning to understand her. *She needs more support or she's going to lose it.* Bryant moved to sit on the arm of her chair and put his along the back of it. "You're overthinking this. Ask Lon how his day is going."

"Tadeas," Delinda implored but received no support. "Lon, how is your day going?"

"Horrible. I'm still hungover from last night," he answered without missing a beat.

She blinked slowly before answering. "Well, that's not—" She stopped. "I hope you at least—" She stopped again. She turned to Bryant. "I can't look him in the eye and pretend to condone that behavior."

Tadeas took the chair across from her. "I see what Bryant is trying to do. Delinda, you and I have lived with the pressure of constant scrutiny. We want the ones we love to avoid the same mistakes we made because we don't want them to be hurt as we have been. This isn't about lying. If anything, it's about being more honest."

She let out a delicate sigh. "Lon, you're important to me. When you talk about drinking, I can't help but worry about you, but that doesn't mean you can't tell me about your life. I want to hear about it. Are you currently seeing anyone?"

"No one person. I prefer threesomes. It keeps things less complicated and clear that I'm not looking for anything serious."

Bryant coughed back a laugh. Talking to Nicolette would be a breeze after this.

Tadeas also made a strangled, amused sound.

Delinda's chin rose, and she steepled her fingers. "I love your shoes. Italian?"

Lon smiled. "Yes. Good shoes are something I could never afford as a child. They are the one luxury I now couldn't imagine going without."

"I completely understand that. I must tell you that I was relieved when my doctor recommended I start wearing flats. High heels are torture devices that I now gladly leave to the next generation."

Lon expression relaxed. "So how many grandchildren do you have?"

Delinda puffed with pride. "Five—well, five originally. Most are married now and having children of their own. I'm so proud of them. They are all different but gifted in their own way." She paused. "Do you have grandparents?"

"No," Lon answered abruptly. "I don't have any family, at least none I know of."

"You have Bryant," Delinda said in a sincere tone. "I have a dear friend, Alessandro, who has taught me a lot about family. He has a flexible definition of it that I wholeheartedly agree with now. At the end of the day, family is more of a choice than something that happens by chance."

Bryant and Lon shared a brief look. *Yep. We're family.* It didn't need to be said.

"How am I doing?" Delinda asked, as if she genuinely wanted to know.

"Not bad," Lon said. "I guess old dogs can be taught new tricks."

Delinda gasped and straightened, looking as if she were about to say something scathing. Instead, she folded her hands again and smirked. "Watermelon."

One by one, they broke out laughing.

Who knew Delinda had a sense of humor? Alessandro had. It was reassuring to see the side of Delinda he had assured Bryant was there.

Satisfied, Bryant said, "Delinda, I do believe you're ready."

Still smiling, Lon stood. "That sounds like my cue to go. Good luck, Mrs. Westerly. I hope everything works out for you."

"Please, call me Delinda," she said as Tadeas helped her to her feet. She walked over to Lon and laid a hand on his arm. "I would love to have you visit my home near Boston. Something tells me we could be great friends. There is nothing quite like Thanksgiving in New England with a view of the Atlantic as a backdrop."

Lon gave her hand a pat. "If Bryant and Nicolette ever get together, I might take you up on that."

With a shake of her head, Delinda said, "Oh, don't hinge your acceptance on that. I heard Jordan Cohen flew out to see Nicolette today. She once asked him to marry her, so it might already be too late."

Wait? What?

Bryant's gut twisted. "They're only friends."

Lon shrugged. "It often starts that way."

In a suspiciously innocent tone, Delinda added, "My source said he's even staying at the same bed-and-breakfast."

Bryant tried to play it cool, then growled, "I have to go." He stormed out to inform his secretary to once again clear his schedule for the week.

He was a patient man—but no way in hell was he going to sit back while another man swooped in.

No way in hell.

Chapter Ten

Nicolette was sitting on a porch swing at the bed-and-breakfast as evening fell, typing in notes from the day. Paisley and Jordan had driven her back, then gone out. She hadn't heard from either since, but she was happy for them. Jordan deserved someone who got his jokes, and Paisley had found a person with the same loyal heart she had. Nicolette hoped things worked out for them.

Nicolette had made good use of her time alone. She'd called everyone she thought might know someone with social media influence. Bloggers. Fellow photographers. YouTube influencers. Photojournalists in the travel field. She was surprised at how much she enjoyed reconnecting with old friends. After an awkward moment or two, it was as if no time had passed at all. Nicolette was confident that not only would she be able to create a buzz about MacAuley, but that by doing so, she was starting to build the life she wanted for herself.

Before Iowa, I would have given up in those first two minutes and thought there was no way back. Before Bryant, I didn't understand the power of yet. Believing that a positive outcome is possible changes everything.

I really can do this.

She compiled a list of websites that promoted attractions in Iowa and cross-referenced the descriptions with attractions that seemed to bring in the most tourists. She used that information to tweak what she planned to write about each photo. Some of the sites had newsletters. She signed up for them so she'd have a better idea of how to create her own.

There was a lot to learn about: affiliate links, referral bounties, kickbacks. The more she read, the more she learned that her content needed to appeal not only to tourists but also to those who catered to certain interest groups. There were regional tours that concentrated on historical buildings, food and wine, supernatural activity, even quilting, and there were ways to encourage them to want to post about MacAuley.

She designed tantalizing bread crumbs to sites to guide users to specific offerings on the town website. Whatever people were seeking, they could find it in MacAuley. All that and ice cream so good it was worth coming home for.

Or something like that.

The crunch of car tires pulling up the driveway caught her attention. She didn't recognize the dark sedan. She stood and placed her laptop on the table beside the swing.

She recognized the driver, though: *Bryant.*

He slammed his door and took the steps up the porch two at a time. "Nicolette." He stood over her with fire in his eyes that sent a wave of excitement through her. His gaze caressed her from head to toe, leaving her nearly breathless.

Her mouth went dry. Her stomach fluttered. "I thought you were back in New York."

"I was." He stepped closer. "But I left something important here."

"Oh." Disappointment nipped at her. *What did I think—that he flew all the way back to New York only to turn around for me?*

"You."

Wait, what?

149

He dug a hand into her hair and pulled, hauling her to him, one hand cupping her ass while he gave her a kiss unlike any they'd already shared—no hesitation, no coaxing, but a passionate claiming with a hint of anger. Nicolette melted into it. His rough touch felt naughty but oh so good. His tongue demanded entry, plundered, and drove all thoughts of resistance from her.

She gripped his shoulders, opening her mouth wider for him. He lifted her so her jeans-clad legs wrapped around his waist. She wound her arms around his neck. Those powerful hands of his gripped her ass as he carried her across the porch.

The door opened and closed behind her. She clung tighter. She'd done the right thing. She'd sent him away.

And she'd spent the night wishing he'd fought a little harder to stay.

And there he was. Back. Her body came alive for his in a way that made it impossible to see this as wrong.

Mediocre sex—now *that* was easy to walk away from.

Passion that curled one's toes? Heat that had one's sex clenching and yearning? When one finally felt that kind of hunger—*no* wasn't an option.

Every reason why she should tell him to stop, every question she had would have to wait until after this tsunami passed. For now all she wanted to do was hang on, ride it out, and believe in possibilities.

Her shirt came off at the bottom of the stairs, along with her bra. His shirt followed.

She balanced back against the banister as he trailed kisses down her neck to her breasts. His tongue worshipped one before moving to the other. She whimpered from the pleasure of it and clung to him.

He pulled her upright again and carried her up a few more steps. With a groan he stopped, lowered her to stand on a step, and his hands went to the fastening of her jeans. Their tongues danced intimately while he finished undressing her. "So fucking beautiful," he growled and threw her clothing over the railing.

She stood there, feeling wanton and free. Where was the sweet man who had asked before taking?

She didn't need that man—not right then. She wanted to be taken, unapologetically, with all the abandon and power his kiss promised. She ran a hand down her own chest, down her stomach to the mound of her sex, and dipped a finger into her wetness. God, she was ready for him. She raised her finger to his lips, teasing, loving how his eyelids lowered and his nostrils flared.

"Is that what you want?" He dropped to his knees, threw one of her legs over his shoulder, and kissed his way up her thigh. Gripping the banister with one hand and his shoulder with her other, Nicolette shuddered as he claimed her sex with his mouth.

Oh God, yes.

The men she'd been with hadn't been into oral sex. Bryant cast a spell over her with his flicking tongue, his strong fingers. When she'd fantasized what he'd be like, she'd imagined him gentler, more tentative.

His confidence was electrifying.

She dug a hand into his hair. His grip on her ass tightened. With his other hand, he swirled a thick finger inside her. She clenched around it, loving the second finger that joined the first as he pumped in and out.

Heat built within her, and she began to beg him not to stop. Nothing mattered beyond the crest of pleasure that was just a few pumps away. *Yes. Oh yes. Just like that. God, don't stop. Just like that.*

She shuddered as an orgasm rocked through her, and she would have sat back on the stair had he not still been supporting her. He lowered her leg, stood, and flipped her over his shoulder like some conquering soldier stealing her away.

He made quick work of the remaining stairs and the short walk to her room. When he tossed her down onto the bed and slowly finished stripping, she nearly came again from the anticipation. He sheathed his cock in a condom, bringing her focus to the rock-hard beautiful promise of it. Like the rest of him, it was perfect. Laid bare on the bed for him, she could have felt vulnerable, but she wanted him as out of control as she felt.

She went up onto her elbows and tossed her hair over her shoulder. Her breasts bounced, and she loved how it drew his attention. She spread her legs just a little, and the wait was over. He dropped onto the bed beside her, rolling her over so she was straddled above him.

She bent so he could work his magic on her breasts. She aligned herself so his tip was poised just below her wet sex. His mouth found hers again as his hands settled on her hips. His upward thrust was powerful, as was his second. She gasped into his mouth, loving how he filled her.

She clutched at him, wanting to feel more of him. Needing all of him.

They rolled so he was above her, still within her. Her legs rose at his sides while he pounded into her. So deep. So good. All the while, his tongue fucked her mouth in a way that left no room for resistance or thought. She was his, all his.

They found a rhythm, then went beyond it as it became more primal. Harder and faster. Deeper and stronger. His hold became rougher. Her pleas more desperate.

Had he stopped then, she surely would have wept. It was that kind of good. The kind of good that can't last, but so consuming in the moment that the future doesn't matter.

His hands adored her, ruled her, brought out a wildness in her she didn't know was there. She dug her nails into his shoulder, cried out for him to fuck her harder.

And he did—so long and so good that she almost lost her mind.

"Mine," he growled into her ear, and she came for a second time with all the profanity she knew. He continued to thrust, then joined her with a guttural sound of release.

They stayed connected while they both came back to earth. "That was so fucking good," he murmured against her kiss-swollen lips as he withdrew.

She wrapped her bare body around his when he returned after cleaning off. "Yes, it was."

He ran his hand through her hair. Her body started to rev again at his hot grin. "I guess I don't have to ask you if you're happy to see me."

Her hand went to his already reawakening cock. It pulsed back to full staff beneath her touch. She ran her hand down his shaft to cup his balls, then back up to encircle and pump him. "Me either."

He kissed her on the nose. "You have quite the filthy mouth, young lady."

She teasingly broke contact with his cock, feigning offense. "Sorry you don't like it."

He rolled her under him, sliding his bare tip between her folds, then back and forth over her clit. Into her ear, he growled, "I fucking love it. You're so goddamn perfect."

She moved her hips with his, half closing her eyes at the pleasure of his full shaft sliding intimately against her. His chest was hot and hard against hers. It wouldn't take more than a small shift for him to be inside her again. "Do you have another condom?"

He rested his forehead on hers. "No."

She closed her eyes. This couldn't go any further. "Too bad."

He moved back and forth against her. "Yeah, I could go for a second round."

Heat flooded through her. He felt so damn good against her clit. Back and forth. So hot. So hard. Oh God. Things couldn't go further, but they felt too good to stop yet.

She kissed his neck.

He suckled her breast.

Back and forth went his thick cock over her clit. She was wet and writhing, he so hard and ready.

"We need to stop," he whispered.

"We do," she said, but her legs parted wider for him. Clear thinking was impossible.

His tip dipped inside her, bare and wrong, but oh God.

She dug her heels into the back of his thighs and thrust upward to welcome him. It wasn't enough. He didn't go fully in. His tongue thrust in her mouth, circling her own. With a groan, he withdrew.

He was going to stop.

She knew they should.

As if acting on a will of their own, her hips rose again, bringing him deeper this time. *Yes. Yes. Yes.* So good. So full.

Fuck me. Just do it.

He rolled off her.

And she hated him for it.

Loved him a little.

Hated him more.

They lay there side by side, sucking in air like they were competing for the last of it. Nicolette's confidence wavered. Iowa was her fresh start. She was supposed to be smarter, stronger.

Unprotected sex would have been stupid.

Life-alteringly dangerous.

Even she wasn't that irresponsible.

No, correction—Bryant isn't. I'm still making bad choices.

He wasn't touching her, wasn't even looking at her. On his back with one arm tossed over his face and his dick still at full mast.

Something that had just been beautiful was now marred by Nicolette's embarrassment. The only way it could get worse was if he . . .

She closed her eyes. *Please don't say you're sorry.*

"I'm sorry, Nicolette."

Fuck you.

"No reason to be," she said without opening her eyes.

"I didn't think we were at this stage yet, or I would have stopped and picked up more."

Yep, that makes me feel better.

He kept talking. "I know there's a lot we could do besides that, but I lose my head around you, and I didn't want to—"

"Please stop."

"Look at me." His arms folded around her again.

She frowned but opened her eyes. "What?"

He smiled, which didn't make her feel better. There was nothing funny about how she felt. "I wanted it just as much as you did."

"I'm about to punch you in the nuts."

"Hey, now. That's not something to joke about." He frowned.

She sighed and shook her head. She wouldn't actually do it, but it had felt good to say.

He glanced down at his erection. "Now you're going to have to apologize to him. He thinks you hate him."

She rolled her eyes. "He'll get over it."

That sexy grin was back. "You could kiss him and make up."

She glared at him.

He laughed. "Maybe later."

"Maybe." A reluctant smile pulled at her lips. It was hard to feel anything but good when Bryant looked at her that way.

He nuzzled her neck. "I'm glad I came back."

Her cheeks flushed as she remembered how nearly all of this had happened on the stairs. "Me too."

"I left because you asked me to. I respect you. But as soon as I heard . . ."

She tensed. "Heard what?"

"It doesn't matter. Not anymore."

Pulling a sheet up over her, she scooted into a seated position. "It matters to me. What did you hear that made you come back?"

"I'm sure it's not a problem."

"What?"

"In fact, now I feel a little silly."

Silly was not at all how Nicolette felt. "What did you hear?"

"That Jordan was here."

Her mouth dropped open. "Wait, what? Where did you hear that?"

Not covering himself at all, he sat up as well. "Honesty is always the best policy, but I also believe that there are optimal times to say some things."

Nothing he'd said had made her feel better. Someone had told him that Jordan was with her, so he'd run back to . . . what . . . fuck her first? And who would have known Jordan was there? Spencer? He didn't know Bryant, did he?

Nicolette stood and took the blanket from the bed with her. "Who told you he was here?"

"Your grandmother."

"Delinda? You went to see my family?"

"Technically she came to see me."

"I'm going to kill her." Nicolette paced the room, wrapping the blanket tighter around her as she did. "Did she threaten you?"

Bryant rose out of the bed to stand beside Nicolette. "It wasn't like that."

"She doesn't want us together, so she told you I'm seeing Jordan?" Bile rose in her throat. "That's it, isn't it? But instead of driving you away . . . you came here because . . ." Her eyes narrowed. "Why did you come?"

He grimaced and took a moment to choose his words. "She didn't threaten me. I came because I didn't like the idea of you and Jordan—"

Her hands went to her hips. "I told you we are just friends."

"And then he came here."

"So that means something would definitely happen between us. Is that it? All a man has to do with me is show up?" Something he'd said earlier came back to her, and her temper flared even more. Her hands fisted. That's all Bryant had done. "I'm an idiot." She stormed out into the hallway.

He followed her. "Nicolette—"

A battle was waging within her. Part of her wanted to believe that good things were possible and that Bryant was there because he cared about her. Seeing her clothing strewn all over from the door up the steps didn't make her feel any better. She could have waited, talked to him, found out why he was there instead of . . . *No, I said I wouldn't beat myself up like this anymore.*

He followed her, making it about halfway down the stairs before stopping. Not that she could blame him. She was swearing as she picked up her clothing. *I'm an adult. If I want to fuck someone on the stairs, I will. And if that says something about me—then I can't do anything about that.*

Delinda's voice echoed in her head. *"How could I be expected to condone this?"*

You don't have to, Delinda. Your opinion of me no longer matters. Shoes in hand, Nicolette glared at the naked man who looked at a loss for what to say. When their eyes met, he smiled, and her heart thudded wildly in her chest. Their connection affected him in a way that he didn't try to hide.

I don't even know why I'm angry with him.

And then she did.

I'm not ready to believe in anything this good yet. I'm going to destroy it before I even know what it could have been. I need more time. "Go back to New York, Bryant. This was a mistake."

In his full naked glory, Bryant took another step down the stairs. "It wasn't. Talk to me, Nicolette. What are you worried about?"

Her body quivered. It was ready for round two.

Stop it, stupid body.

He took another step, his gaze holding hers as he did. In a blanket, clutching her clothing to the front of her, she felt powerless to do more than wait for him. Right or wrong, the pull of him consumed her.

"Who the fuck are you?" a voice boomed from behind Nicolette.

"Bryant Taunton, sir."

She spun, too, and felt her food start to travel back up from her stomach. "Dad?"

In a tight voice, Dereck Westerly said, "I'll talk to you in a minute, Nicolette. Right now I'm wondering how long it'll take that naked prick to realize he should start running."

"Oh shit," Bryant said and grabbed a small rug from the floor, using it to cover himself. "This isn't how it looks."

"What are you doing here, Dad?" Nicolette asked, the embarrassment she felt outshone by awe that he was there. She'd dreaded Delinda's eventual arrival, but she'd long ago stopped thinking that her father would chase after her if she ran.

"I came to see you." Dereck shot death looks at the man behind his daughter. "I did not come to see *that*. Young man, if you don't want to swallow my fist, I'd suggest you go find your clothing."

"I'll be right back," Bryant said, making his retreat to his pants. Only his pants. His shirt and shoes were too close to her father.

Once he was gone, Dereck's attention returned to Nicolette. "Are you okay?"

"Um, yeah." Not really. In all the variations of how she'd dreamed her father might one day show up and want to see her, she'd never imagined this one. She could tell herself a thousand times over that his opinion of her didn't matter, but it did.

She was still trying to find her voice when her father added, "He didn't—"

"No, he's a good guy, Dad. I'm the one who's fucked-up." Tears began to pour down her cheeks.

"Oh, baby." Her father pulled her to his suited chest—blanket, pile of clothing, and all. "I'm so sorry."

More tears poured out, and she let them fall. "What are you sorry for?"

"Everything." He hugged her tighter, then stepped back. "Go get dressed. There are some things we should talk about."

She sniffed, still too shocked to move.

Bryant returned, bare chested. A less confident man would have stayed out of sight. He walked down the stairs and right up to her father as if he would be greeted with a handshake. "Mr. Westerly."

Nicolette watched a vein pulse at her father's temple. She turned to Bryant. "You should go."

"Yes, you should," her father said in a tone that could kill.

"I'm just going to grab my shirt." Bryant said, picking it up off the floor only a foot or so from her father. "And my socks." He grabbed those from near the bottom of the banister. "Oh, and my shoes."

"Get the fuck out," her father growled.

Bryant smiled at him like a man who didn't get the awkwardness of the situation. "I'm really glad you're here, Mr. Westerly." With a boldness that took Nicolette completely by surprise, he kissed her. One deep, toe-curling, quick kiss. Then he said, "I'll call you." And walked out the front door.

In the silence that followed, the enormity of the scene her father had walked in on sank in, and Nicolette's cheeks flamed. "I'll be right back."

Her father nodded.

She made it all the way to the top of the stairs before turning, half expecting her father to be gone. "Please don't leave, Daddy." Even to herself, her voice sounded like a plea from a much younger her.

"I'm not going anywhere."

She turned and hastily made her way back into her bedroom. She threw on her clothing but paused for a moment beside the tousled bed. She didn't understand Bryant any more than she understood herself when she was around him. How could she feel so good and so bad at the same time?

He'd actually looked happy about her father's arrival. It didn't make any sense.

What kind of man came to see her after meeting with her grandmother? He wasn't the first she had confronted, but the others had run for the hills. Delinda was a force not many dared to tangle with.

Was Bryant there because he cared about Nicolette more than he cared what her grandmother might do? Or was it what Rachelle had suggested? *Is he using me to get back at her?*

Flashes of their romp came back to her, warming her from head to toe. She wanted to believe in him and in her newfound positive attitude.

He said he'd call me.

Isn't that what a man says when he doesn't plan to?

It wasn't as if he could have stayed.

Dad.

Putting her questions about Bryant aside, Nicolette brushed out her hair, made sure her clothing was all in place, and rushed back out into the hallway.

Her father was downstairs.

He'd come for her.

She blinked back fresh tears. She'd messed up in London and probably ruined whatever chance she might have had with Bryant.

But somehow Iowa was delivering something she'd stopped praying would happen. Her father had come for her.

And he wanted to talk.

Chapter Eleven

Dressed again, Bryant sat in his car in the driveway of the bed-and-breakfast. Two things remained certain: sex with Nicolette was amazing, and he should have introduced himself to Dereck Westerly in London, because a naked boner didn't make the best first impression.

He dialed Lon. Not that he expected to receive much encouragement from him, but Lon only worried about something when he cared. He deserved to know Bryant had just made up his mind—Nicolette was definitely *the one*.

Lon picked up on the first ring. "Hey, we were just talking about you."

"We?"

"Me and your father. He was pretty pissed that you stood us up, but I explained that you're chasing booty. What man can argue with that?"

"Tell me you're joking. You're not actually with my father."

"Sure am. Want to say hello?"

"What the fuck are you doing, Lon? I thought you were joking when you said you texted him."

"I am a ballbuster, but no, I really did, and he really came. I showed him around your office. He was impressed."

"Enjoy your time together."

"You're heartless, Bryant."

"Ask my father where I got that from."

"Hang on," Lon said in a mock serious tone. "Sir? Where did Bryant learn to be such a pussy? Oh, he was born that way? Your father said you were always like that."

"Fuck you."

"He wants to talk to you. Are you okay with that? I don't want to make you cry or any shit like that."

Before Bryant had a chance to tell Lon off again, his father's voice came across the line. "Tell me, is dating a Westerly your newest attempt to piss me off? Why are you hanging out with that trash?"

"This conversation is over. Tell Lon I said thank you. Good talk."

"Don't be a little bitch. Westerlys are bad news, and you know it. They ruined my father. They tried to ruin me. If you think they won't come for you, I've overestimated your intelligence, and my estimation of it was already pretty low."

Lon was back. "Holy shit, sorry, Bryant. I get it now. Mr. Taunton, we need to talk. You've got serious parenting issues." After a brief pause, Lon added, "Easy, old man, I don't fight people twice my age. Ouch. That's rude. What happened? You were so normal until a minute ago. Westerlys suck. Got it. Stole your money. Yep. Delinda's Satan incarnate. That's a bit harsh, but I can see why you'd think that. No, I'm not trying to be funny—it comes naturally. Bryant, your father is going to have a stroke if he doesn't calm down. He wants to talk to you again. Hold on. I've got this." Bryant heard his father swearing in the background. "You're not helping your cause, Mr. Taunton. Do you want to have a relationship with your son? You don't care? Cold. But not really true or you wouldn't be here. He needs to stay away from the Westerlys? Hey, I told him that like five times already. If he won't listen to his best friend, he's not going to listen to a father he doesn't even talk to." There was the sound of a door slamming. "So your dad just left. I don't think I'm as good at the whole reconciliation thing as you are."

Bryant groaned and laid his head on the steering wheel of his car. The only consolation was that, no matter what Lon did, it wasn't as if he could make things worse between him and his father. "Thanks for trying in your own special way, but next time—don't."

"Yeah," Lon said with a sigh. "So how's Iowa?"

"Good. Great. Fantastic." Bryant remembered he was still sitting in his car outside the bed-and-breakfast, and said, "Confusing."

"Did you see your true love again?"

Bryant glanced at the window of her bedroom, and the front of his trousers tented. "I did."

With a chuckle, Lon asked, "Did she ask you to leave again?"

Bryant frowned. "She did."

"I don't want to be a cold slap of reality, but I'm sensing a pattern here. You go see her. She tells you to leave. You go back. She tells you to leave again. What does that usually mean? Let me think about it for a second. Hold on . . . she's not that into you, dude."

"Oh, I'm pretty sure she is." Memories of how she'd nearly begged him for round two had him shifting uncomfortably as his dick began to throb.

"No. No. That's how you become a stalker. Strike three. You're out. Come back to New York. Trust me. I hate to do this, but I'll even share Tamara and Lynn. Normally, that's my private stock, but I'm worried about you."

Never really sure how much of what Lon said was serious, Bryant ignored his offer and said, "She was happy to see me. I'd still be with her, but her father showed up."

"No shit."

"Yeah. I guess my talk with Delinda worked."

"Wow. Good for her. Good for you."

"They're in the house talking right now."

"And where are you?"

"In the driveway. In my rental car."

"After she asked you to leave?"

"Yes."

"Just hanging around. Like a *stalker.*"

Bryant started the car. "They do need time alone to work things out."

"And she asked you to leave."

"Yeah."

"Come back to New York."

Pulling out onto the street, Bryant started to drive toward the airport. "I probably should."

"Yes, you should."

Nicolette filled his senses. The scent of her was still on him. The taste of her on his lips. As he drove, he fought to concentrate on the road rather than the images of her lying on the bed waiting for him. He could still feel her tight, wet heaven. Still hear her cry out in pleasure, swear like a sailor during her orgasm. "I think I'm in love, Lon."

"But you're driving away, right?"

"Yes."

"Good."

After hanging up with Lon, Bryant contacted his pilot. Although Bryant had told him to be prepared to stay a few days, he would be at the airport in minutes—the perk of having a pilot on a generous salary was how readily he agreed to meet him.

Leaving MacAuley was harder than it had been the first time, but it would have been selfish to stay. Nicolette needed time with her father. Had he known that Dereck would be heading to Iowa that day, he would have waited . . .

Or maybe not.

Although Bryant wasn't normally a jealous man, he wouldn't have been able to stay, knowing that Jordan was at the same bed-and-breakfast.

At the same bed-and-breakfast—that part hadn't changed.

Bryant slammed on his brakes and pulled over to the side of the road. The arrival of Nicolette's father didn't change the fact that Jordan was still going to be sleeping under the same roof as Nicolette.

Sharing breakfast over the same table.

Possibly exploring the town with her.

Not going to happen.

A car pulled up behind Bryant's. Shit, the sheriff. Great. Bryant lowered his window.

"Problem with your car?" the uniformed man asked.

"Thought there was, but everything looks fine, thanks, Officer," Bryant said.

"You that guy from Boston?"

"New York."

"I thought I heard there was a guy here from Boston."

Rub it in, buddy. "I believe there is, but I am not he."

"What are you doing in these parts?"

"I came to see a friend."

The sheriff tipped his hat back. "Anyone I'd know?"

Lon, if I actually get arrested for stalking, your ass is bailing me out. "My friend is staying at Paisley's bed-and-breakfast. She's not from around here, either."

"Miss Westerly. Haven't met her yet, but I hear good things about her. Who knows, she might even save my job."

"Save your job?"

"If this town gets annexed into McGregor, I'll be applying to their department. Never can tell if they'll honor my time in or give my job to someone's cousin." He tapped his thumb against the gun on his belt. "Wait, are you that guy who came to see the Miller factory? Taunton, right?"

"That's me."

"So what did you think of it?"

"It didn't actually work out for me to see the place."

"That's a shame. It isn't in bad shape at all. We sure could use a business relocating out here."

"Yeah."

"The site is only a few miles out of town. Why don't you follow me there? I'll give you a quick tour around."

"You have the keys?"

"I know how to get in."

"Isn't that illegal?"

The sheriff smiled for the first time. "Who're they gonna call?"

Bryant chuckled. "Good point." There was no reason for him to go see an empty factory—on the other hand, he also wasn't keen to return to New York. He couldn't go back to Paisley's—not yet. Why not? "If you're up for it, I'd love to see the Miller factory."

An hour later, Sheriff Todd concluded a surprisingly detailed tour of the closed factory that finished with him explaining that the land was now owned by one of his cousins, a fact that made Bryant less concerned about using a hidden key for access.

It could have been his own reluctance to leave Nicolette and his desire to help her, but he could now picture how the factory could be adapted for robotics assembly. The price was cheap enough. The location was private but within good proximity to universities capable of supplying qualified workers.

Making an offer wasn't completely out of the question anymore.

"So what do you think?" the sheriff asked.

"It has possibilities. I'd have to read the property disclosures before I'd feel comfortable bringing it up to my business partner."

"My wife would be able to answer most if not all of your questions. She's a real estate agent."

Of course she is. Am I out of my mind? Lon is definitely going to think so. Iowa?

The idea seemed less crazy a short while later when Bryant was seated across from Pat, the sheriff's middle-aged wife, in their home office. The tall, slender brunette dressed sharply but in an understated way—reflecting the hidden depths of everyone he'd met in MacAuley. She had a confidence about her that he looked for in his employees.

She had just listed the number of major tech companies the area had recently courted with state and local incentives. Although Bryant's arrival had been unexpected, she'd pulled together an impressive amount of information while her husband cooked dinner for them.

"MacAuley has the land and the government funding. This area is ripe for economic development," she said.

"I agree. I just want to make sure I'm considering the area for the right reasons."

She closed her computer, putting it aside, and said, "What's the wrong reason?"

From the doorway, Sheriff Todd said, "Dinner is ready, and the wrong reason is always a woman."

"That's not what you told my father," his wife said with a cheeky smile.

Without missing a beat, the sheriff replied, "We all stretched the truth back then. You told me you loved to cook."

Pat stood, waving for Bryant to join her. He did. "Did I say cook? I meant eat. What smells so good?" She kissed her husband as she passed him.

Sheriff Todd's chest puffed with pride. "Stuffed chops." He nodded at Bryant. "You ever had them?"

"Not that I recall," he said.

"I use apples, corn, honey, and a secret ingredient I'd have to kill you over if I told you."

Bryant's eyebrow rose. "That is funny only because you're no longer wearing a gun."

Sheriff Todd laughed. "You ever try apple-pie moonshine?"

"No, but I keep hearing about it."

"Then take a seat. Nothing goes better with stuffed chops than Lily and Lucy's moonshine."

"Is that the recipe from the cemetery?"

The man's face lit up. "It sure is. Look at you, already an expert on MacAuley history."

Bryant sat down at the table and took a whiff of the steaming center plate of pork chops. "It smells delicious."

Pat sat down next to him and poured a shot for each of them. "Careful, this moonshine is deceptively smooth. It'll kick your butt if you underestimate it."

Her husband took a seat at the table and winked at her. "Just like a good woman."

Bryant chuckled and raised his shot glass. "Here's to good things happening for a town that has also been underestimated. Hopefully that's about to change."

They all drank to that.

When Pat went to pour him a second, he put a hand up. "I'm already muddled enough sober, but it was surprisingly good."

Sheriff Todd asked, "Were you heading toward the airport when I came across you?"

"Shit, I forgot about something. Hang on." He took out his phone but hesitated before texting his pilot. He should say that he was delayed and would be there shortly, but the truth was, he didn't want to leave MacAuley.

"What's her name?" Pat asked.

"Nicolette," Bryant said without looking up.

"The one I told you about, Pat. The Westerly woman." Sheriff Todd held out the plate of pork chops toward Bryant. "Shelby said you make a nice couple."

He took one and passed the plate to Pat. "We're working on it."

"Then why are you leaving?" she asked.

"That's what I'm asking myself. It's complicated, though. Her father just arrived, and I don't believe I am presently his favorite person."

Bryant was passed a basket of corn muffins. "I've been there," said the sheriff.

Pat poured glasses of water for everyone. "Yes, he has. My father was a farmer. His father was the sheriff. They both had strong opinions that didn't always match. I went away to college, and my father thought my coming back to MacAuley meant he'd wasted a lot of money. Todd and I eloped and pissed them both off. Our first Christmas together was lively, but they got over it."

"I'm optimistic by nature," Bryant said, "but I don't think I can see our families working out as well. It doesn't matter, though, because I don't see much of my father."

"Why not?" the older man asked, seeming genuinely interested.

Normally Bryant would have said, "He's a dick," and left it at that. But needing to dig deeper so they would understand, he added, "We had a falling-out when my mother died. I didn't think he did enough for her. It wasn't a pleasant time for either of us, and we never came back from that."

"That's a shame," Pat said. "But it happens."

Sheriff Todd made a circle with his hands. "Shake her family tree enough, and all kinds of assholes drop. We keep the holidays small."

She rolled her eyes but didn't look bothered. "Really? That's why? I'm not the one who has a cousin with sticky fingers. Imagine, a sheriff who gets robbed on a regular basis by his family."

Sheriff Todd grimaced. "I can't arrest my cousin. At least not until I catch him in the act."

"Family," Pat sighed. "You can't pick them. All you can do is lock your shit up and hide the moonshine."

It was refreshing to hear family issues discussed without anger. Most people he knew tried to sell their situations as perfect. In reality, everyone was dealing with something. He looked down at his phone again. "Is there somewhere to stay nearby besides Paisley's?"

"We have a spare room," Sheriff Todd said. "I don't make breakfast, though."

"I don't want to intrude. Is there a hotel or motel?"

Pat tapped her husband's arm. "Looks like we're not good enough for him. He's one of those city types who needs his pillows fluffed."

With a grin, Sheriff Todd said, "Guess no one ever warned him about what happens when you offend small-town law enforcement."

Bryant looked back and forth between them, trying to gauge how serious they were. "Oh, that's where we're going to take this?"

Pat shrugged, looking innocent.

Her husband's grin widened.

"Fine," Bryant said. "I'd love to see your guest room." He sent two quick texts out—one to the pilot and one to Lon to tell him not to expect him back just yet.

They spent the next few hours swapping stories like old friends.

To give her shaking hands something to do, Nicolette made a coffee for her father, and the two sat at Paisley's kitchen table, having a conversation every bit as painfully awkward as every other one they'd had—times a million.

Her father's expression remained tight, but she wasn't sure if that was because of what he'd walked in on or a sign of what he was about to say to her.

"I didn't know you were coming," Nicolette said, twisting her fingers painfully on her lap.

"That was obvious," he said.

"Bryant—"

"I didn't come to talk about him," her father cut in.

"Of course."

They sat in silence for a few minutes. Dereck took a sip of his coffee. Nicolette told her churning stomach to calm.

"Nicolette, your mother and I are working things out—things we should have addressed long ago."

Like me? She didn't ask him aloud. There was so much she wanted to say, but it was all bottled up inside her. She felt if she said anything at all, it would all pour out and end whatever chance they might have at a conversation. She knew all her issues—what she needed to hear was whatever he'd come to say.

He cleared his throat. "When we are children, we see our parents in unrealistic terms. They are supposed to know everything, *be* everything to us. The reality is, they aren't perfect. They make mistakes. They lie. They disappoint."

"Yes," she said in a tight voice.

"Your mother made mistakes, and they have come back to haunt her—haunt you—but she loves you."

"Her definition of love and mine don't match." It was no more than the truth.

He rubbed a hand over his forehead. "You're angry."

"Yes."

"I know that feeling well."

Nicolette's heart softened toward the man across from her. "Why did you let all of us believe you were the one who had cheated?"

He took a deep breath. "I will always love your mother. To me, she will always be the woman I fell in love with in college. We were young. She made me so happy. The life I imagined with her was full of laughter, kids, travel. Easy."

"Then your father killed himself." Nicolette had heard this part of the story.

"And everything changed. No—I changed. I no longer had the luxury of coming home to share a meal with her. My time, my energy, my soul, were required to save the family business that my father had lost control of. My mother pushed me because she didn't want me to fail, as my father had. I became a very different man than the one your mother married. So I was the first one to break our wedding vows. I didn't cherish her."

Nicolette wiped at the corner of her eyes. "You did what you had to do."

"Maybe. A relationship—any relationship—requires investment from both sides. She was faithful to me for years and suffered in lonely silence. I knew she was unhappy, but I was equally miserable. My mother saw Stephanie as unsupportive and draining, so she tried to drive a wedge between us."

"She succeeded."

"But it didn't have to be that way. I could have—I should have—chosen Stephanie. The truth is, I was afraid I would become my father. I didn't know if I had what it took to turn the family company around. I made unconscionable deals and became someone I didn't recognize. I saw Stephanie pulling away, but I didn't fight for her. I begged her to stay, but I didn't make any changes. The family fortune was secure. I knew what it took to succeed, and I wasn't willing to risk breaking my stride . . . not even for her." He swallowed hard. "Not even for my children."

Nicolette shook her head. "At least you were honest with her. She lied and would have continued to lie had the truth about Spencer not come out."

He stared down into his coffee for a few long moments. "She is not without flaws. Nor am I. When she finally did divorce me and marry the man I was pretty sure was Spencer's biological father, I couldn't stomach it. I couldn't go to their new home to pick you up, see that man with the woman I still loved, not hate him for being able to make her laugh again." He looked up with such pain in his eyes, more tears instantly filled Nicolette's.

"I understand. You weren't sure if we were even yours."

His mouth pressed in a tight white line before he said, "That never stopped me from loving you, Nicolette. I never asked for a blood test, because you and Spencer were mine. I was there when you were born. I held you first. I should have put aside my pride. You shouldn't ever have waited for a father who didn't come—not once. That you did, that you thought it meant I didn't care—that's my greatest mistake."

Nicolette's body began to shake. She refused to reduce to tears in the middle of what might be one of the most important conversations of her life. She needed to hear what he had to say, and she needed him to hear her as well. "I did think it meant you didn't care."

His hands gripped his coffee cup. "I know." He took out an envelope. "I gave a sample of my DNA to this clinic. If you want to know, all you need to do is contact them and provide a sample of your own. But before you do that, Nicolette, know that I don't care what the results are. I am your father. Maybe not the one you needed. Maybe not the one Mark would have been, or was, but I love you, and I want to be part of your life and to take care of you."

Nicolette accepted the envelope with a shaky hand. "I don't want your money—no matter what the results are. This isn't about that."

He laughed without humor. "God, you are every bit as proud and stubborn as I am. I hope you see that before it costs you as much as it did me. The walls you use to protect yourself, they don't just keep people out—they trap you in."

Nicolette buried her face in her hands for a moment. That was exactly how she felt. Trapped by her own choices. "I don't want to be you, Dad." She looked up as she realized how that must sound. "I don't want to be me, either. I have been pushing people away." A tear rolled down her cheek. "I see that now. When I get scared, I get defensive and pull back."

He placed his hand over hers. "And you doubt you're my daughter? It's like looking in a mirror."

"Are you here to cheer me up or depress me?" she asked with a half laugh.

His mouth twisted in a semblance of a smile. "I'm here because my daughter needs me, and I may have failed her in the past, but that's the past. This is a god-awful uncomfortable conversation to have, but I'll have it every day until you believe me. I love you, Nicolette. You're my daughter. No test result could ever change that."

Her eyes filled with tears again. She was ready to take a leap of faith. "Can I hug you?"

He stood up, blinking back his own tears. "Come here."

She walked into his arms and cried. "I'm so sorry, Dad."

"Oh, baby. So am I. We can't go back—but we can go forward."

She wept for the little girl who had stopped believing this moment would ever happen. Wept in release as she finally let that girl go.

When she finally calmed down, she walked to the kitchen sink, blew her nose, and wiped a wet paper towel over her puffy eyes. She felt like she'd been through a wringer, but a necessary one. She turned around, resting back against the sink. "So are you flying back tonight?"

He looked around. "I was planning to stay here. I'd like to help with whatever you're working on."

"Stay here?"

"If there is a room available."

While Nicolette was still processing that, Bruce and Tera burst into the kitchen. They were laughing over something, but both stopped when they saw her father.

Nicolette sniffed, smiled brightly, and said, "Dad, this is Bruce Russo and his daughter, Tera. Bruce's sister, Paisley, owns the bed-and-breakfast."

Bruce and Dereck shook hands.

"It's a pleasure to meet you," Dereck said.

Bruce responded in kind.

Tera put a hand on her hip. "You're Nicolette's father?"

Without hesitation, Dereck said, "Yes."

"Holy tomatoes," Tera said and strode over to him. "Finally, some-one who knows Water Bear Man. My name is Tera. I'm going to marry your son, so that will make you my father-in-law. Right, Dad?"

Dereck started to say, "My son Eric is—"

"She knows." Bruce put his arm around his daughter. "Tera, we'll talk about this later."

"But he can get Water Bear Man to come here." Tera pouted.

Nicolette winked at her father. "She's hoping by the time she's old enough to marry, Mrs. Water Bear Man might be . . ." She made a hatchet sign across her neck.

Dereck chuckled and went down to eye level with Tera. "You do realize that by the time you're that age . . . he'll be as old as I am."

With a gasp of horror, Tera exclaimed, "*That* old?"

In a somber tone, Dereck suggested, "You might want to pick a younger superhero."

"I will, thanks." Eyes wide, she nodded with an insulting amount of sincerity.

Dereck straightened and winked back at Nicolette.

She smiled.

For the first time in her life, it felt like they were on the same team. Two people sharing a common cause. *Magic.*

Her cheeks warmed as she remembered the scene on the stairway. Could they work past that as well?

"Have you seen Paisley lately?" Bruce asked.

"She and Jordan went out for a drive," Nicolette answered.

Her father asked, "Jordan Cohen? I didn't know he was here as well."

"He came by to check in on me."

Bruce frowned. "Paisley's not answering her phone."

"I'm sure everything is fine," her father said with confidence.

"I hope I don't have to kill him," Bruce said.

"I know exactly how you feel," Dereck added without missing a beat.

Bruce looked from her father to Nicolette. "Bryant Taunton? I've met him. Seems like a nice-enough guy."

Dereck's nostrils flared. "Meeting him was eye-opening."

Nicolette rushed to her father's side. "Dad, let's see if we can find a local hotel for you. I'm sure you'd be much more comfortable in a place like that."

Bruce scoffed at the idea. "There's plenty of room here—Paisley would love to have the house filled up."

"Nicolette's grandmother is considering flying in tomorrow. Will there be room for her as well?"

Nicolette groaned. *Say no, Bruce. I will give you my inheritance if you do. Just say no.*

"Absolutely," Bruce said. "I'll come by tonight and help prepare the rest of the rooms. There are eight guest rooms in total. Should we expect anyone else?"

"She might bring her fiancé." Dereck didn't seem to notice how each of his announcements tortured Nicolette a little bit more. "They may share a room. Not sure."

Oh my God. "King Tadeas can't stay here. Doesn't he travel with royal guards?"

"I'm sure they'll work that out," Dereck said.

Bruce's chest puffed. "A king? No shit. This town is getting fancier by the minute."

Nicolette implored her father with her gaze. He had to know they couldn't stay at Paisley's. "Dad."

"Nicolette" was all her father said.

Tera broke in. "Is that the grandmother you did that funny voice for?" And she proceeded to do as good of an imitation as Nicolette had. "A lady doesn't raise her voice. Elbows off the table. A lady doesn't laugh loud." Her voice returned to normal. "You didn't tell me she was marrying a king. No wonder she has all those rules. Duh."

Nicolette shared a smile with her father. "Duh."

Tera lost interest as the conversation turned to what Nicolette was doing for the town. Dereck asked a surprising number of questions of both Nicolette and Bruce. He seemed interested even in the history of the town.

When he heard a car door slam in the driveway, Bruce said, "That's probably Paisley." He shook Dereck's hand again. "I'm going to make sure Jordan knows I'm here and that I'm not going anywhere."

After he and Tera left the kitchen, Nicolette looked up at her father. "Are you staying here because of what you saw earlier?"

Dereck adjusted his cuffs and flashed her a smile. "Duh."

Chapter Twelve

Bryant woke up in a strange bedroom to heavy panting in his face.

"Go away, Titus." He gave the bulldog a pat on the head. The dog tipped his head to the side, lolled a wet tongue out, and climbed onto the twin bed beside Bryant. His open mouth curled in what could have passed for a smile.

Bryant arched an eyebrow at him. "You smell bad." The dog's expression didn't change. Bryant added, "Is this your bed? Is that what you're trying to tell me?" Titus wagged his tail.

Pat appeared at the open bedroom door. "Titus, leave the poor man alone." Titus wagged his tail again in response. "Bryant, we would have let you sleep, but you have a visitor. My husband is showing him around our property, so you have time for a quick shower. We put your stuff in the bathroom across the hall."

"The visitor—is his name Lon?" Bryant asked as he sat up.

"Got it in one. Sounds like he wants to see the factory, too. I can take you both or give you the code and let you show him around." She called Titus to her; then before she closed the door, she said, "Something tells me you and this town would be a good fit. Tell me what you need, and we'll make it happen."

Bryant threw back the bedding and rose and stretched. When he'd told Lon where he was, he should have known he'd fly out to check on his sanity and sobriety. Business and romantic endeavors didn't mix, but this felt different. He wanted to be with Nicolette, but he also felt invested in the future of a town he was growing attached to. He often made decisions that affected the lives of people he'd never met, but this was getting personal.

Maybe having Lon there was a good thing.

A few minutes later, Bryant thanked Pat and headed out the door to join Lon and Sheriff Todd. They were behind the house near a barn full of antique tractors.

Looking as fresh as if he'd just come from a board meeting, Lon met him in a dark-charcoal suit. Sheriff Todd said he couldn't be late to work, so he'd leave them in the capable hands of the region's best Realtor.

Alone with Lon, Bryant shoved his hands in the pockets of his jeans. "You don't have to say it. I know what you're thinking."

"Do you?"

"You think the only reason I'm considering the Miller facility is because of Nicolette, but there is a reason eleven other tech companies have moved to Iowa in the past decade." He rolled his tight shoulders. "Before you say it, yes, I'm acting a little out of character. Normally, you're the one who makes impulsive decisions, and I remind you to assess all aspects before moving forward. I'm not suggesting we buy the factory today, just that we consider it. Pat, Sheriff Todd's wife, offered to show us around."

"How could I turn down a tour by Sheriff Todd's Realtor wife? Do you even hear yourself? Do you really think this is where we need to expand to?"

"I do. This town needs jobs. Keep an open mind until after you see the place."

"Not necessary. Someone already put in an offer this morning."

"Hang on." Bryant's head snapped around. "Someone else put an offer in on the Miller factory? Who?"

"Jordan Cohen. Nicolette's friend from Boston."

"No, he didn't," Bryant growled, and his hands fisted. "Look me in the eye, Lon, and swear to me you are not making this up, because it's not funny."

"Calm the fuck down. This is a good thing. She doesn't want you here. You get to leave without feeling guilty about not saving this little corner of the US, and everyone is happy."

Bryant ran his hands through his hair. "Who the hell is this Jordan guy anyway?"

"First, he's close with Spencer Westerly. He's big in virtual reality. Actually, I'd love to meet him. What he has done for the industry is mind-blowing. Even you could probably learn something from him."

"He's *that* Cohen? Fuck me."

Lon shrugged. "Good news? Nicolette's father is staying at the same bed-and-breakfast. From what I hear, they're all getting along. You've done a good deed there as well. Let's call this a win and go home."

"No, it doesn't end this way."

Lon rocked his head back and forth and said, "It looks like it does."

"I don't give up just because things get difficult," Bryant snarled.

"Okay," Lon said in a tone similar to one a person would use to calm an irate child. "I get that you have feelings for this woman, but there is a time when we all have to cut our losses and move on. It doesn't make you less of a man if she chooses someone else."

Bryant kept pacing and shaking his head. "I don't believe she would choose him. She likes me. I won't explain how I know she does, but let's just say it was pretty clear how she feels."

"You fucked her and think that means she can never be with another man? If that's how it worked, half of the women in Manhattan would be ruined for all other men after being with me. Women move on, Bryant. Even after great sex. For your sake, I'm hoping it was good. There's no comeback from bad sex."

"You need to help me."

"Help you?"

"We need to buy that factory, and I need a room at Paisley's bed-and-breakfast."

"You know you've lost your mind, right?"

"I also need to know what to say to Nicolette's father to smooth things over with him. I was naked when we met, and I don't think that gave him the right impression."

Lon looked around as if hoping someone else was there to witness his friend losing his mind. Finally, he flexed his shoulders and said, "Okay, the local Realtor can show us this fucking factory. You text Paisley and see if she'll even agree to rent you a room again. I'm in, but you need to promise me something right now."

"What?"

"I'm going to be brutally honest about the site, even if you don't want to hear it. And if Paisley says she doesn't think anyone wants you at her place, we're out of here. No argument. No trying to outbid Cohen for a site we don't need. We're done."

"Nicolette has feelings for me."

"She might. I honestly have no idea. But if I was flying off the deep end, I know you'd reel me in."

"I would."

"That's why I'm here. So how the fuck did her father see you naked?"

◆ ◆ ◆

Around lunchtime Nicolette walked into Lily's Breakfast Nook. She'd gone back and forth about whether she should start a new job while her father was there and—gulp—Delinda was likely already on the way over. Having either of them in MacAuley didn't change the reality of how little money Nicolette had. She could ask her father for a loan, or she could keep her pride as well as her original plan.

Besides, she'd meet more of the people from town while waitressing. Wasn't that what she was there to do? She went to the back to tell Lily she was there.

"Well, then, go get something done" was her only response.

So Nicolette did. She made more coffee and introduced herself to customers as they came in. Before she could stop them, most people served themselves. Habits were hard to break. She tried not to get discouraged and instead cleaned the counter area and also washed the floor. When the small lunch rush ended, she'd made two dollars. She sat down in a booth and took out her laptop. If nothing else, she could work on the website for the town.

She threw herself into arranging the website pages and testing that all the links worked. She was so engrossed in it that she jumped when her phone buzzed with a message.

Paisley: Is your grandmother still coming today?

Nicolette: I haven't heard one way or the other.

Paisley: I am so excited. I've never met royalty. I was planning to bake a chicken. Do you think they'll eat that? You do really think they'll stay here? Your father thinks they will.

Nicolette: I'm sure they will. And chicken sounds perfect. They'll love it. They'd better.

Paisley: I feel like this is a dream. My rooms are filling up. I'll be able to pay my bills all in the same month. I don't know how to thank you.

Nicolette: I'm happy it's all working out.

Paisley: How is Lily's?

Nicolette: Honestly?

Paisley: You didn't make anything, did you?

Nicolette: Not true. I have two dollars I didn't have when I walked in.

Paisley: Hang in there. Once we get tourists, you'll be rolling in tips.

Nicolette: That's true.

Paisley: Hey, quick question. Do you mind if Bryant Taunton stays here? He asked if he could. I told him I'd have to check if I had the room. What do you want me to say?

Nicolette: Does he know my father is staying there?

Paisley: I told him he is. And that Jordan is here. He didn't sound happy about that. Does he have a problem with Jordan? How do they know each other?

Alone in a booth, Nicolette started laughing. What else could she do? It was that or cry. The whole thing was so messed up.

Lily came out of the kitchen. "You drinking out here?"

"I wish," Nicolette joked.

Lily blew a curl out of her face, wiped her hands on her apron, and sat in the booth across from Nicolette. "What's got you looking like your world is upside down? You pregnant?"

"No." She shook her head. Now that would be bad. Thankfully Bryant was more responsible than she was.

"I've been reading about your family online. Why would someone like you want to work here?"

Nicolette went forward onto her elbows, burying her face in her hands.

Lily snapped, "Elbows off the table. A lady knows better than that." Nicolette straightened with automatic speed.

"Relax," Lily said, cackling and holding her stomach, then cackling some more. "Tera was in here earlier doing an impression of your grandmother. I had to see if she got it right. Guess she did."

She chuckled. If nothing else, her time in MacAuley was teaching Nicolette not to take herself so seriously. "That kid is a hoot."

"Oh, she's something all right. She can't help it, though. We're a spunky bunch. Now why don't you tell me what has you down?"

"You'll think I'm ridiculous."

"I already do." Lily cackled again. "Girl, if you're lucky enough to get to my age, you'll see that very few things are as bad as we think they are when we're young."

"You're probably right." Nicolette sighed. "I don't know how to talk to my grandmother. I don't know why she's coming here. My father says it's because she cares about me, but I'm afraid of the side of me she brings out. No one can make me as angry as she can." Nicolette swallowed hard. "No one can make me feel as bad about myself."

When Lily didn't immediately respond, embarrassment filled Nicolette. People often asked how others were, but very rarely did they really want to know.

Lily took one of her hands in hers. "I want you to look around. You see anyone in here?"

"No."

"My granddaughter doesn't want to live in MacAuley. My husband passed away. I don't have anyone to take over this place when I die. Four generations of Lilys, and I can't convince my own granddaughter it's worth keeping open. The whole town knows I can't run this place by myself. They help make their own food, clear off their own tables, sometimes even sweep the floor because they feel sorry for me. I spent every last dollar I had in my savings making sure my husband had what he needed in the end. I could feel sorry for myself. I could hate my life here or that I can't afford to move closer to wherever my granddaughter goes. But every single morning, I make a choice to wake up and be grateful. There's two kind of people in the world—those who nothing will make happy and those who everything will. Which one are you, Nicolette?"

The question rocked her to the core, made her take a real assessment of herself. "I don't want to be the first."

"Then try the other way. Hell, there's no greater blessing than a good family. Maybe your grandma is hard on you, but you still have her. That won't always be the case. And if you don't like who you become around her, stop becoming that person. She can't make you feel bad about yourself. No one can. People is people. That might be hard to believe at first. I read your grandma is dating a king or something like that. But that don't make her better than you."

"I know it doesn't." Nicolette's eyes misted. "I just want her to be proud of me."

"Well, the first thing you need to do is quit whining. I just want to smack my granddaughter when she does that. Sit up straight. Look her in the eye. Tell her what you're doing here. If she's like any kind of grandma I know, she'll be proud of you—even if she doesn't say it."

It sounded so simple. So beautifully simple. "I'll do that, thanks."

With a final pat, Lily said, "And no offense, but you're fired. I can't have employees who play on the computer all day."

Nicolette's mouth dropped open; then she started to laugh.

Lily gave a full belly laugh that only had Nicolette laughing harder.

"I just peed myself," Lily announced.

Nicolette laughed so hard she almost did the same.

Lily stood, said she was going in the back to change, and asked Nicolette to watch the restaurant until she came back.

"I'll wash the booth," Nicolette offered.

"See, how could any grandma not be proud of you? Heart of gold, that's what you have." She disappeared out the side door.

Nicolette was still smiling while she disinfected the entire booth. She caught her reflection in a window.

Heart of gold—I like that. Inner voice, we're going to start using that instead of "asshole."

Lily, your page is going to be the best damn one on the town site.

The door of the restaurant opened. "Nicolette." *Delinda. And King Tadeas.*

Nicolette turned from washing her hands. Her first instinct was to become defensive, but she fought the reaction. *She's not better than I am. And she's here for me. According to Lily, either nothing she does will make me happy or everything will. It's my choice.*

"Grandmother."

Delinda smiled and walked farther in with Tadeas on her arm. "Your father said you're working here now."

"Yes and no." Nicolette came out from behind the counter. "I was actually just fired."

Her grandmother's eyes widened. Nicolette braced herself for the lecture she knew would follow, but instead, Delinda looked sympathetic. "I'm sorry to hear that. I'm sure you'll find something else."

"I will," Nicolette said quietly.

Delinda stopped just in front of her. "I know you didn't invite me here, and if you want me to, I'll leave, but there's something you need to know. I'm—I'm sorry for not knowing how to talk to you. I intend to do better in the future. I do love you, Nicolette. You can doubt everything else, but don't ever doubt that."

Nicolette's hands went to her mouth. Could this be real? It never would be if she didn't let herself believe it could be. So instead of holding on to her doubts, she rushed forward and enveloped her grandmother in a long, tight hug. "I love you, too."

Once released, Delinda wiped a tear from her cheek and smiled at Tadeas. "Well, that went better than expected."

He smiled so sweetly at Delinda that Nicolette hugged him as well. *This is what I've wanted, and I see now that the change had to happen in me before it could.* "I don't want you to leave, Grandmother. I'm trying to do something important for this town, and I'd like to show you what I'm working on."

"I'd love to see whatever you want to show me," Delinda said, still dabbing at the corners of her eyes.

"It's on my computer." Nicolette headed to the booth where it was, then picked it up and said, "Why don't we sit at a table instead."

They spent the next twenty or so minutes looking over the website Nicolette was building and conferring on whom she'd contacted about the town. Delinda seemed genuinely interested, as did Tadeas.

"If there is any way that we could help you with this, all you have to do is ask," Delinda said.

She means that.

She wants to be part of this.

Over coffee that she poured for them, Nicolette told her grandmother and Tadeas about how the community was like one big family. "I didn't come here for the right reasons, but I'm staying because I want good things to happen for this town." She told Delinda about Paisley, Bruce, Tera, the Nelsons, and Lily. "Being here is changing the way I look at myself. Lily says happiness is a point of view, and that's what I'm discovering here."

"Lily sounds like a wise woman," Delinda said.

"Oh, I wouldn't say that," Lily said from inside the kitchen. "But I make the best ice cream you'll ever taste."

Tadeas rose to introduce himself, as did Delinda. "I would love to try it."

"Help yourself," Lily said to the king. "The bowls are over there. The spoons are near the freezer. I don't have any waitstaff, so if you want some, you just go get some."

Delinda and Tadeas exchanged a look. Tadeas said, "It would be my pleasure."

After he'd walked away, Lily winked at Delinda. "Now that's a keeper."

Delinda smiled. "Yes, he is. Would you care to join us?"

Lily fixed her hair. "Oh, I don't know. I'd hate to intrude."

"No intrusion at all," Delinda said graciously. "My granddaughter speaks highly of you."

"Maybe just for a moment."

Tadeas returned with two bowls of ice cream and came back with two more. He didn't look at all bothered to be serving the ladies. When he took his first bite, though, he lit up. "This—this is heaven. I have traveled the world, and I have never had any ice cream compare."

Nicolette snapped a photo of the wonder on his face as he took a second spoonful. *Ice cream so good, it's fit for a king. Not a bad tagline.*

He held out another spoonful to Delinda. She blushed and ate it from his spoon. "Absolutely delicious."

Seeing them together like that—not formal at all, just a loving couple—warmed Nicolette's heart. She remembered how natural it had felt with Bryant. "I'm so glad you found each other. Makes me think love is really possible," Nicolette blurted out.

"You'll find someone, Nicolette," Delinda said.

A group of schoolchildren walked in. Lily excused herself to go greet them.

"I have met someone." She was just now starting to believe it herself. "His name is—"

"Bryant Taunton," Delinda and Tadeas said in unison.

Delinda didn't look bothered by the name. "Yes." Not wanting to ruin the mood, Nicolette chose her words carefully. "I heard you spoke to him." There had to be a gentle way to tell her grandmother to leave him alone.

"More like he spoke to me," Delinda said and shared another smile with Tadeas. "I like him."

"You do?" *Okay, who is this, and where is my grandmother?*

"I do."

"Has your father met him?" Delinda asked.

Nicolette blushed straight down to her shoes. "Briefly."

Delinda gave Nicolette's hand another pat. "I heard Dereck is staying at the same bed-and-breakfast as you. Is there room for us as well?"

Since when does she ask?

Nicolette looked down at her messages. "I never answered Paisley. She said Bryant was asking if there's a room available for him."

Delinda's chin rose, but her tone sounded kind as she said, "If there isn't enough room for all of us, Tadeas and I will find other lodging."

In that moment, Nicolette glimpsed something in her grandmother that reminded her of herself. *She's afraid I don't want her, and like me, when she gets scared, she pulls away. OMG, I* am *like her.* "No, Grandmother, I want you to stay at Paisley's. Both of you."

Delinda frowned. "Then what's the problem?"

"What do I tell her about Bryant? I do want to see him again, but having him and Dad and you all in the same house might be—complicated."

"If you're not sharing a room, I'm sure it would be fine."

That wasn't sarcastic. She's actually being nice. "Wait, did you just say you'd be okay with it?"

Delinda's smile was strained, but it was there. "I would make myself okay with it, because I love you and want to be part of your life."

"I want that, too." Nicolette rose to her feet, crossed over, and hugged Delinda again. "I don't know about Dad, though."

"If Bryant is important to you, he'll deal with it," Delinda said.

Nicolette looked down at her phone. She could tell Bryant that now wasn't a good time, but she'd already pushed him away. How many times could she do that before he listened and stayed away? Her life was already littered with casualties of that exact cycle.

Bryant knew her father was staying at Paisley's, and he still wanted to go there.

I can second-guess his reasons, or I can believe in him . . . and me.

She texted Paisley that not only was Bryant welcome to stay at the house, but that her grandmother and King Tadeas would also like— "One room or two?"

Delinda's cheeks flushed.

King Tadeas smiled.

Talk about awkward. Her father would have a stroke for sure.

This is not okay—yet.

An idea came to Nicolette, and she texted Paisley: Do you have adjoining rooms?

Paisley: Yes, I do.

And just like that, the impossible felt very, very possible.

Chapter Thirteen

Waiting for Paisley to text back was slowly killing Bryant. He'd expected a quick yes. Instead, he'd had time to drive Lon to the factory site. It probably was a good idea to take a second look with someone who wasn't emotionally involved in the outcome.

Lon admitted the building was in better condition than he'd thought it would be. The price was definitely attractive. The incentives Pat described as they toured had Lon at least seriously considering the possibility.

She left them alone on the site to discuss it on their own after warning that a serious offer had been put in that morning. "We know," Bryant had wanted to say, but didn't.

"I don't hate it," Lon concluded when they returned to the parking lot. "The proximity to universities is promising as far as a potential workforce. There's definitely enough land for sale in this area if we decide to expand. I see the lure of the place."

"I knew it. I know you don't believe in fate, Lon, but I came here for a reason."

Another car pulled into the parking lot. Lon looked from it to Bryant. "Don't do anything stupid."

"What are you talking about?"

When the driver stepped out of the car, Bryant had his answer. Jordan Cohen still looked like someone had poured Shaggy from *Scooby-Doo* into a suit.

No way he's Nicolette's type.

The confident bastard walked right up to where Lon and Bryant were standing and held out his hand. "Jordan Cohen. The office said no agent was available to come out again today, but I'm glad you're here. I took a preliminary tour, but I want to take a second look at some things. I love the isolation of the area—it'd be perfect for some of our classified projects."

Lon shook his hand. "Lonsdale Carver. I was hoping to meet you while we're here."

"Okay," Jordan said, looking a little confused. "Why does that name sound familiar to me?"

"We're not real estate agents." Bryant shook Jordan's hand with enough pressure to make the other man wince. "Bryant Taunton."

Jordan pulled his hand free and shook it. "Bryant? Are you the guy who said he was interested in the factory but really wasn't? Paisley said something about you. I should thank you. If not for that, I wouldn't have even thought to look around at what was available in this area."

"What brought you to MacAuley, then?" Bryant asked in a low tone.

Lon said, "Bryant, we should head out."

"No, I've heard a lot about Cohen. I'd like to hear his plans from him."

Jordan looked back and forth between the two men. "Am I missing something? Am I supposed to know you?"

"I'm a friend of Nicolette's," Bryant said coldly.

"Well, then, it's nice to meet you, friend of Nicolette," Jordan said, scratching his head. "I'm also a friend of hers. We go back a long way. Her brother Spencer is my best friend."

"Is that why you're here? For Nicolette?" Bryant stepped closer.

"That's why I came," Jordan said with a shrug; then a funny, goofy smile spread across his face. "I was not expecting to want to stay. I'm making some impulsive decisions right now, but they all feel right, you know what I mean? I don't even care. For the first time in my life, I think I'm in love—"

Something in Bryant snapped, and his fist connected with Jordan's nose. Talk about something feeling right . . .

Blood instantly spurted onto Jordan's upper lip. "What the fuck was that for?" Jordan growled, taking a defensive posture.

Lon intervened and said, "You're going to have to excuse my friend. He doesn't usually go around punching people. Don't press charges. I'm bringing him in for a psych eval as soon as I get him back to New York. There's definitely something in the water here that is messing with his brain."

"Stay out of this, Lon. Sometimes a man has to fight for what he wants. You're too late, Jordan. If you've known Nicolette as long as you say you have, you've had your chance. You're not swooping in last-minute, buying this factory, saving this town, winning her heart."

"What the hell are you talking about?" Jordan pulled out a tissue from his pocket and wiped the blood from his face. "Nicolette is like a sister to me. Always has been."

"Then why did you just say you're in love with her?" Bryant snarled.

"You do need help. I never said that. It's Paisley I'm interested in. She's incredible. The only reason I decided to stick around." He sniffed and pocketed his tissue. "But now I see I might also be here to keep Nicolette safe from crazies."

Bryant's anger dissolved. "You're interested in Paisley?"

Lon shook his head and sighed audibly. "Bryant, I told you this woman was trouble from the first time you mentioned her. You're one of the most careful people I know. You're not impulsive. You don't brawl. I want you to take a hard look at yourself and tell me that this woman is good for you."

"You're really not into Nicolette?" Bryant asked.

"Why would I lie?" Jordan threw up his hands. "Okay, because there's two of you, and you both look like you spend more time in the gym than I do, but I know some ninjitsu shit, and I could take at least one of you."

Lon ran a hand through his hair. "No one is fighting anyone. This is literally the stupidest thing I've ever witnessed. Maybe the two of you could have a dance or . . . type-off . . . or some nerd shit that you guys learned in prep school."

"You're right. This is not me," Bryant admitted. "I shouldn't have punched you, Jordan."

"I should have punched you back. If I were writing the scenario into a game, I totally would've coded for a punch back."

"Yeah, just standing there holding your nose is pretty lame. Best counter would have been a roundoff kick."

"Or an uppercut to the chin and a power boost." Jordan touched the bridge of his nose gingerly. "You're big in the robotics field, aren't you? That's where I know your name from."

Bryant nodded. "Everyone has heard of your AI programs. They're genius. Way ahead of what anyone else in the field is doing."

"This is so wrong." Lon looked at the two of them like they were insane. "You'd both be dead where I grew up."

When his phone beeped with a message from Paisley, Bryant smiled. "Looks like there's room for me at the bed-and-breakfast, after all." He looked at Jordan's swollen nose. "Hope this doesn't make things awkward."

"After this, you still think it's a good idea to stay there?" Lon snorted.

Bryant shrugged. "I like her. What would you both do if you thought you'd met *the one*?"

"I'd offer to buy a factory to save her town." Jordan nodded toward the factory behind them.

"Me too," Bryant said. "I'm in the process of putting in a bid higher than yours."

"No shit." Jordan's smile widened. "Because you thought I was doing it to impress Nicolette?"

"I have more business sense than that," Bryant countered.

"He was totally trying to one-up you," Lon interjected.

Jordan scratched at his head. "I really like the property."

"So do I."

Jordan glanced around. "It'd be perfect for some of the interactive programs I'm designing."

"Moving a percentage of our robotics assembly here would provide a large number of jobs for locals." Bryant wasn't ready to give up on the idea of investing in the area.

"I would be providing skills that could increase their employability tenfold."

As I would be. "I would bring stable income to many in the area."

"Do you want me to get a ruler so you can whip them out and compare?" Lon asked dryly. "Nothing would surprise me anymore. Any moment, I'm expecting the two of you to announce a joint venture. Hug. Buy homes side by side. Carpool your kids to school. Or for me to wake up and realize shit like this doesn't happen and I'm still in New York in some kind of coma after being slipped something in a drink."

Bryant and Jordan looked at each other. Bryant said, "AI has a place in the medical field."

"Oh my fucking God," Lon said.

Bryant looked down at his phone and texted Paisley that he'd be staying for an extended period of time and wanted to make sure that was okay. Then he nodded to Jordan. "You've known Nicolette a long time?"

"Yep," Jordan said cautiously. Bryant couldn't blame him; last time, answering with honesty had gotten him punched.

"So you know her father?"

"We've recently become more acquainted."

"Does he come across as an easygoing man or someone who holds a grudge?"

Jordan grimaced.

Before Bryant had much time to reflect on that, his phone beeped with incoming texts. He read both and punched at the sky in victory. "Paisley says she sees no reason why I can't stay there, and Nicolette wants to meet up before I go to the house."

"That could be good or bad," Jordan said.

"It's good," Bryant answered. "Things are aligning. That only happens when something is meant to be."

Lon turned to Jordan. "I'm staying in a hotel in McGregor, but I might switch over as well. I can't miss how this shit turns out."

Jordan balanced his hands like scales in the air. "It could go either way. Nicolette's grandmother is supposed to be arriving today. I might need the address of that hotel you're considering leaving."

"I'm glad you're here." Bryant gave Lon a shove. "Nicolette is the one for me. You'll feel the same once you see us together."

"Is he always that optimistic?" Jordan asked.

"Yes. The pisser is," Lon said, "things tend to work out for him when he gets like this."

A dark memory butted in, nipping at Bryant's confidence. "No one wins every time, but you can't let your losses define you."

"I like that," Jordan said with a nod of approval.

"You would," Lon said while shaking his head in wonder.

Chapter Fourteen

Nicolette started to feel a little foolish as she waited on a bench in a park about thirty minutes from MacAuley. She'd read about the place while researching the area, and the name had seemed fitting.

Determination Park.

Now she saw that there was nothing particularly special about the place. The swings were of the old-fashioned metal-frame type. There was a playground and a plaque dedicating it to a local man who had made the park possible. An article about the man and the park described them both as a testament to how the collective determination of people can overcome hardships.

Its name matched her new philosophy. She and Bryant would work things out, because she finally believed in him, in herself, and that great things happen when a person doesn't give up.

Lost in her thoughts, Nicolette jumped when Bryant sat down beside her on the bench.

Her breath caught in her throat.

Their gazes met, held, and the air sizzled.

"Thanks for coming all the way out here. I thought it was best for us to meet away from everyone else first." His gaze slid down her. She was dressed in her normal jeans and T-shirt, but when he looked at her that way, she felt sexy and exposed. Nothing she concealed was still a secret to him. He had kissed every inch of her. Those hands knew her curves. His tongue knew her taste. She swallowed hard.

He looked as if he would kiss her, then held back. "I asked Paisley if I could stay at her bed-and-breakfast." He watched her reaction closely.

"I know. She told me."

He leaned closer.

As did she.

"And you're okay with me there?" His hand rose to caress her cheek.

She closed her eyes briefly, savoring the feel of his touch. It took that little for her body to come alive for him. When she looked at him again, there was a similar fire reflected in his eyes. "I am. There's something I want to say first, though."

He traced a thumb over her lips. "Whatever it is, we'll work it out."

"How do you know it's a problem?" she asked barely above a whisper as she fell further under the spell of his touch. The park was flanked by private homes. Children were playing in the distance. What she was imagining doing with him definitely required a different location.

He smiled. "It's you."

She ran her hand up his thigh. "So I'm trouble?"

"Of the best kind." He kissed just behind her ear softly. She shivered as a wave of desire rocked through her.

There were things that had felt important to say before he was this close to her, reminding her of how good the rest of him would feel. *What was it I wanted to tell him?* "There's no reason to be jealous of Jordan—he really is just a friend."

"Mmm." Bryant kissed a little lower on her neck, taking his time like she had him just as mesmerized as he had her.

Nicolette caught a mother frowning at them and gave him a little push. "Bryant, I'm serious."

He raised his head, then glanced down at his hand. "I'm not worried about Jordan."

Her gaze followed his. When she saw that his knuckles were bruised, she gasped. "How did you hurt your hand?"

Bryant flexed his fingers. "I can't believe I made it this far in my life without ever punching anyone. Much more satisfying than unfriending someone online."

"You punched Jordan?"

"Violence is never the answer, I know. I just thought he was saying that . . ."

"That what? I can't believe you hit Jordan." She covered her face with one hand. "You know he's staying at Paisley's, too."

"We're good," Bryant said. "It was a misunderstanding."

"And you think I'm the one who would benefit from anger management?"

Bryant laughed. "You bring out a side of me I didn't know I had. I don't like the idea of you with anyone else."

A wave of pleasure washed through her. "Well, that doesn't mean you can go around punching people."

"You're right." He began to nuzzle her neck again. "There are much better ways to spend my time."

Yes. Yes. Yes.

Okay, hang on. I brought him out here to talk.

"Bryant, MacAuley has been so good for me. Meeting you has also been good for me. I'm beginning to see the world in a whole new light."

He growled in her ear, "I want to hear all about it, but what do you say we find a hotel near here, fuck until neither of us can walk, then we spend the rest of the night talking."

Nicolette threw her head back and laughed. *Well, okay, then.* "Shouldn't it be the other way around?"

"Not if you want me to be able to concentrate," he said with a shameless grin.

She laughed again and moved her hand farther up his thigh. "So if I want you to listen, I definitely shouldn't do this?"

He shifted his hips forward, his pants striving to contain his raging hard-on. "You will never hear me tell you to stop."

She kissed her way up his jaw and whispered, "Then take me somewhere where I won't have to."

He was on his feet instantly, dragging her along by the hand. "I drove by a place on the way here."

She doubted her feet touched the earth all the way to the car. Nothing in her life had prepared her for how he made her feel. They checked in to a small designer hotel on the waterfront of the Mississippi River with huge grins on their faces and no luggage in their hands. The older male clerk at the front desk rolled his eyes as he handed them a key card.

On their way to the elevator, Nicolette spotted the hotel store. She glanced up at Bryant. "Do we need . . ."

He pat his suit jacket pocket. "I bought a few on the way." He twirled her into his arms. "Okay, several."

Nicolette blushed, but only because her thoughts were filled with images of them putting those condoms to use. She didn't have to imagine long.

Once inside the door, his kiss turned every bit as sinfully addictive as she remembered. She slid his jacket off his shoulders. He pulled her shirt over her head. They tore at each other's clothing, their kisses getting hotter, their hands getting more desperate as they moved into the room. Bryant bent and grabbed a handful of condoms that had fallen to the floor. He tossed them onto the bed like rose petals.

She laughed and pulled him down onto the bed with her. The rolled together, lost in the ecstasy of being together again. Her hands moved over him with bold confidence. He groaned and kissed his way over every inch of her.

When they rolled again so he was on top, he pinned her hands above her head. Her legs wrapped naturally around his waist. His still-bare cock nudged at her sex. There was a wildness in his eyes that mirrored how she felt. "I like you. You like me. Just fucking say it."

"This isn't enough?" She slid her wet sex along the length of him. He shuddered.

"With anyone else, yes." He groaned when she did it again.

She pulled her hands free, pushed him onto his back, and mounted him. She held his hands as he'd held hers. The way he wanted her, the way he didn't try to hide it, made her feel powerful and free. Here, with him, there were no inhibitions—no second-guessing. She took his mouth, claiming him the way he'd claimed her. She kissed her way down his neck, down his chest, loving how he moaned and begged her not to stop.

Just as she'd begged him.

She gave him one last heated look before she took his cock deeply into her mouth, rolling her tongue around it. Hoping she brought him the pleasure he'd brought her, she worked his balls with one hand while taking him deeper and deeper.

He didn't swear the way she did, but he went just as wild. When he finally came, she took all of it, all of him, and loved the pained, guttural sound he made.

He guided her back up to him. The rush of a moment earlier had passed for him, but the hunger in his eyes promised that this was far from over. The things that man could do with his tongue were sinful. He teased her breasts until she was sure she could come from that alone. He pulled her up so she was on her knees directly above his face, then guided her down to the perfect height for—oh, holy shit, heaven.

Swearing wasn't something she thought about—it just happened. When he used two fingers to hold her sex open wider while his tongue increased the speed of its clit flicking, she swore loud and clear enough for someone in the room next door to bang on the wall. It was the first time Nicolette had ever laughed while coming, and it felt fucking fantastic.

She was still catching her breath when he flipped her over, lifted her ass in the air, and sheathed himself in a condom. She braced herself as the tip of his huge cock teased her hole. "Say it, Nicolette. Say you like me."

Then he plunged deep inside her, dug his hand in her hair, and filled her so completely it hurt in a wonderful way. She cried out his name. He pounded deeper, harder, wilder.

A warm heat began to spread through her again. He tugged her head back and growled, "Say it." And ground himself deeper still.

Reaching a place no man ever had. Oh, that mystical, magical place that had fireworks going off as never before. "Fuck yes. Yes, I like you, Bryant," she called out. "I like you so fucking much."

"We know," someone yelled from the other room.

Their audience was forgotten as he took his pounding up a notch. So good. So wildly deep and perfectly positioned for . . . oh, holy fuck . . . she came with a cry. He joined her with a growl and a final thrust.

He withdrew, cleaned off, and pulled her down into his arms. She kissed his smiling lips. A television next door blared.

"Jealous bastards," he joked and tucked her closer.

She buried her face in his shoulder. "I should be mortified." She met his gaze. "Instead, I'm just happy."

"Me too." He reached behind her and grabbed more condoms. "Let's really piss them off." The grin he gave her was irresistible.

She ran a hand down his cheek. "I do like you, Bryant."

He kissed her deeply. "I know." Gently, he threaded his hand through her hair. "I'm almost ready to listen to your epiphany, too."

She shook her head and smiled. "Almost?"

He traced a finger from just behind her ear to circle one of her nipples. "I suppose I can try. You speak, and I'll just entertain myself while you do."

Nicolette closed her eyes as her tip puckered for him. His warm breath teased her other breast. "I realized that I've been looking at things all wrong. Everything in life—either everything makes you happy or nothing does . . ."

He tugged on her nub with his teeth, then started making circles with his tongue while his hand moved down to her sex and began to mirror the move on her clit. She shifted her legs to give him better access and tried to remember what she was saying.

"Does this make you happy?" he murmured, then slipped a finger inside her, pumping it slowly in and out of her while moving his thumb back and forth over her clit.

"Oh yes," she gasped as he thrust a second finger in. "Anyway, it's up to me how I see things." He moved his hand so his fingers went deeper still. "So from now on . . ." His finger found the spot that had been elusive to her previous lovers. "Holy fuck, don't stop."

He raised his head with the sexiest smirk on his face. "I'm listening."

She dug her hand into his hair and dragged his mouth back to just above hers. "We'll talk later."

◆ ◆ ◆

With a sleeping Nicolette in his arms, Bryant shifted to peel one of the few unused condom packets from his back. He tossed it on the floor beside the bed and chuckled as he draped his arm once again around the woman who had rocked his world.

He brushed a loose hair off her forehead.

As good as life could be, it was also full of things Bryant struggled to wrap his head around. The daily news was a constant barrage of the unexplainable and unconscionable. Thinking about death, suffering, and the state of the environment on a global scale could overwhelm him if he let it.

Caring for his mother had taught him to focus on what he could do, the positive he had the power to bring. Cancer didn't care that Bryant had gotten a solid education or how much money he was set to inherit. It didn't ease when he prayed, didn't go into remission because he sought out the best doctors. Cancer didn't even bring out the best in the people who surrounded his mother.

His mother, however, had been strong even in the end, and that still inspired him. The day she'd decided her fight was over, she'd called him in to hold her hand. Her last words would never leave him. "I'm tired, Bry. If I'm not here tomorrow, you didn't fail. I didn't fail. This is part of life that we all eventually face. It can scare you, or it can free you. I don't know what comes next, but I don't regret how I lived my life. Live yours in a way that you can say the same."

There was a different look in her eye that day—she knew. "I'll get Dad," he'd said.

She'd smiled and closed her eyes. "This isn't a journey he could go on with me. Forgive him for that, Bry."

So Bryant had, at least to the extent that he could.

As he watched a sleeping Nicolette, he realized why his mother was so vivid in his thoughts then. Caring about anyone involved risk. But in the end, there was nothing more important—nothing.

The woman in his arms would one day be his wife.

He believed that just as surely as he believed the sun would come up the next day.

Nicolette stirred, and her eyes opened. "Are you watching me sleep?"

"Sorry."

She wiped a hand across her dry lips. "Am I drooling?"

He kissed that sweet mouth of hers gently. "No. I was just thinking." Then he smoothed her hair away from her face again. "Do you want to talk now?"

"Uh." She rubbed a hand across her eyes. "Okay."

"I liked what you were saying you learned in MacAuley."

She smiled and traced his jaw with her fingers. "I didn't think you were actually listening."

He grinned. "I was trying to, but you're a formidable distraction. Forgive me?" He kissed her bare shoulder.

"I suppose I can't blame you. I *am* irresistible." Her sweet, sexy smile was one he'd gladly wake up to every morning.

Hugging her tighter to his side, he said, "I want to hear everything. Did you and your father talk things out? What did you do today?"

She ran her hand down his arm. He flexed, because at the end of the day, he was a man, and he liked to know he pleased her the way she pleased him. "Why do I get the feeling you had something to do with him being here?"

He tried to look innocent. "Me?"

"I spent some time with my grandmother today, and she said you had spoken to her. Something about the way she said it made me think that the conversation didn't go the way I'd thought it would. It wasn't about her threatening you to stay away from me, was it?"

"No, it wasn't."

Her eyes met his. "You told her what I said about my father, didn't you?"

It was hard to determine what she was thinking, but he wasn't about to lie. "I did. If you're upset about it, I can understand, but I thought—"

She cut off his words with a kiss, then placed a finger softly over his lips. "Thank you."

He smiled against her touch, then kissed her finger. She lowered her hand. He said, "I didn't know if it would work, but Alessandro kept saying that Delinda and Dereck love you. I thought they deserved a chance to prove it."

A shadow passed over her face. "What are we doing, Bryant?"

He could have said a hundred different things. So many responses leapt to the tip of his tongue. Some were sexy. Some were witty. She didn't need any of those, though. Looking into her eyes, he knew that more than anything else, she craved the truth. "The best we know how to." He rolled onto his back and looked up at the ceiling, seeking a way to describe how he felt without diminishing it or scaring her off by saying too much, too soon. "From the moment I saw you in London, I knew my life would never be the same."

She wrinkled her nose at him. "Because I looked good in that stupid dress?"

He kissed her jaw. "I thought you were hot, yes, but that wasn't all that drew me to you. I've been lost. I've been lonely. Angry. I felt your pain."

She shook a little against him. "And then I got shitfaced."

Bryant looked back up at the ceiling again. "I didn't care. I wanted to be there for you."

"And you wanted to fuck me." She hugged him tightly.

His eyes flew to hers. She was smiling, thank God. "That, too."

With a flat hand, she caressed his chest. "I wasn't ready for you. Not even when I came here. I was so confused."

"I know."

Her hand stilled. "Watching the people in this town take care of each other, seeing how connected they all are, made me want that. I don't want to be alone. I do want to work things out with my family." There was a light in her eyes that hadn't been there before, something that made his heart thud loudly in his chest. "And I want you."

It was more than he'd expected her to say. "From the first moment you saw me. Admit it."

She chuckled. "It's your humility that I love the most."

"Did you just say you loved me? Fitting. You were the one who asked me out. When it comes time to propose, should I buy the ring, or will you?"

"You're such an ass."

He kissed her forehead. "But I'm an ass you love."

Did she? Could she? That kind of leap of faith would have terrified her before she met him. "I do see us headed there."

He reached behind her, picked up a few condom packages, and threw them up in the air. "Woo-hoo."

She slapped his chest, then kissed it. "You're so—so—"

He narrowed his eyes at her. "I believe the words you're looking for are *charming, sexy—the kind of man a woman gladly drops to her knees for.*"

She laughed. "Yes, that's exactly the way I'd describe you."

His chest rumbled with laughter. "I thought so."

"So what did you do today?" she asked after a pause.

He told her about the factory, about Sheriff Todd and Pat, about how he felt when he heard Jordan had put in a bid for the site. She didn't let him skip a detail of what had led up to him punching her friend.

"You were jealous," she said as if that weren't a common human condition, as if no man had ever fought for her before.

"To the point of making an ass of myself. We talked it out, though. Thankfully, Jordan understands my pain."

"Because of Paisley."

He told himself he wouldn't say anything, but it just came out. "Delinda said you asked Jordan to marry you."

"For my inheritance. A few years ago, my grandmother sent out a decree that if any of us married and invited everyone in our immediate family to the wedding, we'd get our inheritance early. Spencer immediately got engaged just to get the money, and even though that didn't work out the way he thought it would, it felt like a good idea for me to do the same—for a moment. There has never been anything but friendship between Jordan and me. I'm glad I didn't mess that up. He came here to help prepare me for the arrival of my family. Just knowing that someone cared that much—and understood—helped. And now, seeing him with Paisley makes me think you just might be right . . . maybe things do start to align and work out when you share a common vision. Like you said—magic."

"It's all about seeing that you don't have to go on the journey alone."

"Yes. I can't believe I'm asking this, but are you bidding for that factory to help MacAuley or me?"

"Both. Honestly, I don't know if I'm going to bid against Jordan or with him. I have a feeling we have a shared vision, also."

She took a moment to weigh his answer. "Before I came here, I wouldn't have believed you came here just for me. I didn't see myself as someone who could inspire that kind of action."

"And now?"

She shook her head in wonder. "You're a lucky guy, Bryant Taunton, because I'm pretty fucking wonderful."

He kissed her briefly. "That's what I've been saying."

"I can finally look myself in the mirror and like what I see. And it feels pretty damn amazing."

Time to lighten the mood. "You know what else feels amazing?" His eyes lit with desire.

"I do need to be able to walk tomorrow," she said with a laugh.

"Such a shame. I bet they're missing us." He motioned toward the wall behind the bed.

At the top of her lungs, she yelled, "Oh yes. Do me like the stallion you are. Don't stop. Yes. Yes. Yes."

They laughed, kissed. Waited. Didn't hear a knock of protest. Laughed more.

Just as Bryant was about to yell something out, there was a thud against the wall, then another. It took on a rhythm any couple would recognize.

Nicolette's eyes widened with comical wonder; then she whispered, "They're so quiet."

He picked up a condom and twirled the packet between his fingers. "Want to show them how it's done?"

She took the packet from him and tore it open with her teeth. He chuckled, but his cock was twitching in anticipation. There was no trace of defensive, withdrawn Nicolette. She was all humor, trust, and confidence. No matter what the future held for either of them, he would do everything in his power to keep that look in her eyes.

Chapter Fifteen

The sun had already come up by the time Nicolette woke to a text message beeping on Bryant's phone. She slid out of bed, retrieved it, and read the message.

Dad: Are you up?

Nicolette considered waking Bryant, but she thought about what he'd done for her with her family as well as the game they'd played with their phones. Technically, she still had a pass to answer one of his messages. She'd never taken her turn.

She typed: Yes.

Dad: First you stand me up. Now you're not answering my messages?

Okay, so answering him again might be considered sending a second message, but Bryant had met with her grandmother in person. This was just a text: Busy. I'm out of town.

Dad: Don't tell me you're with that Westerly woman.

Nicolette: I am.

Dad: That family is pure evil. They'll act like they like you, then do everything they can to ruin you. If you need proof, I have it in spades.

Nicolette brought a hand to her mouth. *I don't want to know what that means.*

Nicolette: That's not who they are today.

Dad: You're a fool if you believe that.

What would Bryant do if our situations were reversed? What would I do if I refused to be afraid? Nicolette: I'm in MacAuley, Iowa, with the Westerlys. I know our family's history with them, but it's time to put the past behind us.

Dad: Sorry, unlike you, I live in reality. I'd come if I were in a position to destroy them. Sadly, I'm not. I'm too busy still trying to rebuild what they stole from us.

Nicolette took a deep breath and followed her heart.

Nicolette: Then come for me. I want you in my life even if I'm living one you don't agree with.

He didn't respond.

Nicolette tucked Bryant's phone back into his jacket pocket. She could have deleted the messages, but that wasn't how she wanted things to be with Bryant. She was going to make mistakes. So was he. If they didn't hide them from each other, maybe, just maybe, they'd work through them—together.

Her phone buzzed next. She scrambled for it.

Delinda: Your father and I have had a wonderful breakfast with Jordan, Paisley, and Lon. Can you guess who was missing?

Her past response to that text would have been to instantly jump to defend herself because she would have felt she needed to. *Delinda loves me. My father loves me. I can be myself and not feel bad for it.*

Nicolette: I'm with Bryant.

Delinda: Will you be returning before or after your father has a stroke?

Nicolette actually laughed at that. Something amazing happened when she didn't instantly become defensive . . . she actually got her grandmother's sense of humor. Nicolette was beginning to see that although nothing had actually changed, everything had, simply because her perspective was different. She texted, We'll be back in a few hours. Could you help Dad handle seeing Bryant again? They had a rough first meeting.

Delinda: I'd rather not know the details.

Nicolette: Perfect, because I'd rather not share them. All you need to know is that Bryant and I are together, and he's important to me.

Her grandmother's response was instantaneous: Then he's important to us as well. I'll talk to your father.

Wow.

She almost decided not to push her luck, but living fearlessly and honestly meant not avoiding uncomfortable topics. If Bryant was willing to stay at the bed-and-breakfast regardless of how her father handled it, she could be just as strong for him.

Nicolette: Grandmother, I have a favor to ask of you.

Delinda: Anything.

Gulp. Nicolette: If Bryant's father comes to MacAuley—or if you ever see him anywhere—could you be kind to him?

Delinda: Is he coming here?

Nicolette: I don't know, but if he does . . .

Her grandmother didn't text for several minutes. Long enough for Nicolette to have a mini panic attack.

Delinda: I'm proud of the woman you've become. It is time to put the past to rest. I'll speak to your father about that as well.

Nicolette wiped a tear from her cheek and texted, Thank you. And I'm proud of the woman you've become as well.

Delinda: Yes. Yes. Well, do us all a favor and shower before you come back. The less you look like you spent the night doing what we all know you did, the easier it will be on your father.

Nicolette smiled. She decided to test this new grandmother she was getting to know.

Nicolette: How are you enjoying your room selection?

Delinda: As quietly as possible.

Nicolette's burst of laughter woke Bryant. He rolled over, felt around the bed, then sat up with a frown. "Everything okay?"

Naked, sitting cross-legged on the floor of a hotel room with Bryant, laughing over something her grandmother had said, Nicolette nodded. "It has never been better."

Nicolette: I love you.

Delinda: I love you, too.

She quickly texted that she had to go but that they'd be back soon. Before returning to the bed, Nicolette dug through Bryant's jacket. With both phones in hand, she sat beside him and said, "I did something this morning that I hope you'll see in the light of what we've been discussing."

She handed him his phone first and instructed him to read his messages. As he did, his expression tightened. Then she handed him her phone, and an expression entered his eyes that warmed every inch of her. He said, "You are truly the most amazing woman I've ever met."

She laid a hand on his shoulder. "Do you think he'll come?"

Bryant put the two phones aside. "No, but we don't have any control over that. Come here."

She fell back into his arms.

His kiss tasted like—forever. She choked back a sob, then a laugh. He raised his head. "That's exactly how I feel."

◆ ◆ ◆

A few hours later, Bryant and Nicolette, along with her father, grandmother, King Tadeas, a blushing Paisley, a smitten Jordan, and Lon were following Shelby and Jackson Nelson around Friendship Cemetery. It was much more enjoyable than sitting in the living room of the bed-and-breakfast beneath the sustained stare of Dereck Westerly.

Everyone, including His Royal Highness, seemed as enthralled by the history of the cemetery as they were with Shelby and Jackson. It was a good sign. Nicolette snapped countless photos as they went along.

When the group moved forward to read a specific headstone, Dereck hung back and said, "Bryant."

Bryant stopped and turned, then reassured Nicolette that he would be fine if she went on. There was no warmth in Dereck's expression, but considering it hadn't yet been forty-eight hours since he'd been given a good look at Bryant's balls, it was understandable. *Time to show him I have attributes he will actually approve of.* "Yes, sir?"

"I've been asking around about you."

"And?"

"You have a reputation for putting compassion above profit."

Bryant nodded.

"However, everyone seems to know someone you've slept with."

Ouch.

Several off-the-cuff responses came to him, but he kept them to himself. What he did or with whom he did it before he met Nicolette was frankly none of her father's business. He could have said that as well, but he wasn't looking for a fight. He let the directness of his gaze be his answer.

Dereck continued, "I would do anything for my daughter. Die for her. Kill for her."

That's as clear as it gets. "I'd explore other options before settling on either of those extremes, but I feel the same."

"You think this is fucking funny?" Nicolette's father growled.

"No, sir." *Awkward. Deserved. Not funny.*

Dereck said, "What are your intentions? Are you serious about Nicolette?"

Bryant pocketed his hands and rocked back on his heels. Unlike with Nicolette, it was not too soon to tell her father how he felt. "If she'll have me, I see myself married to that woman."

The man's eyebrows rose, then met in a line of irritation. "You'd better not be bullshitting me."

In a world where many people danced around what they were trying to say, Bryant had an appreciation for directness. He also liked what this conversation said about Dereck. He was finally becoming the father Nicolette yearned for. He looked forward to being able to tell her about his death threat. It was heartwarming, really.

He kept that thought to himself as well, though.

Dereck added, "What is between you and Jordan? First you're in competition over Nicolette, then over an abandoned factory?"

"We'd both like to do something to bring jobs to this area, and we're both in the position to do it. Nicolette was never a concern."

"You broke Jordan's nose over her."

"A misunderstanding that was quickly resolved."

Dereck cleared his throat. "My mother told me you were the one who sought her out and recommended I come to Iowa."

He held Dereck's gaze. "Your daughter told me she needed her family but didn't know how to reach them. On the outside she's all fire and fight, but beneath that she loves deeply and hurts easily. How could I not try to help?"

"Alessandro said he sent you to her."

"I would have come to her anyway. Not while she was on the run, perhaps, but eventually. All he did was give me a nudge."

"He also told me about your mother. I was sorry to hear that."

"Thank you."

"I'm sure you're aware that I've had a few tangles with your father."

There was nothing Bryant could or would say to that.

Dereck rubbed his forehead. "Be good to my daughter." He held out his hand.

Bryant forgave him for crushing his hand bones together. He would have done the same. "That's all I want to be."

Just before releasing his hand, Dereck leaned in and growled, "And keep your fucking clothes on."

He flexed his hand and smiled, "Yes, sir." *At least in public.*

Lon strolled over, sized up the mood, and said, "I don't say this often, so I don't want either of you to think you'll ever hear me say it again, but I was wrong, Bryant. Now that I've seen you and Nicolette together, I don't think you're crazy anymore." He winked at Dereck. "I don't think you're crazy *any less*, but the two of you do make a nice couple."

Dereck smiled. *Wait. They get along?*

He must have said it aloud, because Lon laughed. "Dereck and I are tight now. We've bonded. Mostly because I wasn't the one who stayed out with his daughter last night."

Dereck shot a glare at Bryant seemingly out of reflex.

Lon grinned.

Payback would come one day. No one could hide in threesomes forever.

A police vehicle pulled up beside the cemetery. Sheriff Todd sauntered across the grass toward them. "Which one of you is a king?"

Tadeas stepped forward. "King Tadeas of Vandorra."

The sheriff tucked his thumbs into his gun belt. "Lily said you liked her ice cream."

"That I did," Tadeas responded graciously.

"What do you think of our town?"

The king looked around before answering. "It reminds me of one in my country. Magnus spent a good portion of his young years in a small town because I wanted him to experience what it means to be part of a close-knit community. Titles don't matter there—character does. I have the sense the same is true here."

"You got that right," Sheriff Todd said with a satisfied smile. He greeted Bryant with a handshake. Bryant introduced him to the rest of the group.

Delinda expressed an admiration for his service to the town, which also seemed to please the man.

Before he left, Nicolette asked the sheriff to take a photo of their group. Their first pose was a serious one, formal enough for even a royal gallery. Then Delinda said, "Let's move this tour along, shall we? At my age, there's always a risk that if I spend too much time in a cemetery, they may not let me back out." The group broke out in laughter as the sheriff continued to snap another photo.

Bryant imagined one day he'd show the photos to his children and say, "And this is the day I fell in love with your mother's family."

Chapter Sixteen

Two months later, Nicolette sat at a table in Lily's Breakfast Nook sipping a coffee with Paisley. "It's so good to have you back," Paisley said.

"It's good to be back."

"What did you think of New York?"

"Busy. Invigorating. Chaotic. I spent a good amount of time at Bryant's office, and it was exciting to see him in that world, but coming here feels like—coming . . ."

"Home?"

It felt strange to say it to someone whose family had lived there for generations, but, "Yes. That's exactly how it feels."

Paisley's face lit up. "When I contacted you, I never imagined how much you'd become part of my life. Imagine, if I hadn't sent that one email . . . none of this would have happened."

Nicolette didn't want to imagine that at all. "I prefer to think we would have all ended up together anyway. This was meant to be. Now that the factory is a done deal, I'm ready to be here full-time. Did I tell you I took an entry-level position in the visual department at the factory?"

"Jordan told me. That's great. He said he would have given you department head, but you insisted you wanted to earn your way up. I like that. Oh, I have bad news."

Time slowed. "What is it?" No, please don't let it be her health or anything on that level.

Instantly apologetic, Paisley must have seen where her thoughts had taken her, because she leaned forward and said, "I shouldn't have said bad . . . it's actually good. Jordan is moving in full-time with me, which means I'm closing the bed-and-breakfast to make it into a home for us."

Nicolette reached across the table and grabbed one of her hands while letting out a happy squeal. "That is fantastic."

"It is. I think this is it, Nicolette." She brought her left hand around and held it up. "In fact, I know it is. He asked me to marry him, and I said yes." A red stone shone from the middle of a circle of diamonds.

"Gorgeous," Nicolette said with a smile. "Is that a ruby?"

"A red diamond." Paisley tipped her hand back to admire the ring herself. "I didn't even know there was such a thing."

"How did he ask you?"

Paisley's eyes widened. "He installed the strangest high-tech closet in my house."

"One of WorkChat's simulator rooms."

"That's it. Glad you know what it is, because I didn't know what to think when he took me inside. It was incredible, Nicolette. We traveled the world together . . . I mean, I felt like I was really in each place he took me to. Then we were on the main street in MacAuley while still in my closet. So realistic it blew my mind. Then he asked me marry him and said he could be anywhere, but the only place he wanted to be was wherever I am." She lowered her voice and dipped her head down. "If you've never had sex while feeling like you're flying, you have to try it." She bit her bottom lip. "You'll need to get your own closet, though. Ours is booked for the foreseeable future."

Nicolette laughed. "I love it. I love everything about this. Congratulations! Why didn't you tell me as soon as it happened?"

"It happened the week you went to Vandorra to celebrate the birth of your new nephew, and it's more fun to tell you in person. A royal birth must have been something."

"It sure was. Rachelle asked me to be there in the room during the delivery. I held one of her hands while her husband held the other. I am so glad I went. All our petty arguments fell away, and it was exactly the way it should have been—just me and my big sister." Nicolette wiped at her eyes with a napkin. "When I think about how close I came to missing that . . ."

"But you didn't."

Nicolette sniffed and nodded. "No, I didn't. Bryant flew over with me but stayed with the rest of the family in a private waiting room. You should have seen how calm he was through the whole thing. He's good for my family. Good for me. My father actually said that—can you believe that?"

"I can. Your father's right."

"My father." Nicolette still loved the sound of it. "I finally did the blood test."

Paisley's mouth rounded. "And?"

"And the truth didn't change anything." Nicolette smiled as she remembered how supportive Bryant had been through the entire process. "Family is a choice."

"So is he . . . are you . . . Tell me if it's none of my business, but . . ."

"What do you think the result was?"

Drumming her fingers on the table before answering, Paisley finally said, "You have your grandmother's eyes."

"I do. She says I also have her spirit. I didn't see it until I started spending more time with her. Now that I know more about her life, I don't see her as strict and judgmental. She's the person she had to be to survive—strong, resilient, and loving in the only way she knew how to be. She calls herself a work in progress, and that's how I see myself, too. There's always more to learn, always room to grow. I'm not afraid of either anymore."

"See, and you thought I wrote to the wrong Westerly. Look around—Lily has real waitstaff now. Her granddaughter already came home for a visit with her friends, who all fell in love with her and her well of advice. Memes of her are going viral, and we've had tours come through simply because they want to meet her and to taste ice cream that's fit for a king. She's loving every minute of it."

There was a time when Nicolette wouldn't have been able to believe so much good news was possible, but it was like Bryant said . . . when people started caring about the same thing—like saving a town or helping a runaway heiress find her way home—things started working out and . . . magic.

The door of Lily's restaurant opened. Tera stepped in holding the hands of two superheroes, Mr. and Mrs. Water Bear Man in all their gray spandex glory. "Lily," the young girl called out, "come meet my friends."

A hush fell over the restaurant as people turned and realized they were extras in a scene that their friends and family would never believe. Lily came out of the kitchen. "Well, look who we have here. Welcome to Lily's."

Eric Westerly flexed his muscles and put his hands on his hips. "Mrs. Water Bear and I have traveled all around the Milky Way seeking the perfect ice cream."

Sage mirrored his stance and, in a booming voice, added, "Our friend Tera said you have what we have been searching for."

A slow smile spread across Nicolette's face. "Paisley, I told Eric and Sage about Tera, but I didn't think they'd really come."

Bruce and LeAnne entered behind them, pulling up chairs beside Nicolette and Paisley. LeAnne leaned in and said, "Nicolette, you have no idea how much this means to Tera. He said he'll stay in his costume long enough for all the children to meet him after Bryant . . . I mean, after this."

"I'll be right back," Nicolette said, rising to her feet. She walked up to the big-screen superhero who was flexing for the crowd and threw her arms around him. "Thank you. Thank you so much for coming."

Eric hugged her back tightly. "Of course we came. We're family."

Nicolette hugged Sage next. "I still feel bad about . . ."

Mid-hug, Sage said, "Don't. You're exactly the family I always dreamed I would have."

They stepped back, both smiling. Tera announced she no longer wanted to marry a superhero . . . she wanted to grow up to be one. "That can be arranged," Eric said with a wink at his wife. "We do want children. How hard would it be to write one into our next movie?"

Jumping up and down, Tera stopped only long enough to call out to her parents, "Mom? Dad? Can I be famous?"

"We'll talk about it when we get home," her mother called back.

Tera made a face. "They said the same thing about me getting a puppy, but this is so much cooler. Don't worry, they will say yes."

Ever the pragmatist, Lily said, "Let's get you in a booth, and you can sort the rest out later."

As she returned to the table with Paisley, Nicolette checked the time on a clock on the wall. Bryant had left early that morning for a meeting, but he'd asked her to meet him at Lily's at noon. He was late.

Bryant was never late.

During the two incredible months they'd been together, Nicolette had learned that he didn't do anything halfway. Business deals. Friendships. Sex.

When he said he would be somewhere—he showed up. She didn't want him to miss this moment, but if he wasn't there, she was sure he had a good reason.

But where was he?

Her stomach flipped when she checked the clock again. Thirty minutes late? She sent him a text.

Oh my God. He's dead. I knew it. I knew nothing could stay this good.

I finally fall in love with a man, and he dies before I get a chance to even tell him.

I should have told him.

I'm going to be sick.

The door of the restaurant opened. Her grandmother and Tadeas walked in. With Brett and Alisha? Spencer, Hailey, and their daughter walked in behind them. Then Rachelle with her baby and Prince Magnus? More and more of her family and friends from the town walked in. Jordan and Lon joined Paisley. Nicolette's mouth dropped open when her father strolled into the very crowded diner holding hands with her mother.

Why are they all here?

She swayed on her feet.

Bryant threw open the door. "Sorry I'm late—this is a tough crew to organize."

She blindly greeted her parents and siblings with hugs as she made her way to the man she couldn't imagine her life without. When she reached him, she swallowed her nervousness. "What are you doing?"

He grinned at her gathered family. "What I've wanted to do from almost the first moment we met."

She took a few deep breaths and blinked back tears.

He dropped onto one knee and opened a small box. A three-plus-carat white diamond flashed up at her. "Nicolette, some things are meant to be—like you and me. Marry me. We'll buy a house here, teach my robots to change diapers, raise our children all wrong, and justify our decisions when they drag us into therapy when they're adults. It'll be a wild ride, but if we're together, we'll laugh our way through anything life throws our way. Even the first time we catch our kid with marijuana. We'll deal with it—together."

Yes. Still, she didn't want to make it too easy for him, so she cocked her head to the side. "You've got this all planned out."

"I do. All you have to do is say yes."

With her heart thudding with love for the man on his knees before her, she said, "No robot is changing a diaper in our house. Our children will be just fine, because whether we raise them here or anywhere, they will know they're loved—and I wouldn't laugh if I caught our child with drugs of any kind."

Bryant's smile only widened. "What you're saying is—yes, you'll marry me." He took out the ring and held it out.

She slid her finger into it. "Exactly."

He rose to his feet and kissed her soundly while the crowd around them broke into applause. After one long, heart-stopping kiss, their hands linked, and they turned to smile at the crowd. Outside of Lon, they were all from her side. Her heart broke a little for Bryant. As far as she knew, his father hadn't made a single attempt to contact him since the day she'd messaged him. "I wish . . ."

She didn't have to say it—he knew. He bent to say in her ear, "It's okay, Nicolette. I don't care."

She turned and cupped his face in her hands. "You do, and I'm going to spend the rest of my life showing you how okay that is. You've mastered how to be strong for others, but there's nothing wrong with leaning on someone else now and then. And guess what—I'm going to be that person. I will be your rock of sanity just as you've become mine."

He hugged her to him and murmured, "I'll show you another rock—tonight, tiger."

"Bigger than this one?" She flashed the ring at him, feeling alight with love.

"So, so much bigger," he murmured.

"Unfortunately, we can hear you," her father said dryly.

Nicolette and Bryant shared a look, then both broke into laughter. She mouthed, *Sorry*, to Dereck, who just shook his head, but he was smiling. At his side, her mother looked happier than she had in a long time.

Would they all have gotten there without Bryant? Maybe—love was a choice as well, and she knew exactly how she wanted to spend the rest of her life. "I love this man. I love him. I love, love, love him," she yelled.

"We know, know, know," Lily echoed back.

Bryant crooked an eyebrow, and a memory of a similar phrase being yelled through a hotel wall came back to Nicolette. She burst out laughing again. He joined in until they were both laughing so hard they were crying.

It was loud. It was crazy. It was perfect.

Still gasping for air and wiping tears from her cheeks, Nicolette met her grandmother's gaze and froze. What did she think of this side of her grandchild? Delinda winked, and Nicolette nearly burst into tears for an entirely different reason. *She sees me, and she loves me.*

Nicolette tucked herself under Bryant's arm. "She really is something, isn't she?"

He kissed her hair. "She is."

Cuddling closer, Nicolette said, "Thank you for speaking to her for me."

He kissed her forehead. "You can thank me later."

"Really? That's what you're thinking about right now?" She rolled her eyes.

There it was—that shameless, sexy grin that she still found irresistible. "Oh, you wanted deeper than that? Let me see . . . No, I just pictured you naked again. Now what were we talking about? Quick, before . . . Oh, damn, now you're in that red dress again . . . with the gaping cleavage and the cold wind blowing it tight against your—"

She silenced him with a kiss. "You're going to give my father a heart attack."

He twirled her. "He'll forgive me when the grandchildren come."

Not if—when. She liked that.

The future was full of beautiful possibilities.

As well as inevitable pitfalls, but they'd face them together.

And the robots? They'd never change a diaper, but they were welcome to do all the laundry and dishes they wanted.

Epilogue

Delinda Westerly looked out over the terraced gardens of her home by the ocean, watching her children and grandchildren enjoy the warm spring day. They were all there, just as she'd dreamed they one day would be. She hated stepping away from the view, but there was something she need to do.

Turning away, she returned her attention to the gray-haired middle-aged man who was gagged and tied to her favorite Chippendale chair. She walked over and took a seat across from him. The besuited man tossed his head back and forth angrily.

Delinda folded her hands on her lap. "Thank you for coming to see me, Mr. Taunton."

Maddox Taunton growled deep in his throat.

"Your son is an incredible young man, and we are excited to have him join our family. Have you seen how good he and Nicolette are for each other? No? That's a shame. I could not have chosen better for her myself. It was a big step for me. I'm learning to trust my children and my grandchildren to make their own decisions. We can't live their lives for them. They have to be free to make their own mistakes and grow from them, as we have."

Maddox attempted to say something that sounded like profanity, but thankfully it was muffled by the gag.

Delinda tapped her nails on the arm of her chair. "I wish you had accepted Bryant and Nicolette's wedding invitation. This all would have gone so much more smoothly. Now, I have to convince you that your son's happiness matters more than anything that occurred between our families." She let out a sigh. "I also have to acknowledge the role I played in all of this. I blamed your father because I needed a reason to explain the unexplainable. I don't know why Oliver chose to take his own life rather than turn to me for help. I'll never know, but I finally see that it wasn't your father's fault. It wasn't my fault. And nothing I did to your family in memory of Oliver made it better. I'm sorry."

If the look in Maddox's eyes was anything to go by, he wasn't feeling the reconciliation, and what he was attempting to articulate through the gag was probably a threat.

"I understand your anger." Delinda rose to her feet. "Perhaps it's too much to expect you to put it aside, but nothing is going to ruin Nicolette's wedding. Tadeas and I kept our own ceremony private so as not to overshadow hers. Don't worry about not being able to congratulate me now—we have more important matters to discuss. You will attend Nicolette and Bryant's wedding, and you'll appear happy for them both. Please do this because it's what's best for your son and not because I now have royal immunity in most countries. Let's not take this where it doesn't need to go. If you're ready to be civil, I'll remove the gag."

She stepped forward, but as his eyes shot daggers at her, she hesitated. "My only other option is to leak a story to the news that you're on an extended vacation to give you time to come to your senses. The duration of which depends entirely on you."

Maddox looked at the royal guards who flanked his chair. They didn't spare him even a glance.

Delinda tapped her chin. "I did invite you to tea; it was your choice to do it this way. My friend Alessandro told me if I wanted a rose garden, I needed to stop planting weeds. You, Maddox, must decide if you are a rose or a weed."

With a disappointed shake of her head, Delinda spoke to the royal guards. "I'm returning to the party. When he's had a change of mind, return him to his home. If the situation becomes complicated, Tadeas will handle the rest."

◆ ◆ ◆

Tucked into bed in the MacAuley home he'd built after proposing, Bryant woke with a start and sat up in bed. Nicolette woke as well, wrapped her arms around him, and rested her head on his chest. "Are you okay?" she asked.

He hugged her to him, then kissed the top of her head. "Just a strange dream."

Relaxing, he rolled back onto the bed with Nicolette still in his arms. "Did my father really respond that he was coming to the wedding?"

She kissed his jaw. "He did."

"He wasn't happy when I first told him about our engagement."

Her kisses approached his ear, and she murmured, "Maybe he needed time. We all get there when we get there."

The tickle of her breath on his ear was quickly erasing his nightmare. "It's just strange how fast the change happened."

She rained kisses back down his neck. "I don't second-guess good things anymore. He wants to come to the wedding—that's all that matters. Good things happen. All you have to do is believe they can."

About the Author

Ruth Cardello is a *New York Times* bestselling author who loves writing about rich alpha men and the strong women who tame them. She was born the youngest of eleven children in a small city in northern Rhode Island. She's lived in Boston, Paris, Orlando, New York, and Rhode Island again before moving to Massachusetts, where she now lives with her husband and three children. Before turning her attention to writing, Ruth was an educator for two decades, including eleven years as a kindergarten teacher. She is the author of the Lone Star Burn series, the Legacy Collection, the Andrades novels, and the Westerly Billionaire series, which includes *In the Heir, Up for Heir, Royal Heir, Hollywood Heir*, and *Runaway Heir*. Learn about Ruth's new releases by signing up for her newsletter at www.RuthCardello.com.